SKY OF ASHES, LAND OF DREAMS

ERIN JAMIESON

To Mrs. Corinne Smith, who helped me find confidence
in myself and my writing back in high school: thank
you for encouraging me to follow my dreams.

ONE

Winter 1917
Gobi Desert

BOLORMAA IS INTRODUCED to the man she is to marry on her eighteenth birthday, over mutton stew and steaming *buuz.*

Smoke, mixed with a light, buttery aroma—bitter and starchy. She runs to the heated pot too late; the dumplings are already charred on the bottom. Worse, it will take much scrubbing to take away the mess she's made. As she scrapes the dumplings out one at a time, she feels a hand on her shoulder.

"*Ta nadad tuslahgui yu.* Can you help me set the table? They'll be here soon." Bolormaa's mother leans over the pot, her deep-set, honey-colored eyes squinting. "What happened to the *buuz?*"

"I looked away for a minute. They were underdone, and then—"

"It only takes a minute," her mother interrupts. "Always daydreaming! How do you expect to manage a household of your own?" She grabs the ladle. "I'll take care of this. Now make yourself useful and bring everything else to the table."

Biting back tears, Bolormaa sets an overflowing bowl of rice noodles on the worn table near the entryway. The thought of managing a household is stifling. Her mind always wanders, no matter how much she tries to train it. She can't shake the lingering, dangerous idea that maybe she needs something more, that her life could be something different than what her mother has prescribed.

She knows this meeting will end poorly. Not only is she a poor cook with a wandering mind, but she's also plain. Instead of inheriting her mother's high cheekbones, she has her father's round jawline and his slightly stubby hands. Her hair, worn either down or in a simple plait, is difficult to tame, often dry with splitting ends. Neither slim nor athletic, Bolormaa often feels like someone who hasn't quite grown into her body.

These thoughts, she knows, she must keep to herself.

Outside, the wind gusts, and a chill penetrates the felt walls of the tent. Her father built this *ger* last spring. With pride, he'd pointed out the handsome, wooden lattice work, the spacious rounded interior. Handmade benches surrounded a table in the center, near the cooking area. The thick tarp insulates them from vitriolic winds—but only so much on a January day when a few moments of exposed skin can result in frostbite.

On the western side of the *ger* they keep their bridles and *airag*, fermented horse milk, if they had any liquor left. To the east, kitchen utensils. Opposite the lone opening was a modest shrine, as well as a collection of trinkets from occasional visitors. And where they are now, visitors are exceedingly rare.

Which makes the expected visitor, her suitor, even more mysterious.

    Erin Jamieson

To travel on a day like this can mean only one thing, and the realization makes Bolormaa's stomach churn. Her day-dreaming days may be over. You don't travel on a day like today if you aren't serious about making an offer or a proposal.

He comes from a good family, she has been told. His father breeds the finest goats for miles, and his mother is a hard worker. She has been told they are kind, dependable, and loving. Everything a good Mongolian family should be.

Bolormaa does not learn the name of her suitor, in fact, until he arrives an hour later. As her mother lets him in, a sharp wind curls into the *ger*. Bolormaa shivers under her *deel*, wishing she'd been allowed to wear her muskrat shawl.

Reserved for special occasions and strikingly different from the wool layers she wears most days, the *deel* is made of fine silk. A golden collar and cuffs contrast with a brilliantly purplish-red overlay. It's fitted with a gorgeous sash, and Bolormaa has often wondered how much the fabric cost her family.

The extravagance of their clothing signifies the seriousness of the meeting. And it's why her mother is angry about Bolormaa's daydreaming, even more than usual.

The young man introduces himself, glancing at Bolormaa as if she's merely part of the *ger*, or a piece of furniture. Bolormaa bites her lip, irritation spiking when she hears his name.

Ganbaatar. Steel hero.

But then he turns to her, and her irritation fades.

His name suits his appearance. Tall and imposing, Ganbaatar has muscles sculpted by a lifetime of riding. His skin is tanned but not yet leathery, his eyes a liquid brown that reminds Bolormaa of freshly ground coffee. His face is stoic, with high, arched eyebrows and handsome curls framing his high forehead. His smile is kind but stiff.

Maybe he doesn't want to be here?

She runs her fingers through her hair but realizes oil remains on her hands from preparing the food. Her cheeks flush.

This Ganbaatar might be handsome, but that doesn't change anything. Her mother said nothing about his appearance, or the way his eyes crease when he smiles.

Bolormaa's father steps forward, his shoulders tight and his liquid brown eyes stern. Usually quietly confident, he seems strained and not as certain about the meeting as he claims to be.

The men shake hands. Her father's is dwarfed by Ganbaatar, who is not only younger and more muscular but livelier. His eyes dance as if the *ger* is something remarkable.

"Thank you for inviting me." Ganbaatar's voice is smooth, compared to the rough, lower notes of Bolormaa's father. As if he's been practicing for this moment.

And yet—Bolormaa tries to catch his eye, yearning for recognition, a sign that he sees her, that he cares about their fate.

"Why don't you have a seat at the table?" Bolormaa's father says. "I hope you like mutton stew."

He nods and he walks to the table, pausing at the chair where Bolormaa is still standing, frozen. "You must be Bolormaa."

She nods. Her chest flutters. For once, she isn't dreaming about doing something else.

His tone softens when he speaks to her, but his words are formal, like he's practicing a speech instead of talking to her.

"Pleasure to meet you," he says.

Bolormaa smiles, and he just studies her until it becomes

uncomfortable. Does he think she looks silly, with oil in her hair? Is he pleased by what he sees?

He does not offer his hand to shake.

"Let him pass," her mother chides, breaking the spell.

Bolormaa fumbles past the chair, face flaming, and slips into a seat across the table. The door to the *ger* opens, and Bolormaa's three brothers file in, their cheeks wind burnt. After everyone sits, Bolormaa concentrates on the passing stew and dumplings, scarcely noticing what she is putting on her plate.

Her father watches their guest across the table. "I've worked alongside your father," he says. "He's a good man."

"He says the same of you," Ganbaatar answers. He swallows a large spoonful of stew, his jaw moving powerfully as he chews the mutton bits.

"Do you intend to take over your father's livestock someday?"

"Oh, no," he answers, spearing a dumpling. "I am already raising my own."

"I see," Bolormaa's father says. It is impossible not to hear how impressed he is. Bolormaa can't decide if this makes her feel better—at least, they admire each other—or more and more like this meeting is less about how much she likes Ganbaatar than how much her family likes him.

And why can't he look at her, even for a moment? Does he think she's ugly or stupid, or does he ignore her out of politeness or propriety?

Batbayar, Bolormaa's youngest brother, breaks the silence, as usual: "Do you race?"

"Horses?" Ganbaatar grins for the first time, and it transforms him. The stiffness fades and his handsomeness multiplies. He becomes almost boyish.

The boy's words rush out. "Bet I can out race you. Father says I'm the fastest—"

"Batbayar," their mother warns.

"It's all right," Ganbaatar says. "I used to race, but I wasn't fast enough."

Batbayar sits up straighter, puffs out his chest—which, being skin and bones, is hardly impressive. "How old do you think I am?"

"That's enough," their mother chides. "Ganbaatar, would you like more dumplings?"

"Now, Sarnai," her father says, "let him talk. Our son is merely trying to entertain our guest."

"I've had plenty, thank you." Ganbaatar's eyes flicker to Bolormaa. She gives him a small smile, but he quickly turns back to Batbayar. "I'm going to guess you're fifteen?"

"See!" Batbayar says excitedly to Altan, the oldest brother. "He says I look older!" He smiles broadly. "I'm only thirteen," he explains to Ganbaatar. "I like you. I really hope you marry my sister."

Bolormaa nearly chokes on a piece of meat. She coughs, drawing even more attention, and reaches for her glass of *airag*. The sharp sting of fermented milk only irritates her throat, and she coughs more. She reaches for the stew, thinking broth might help, and knocks her glass over.

The effect is immediate: the milk drizzles across the table, stains the front of her skirt, and runs into Batbayar's plate. He stands up and shrieks, claiming his food is ruined. Altan tries to calm him, while Bolormaa's other two brothers scramble to find something to clean the spill. Simultaneously, her mother and father apologize. When no one is looking, Batbayar winks at her. He's causing a stir on purpose.

 Erin Jamieson

But no one will see that, and ultimately, Bolormaa will look like a fool.

She stoops beside her chair, wishing she could disappear, feeling the chill of the ground and hearing the wind howl outside. How lonely and desolate that wind sounds as it travels across the barren land.

"Nothing to apologize for," Ganbaatar murmurs. "Accidents happen. My young cousin always spills things."

His young cousin, always spilling things. The words pierce her. How young and foolish does he think she is? And how old is Ganbaatar himself if he was fifteen "a long time" ago?

"Allow me." Ganbaatar stands beside her, holding a rag brought by her brother, trying to soak up the spilled *airag*. He smells heavily of hay and freshly fallen snow. Up close, his muscles are well-defined; his arm is the size of her neck. Though Bolormaa has spent her entire life with boys and men—from her siblings to the other herders she's met—this feels different.

His hand brushes hers—a mistake, maybe, but long enough that Bolormaa feels the warmth of his calloused skin. She imagines what it would be like to hold his hand, to feel his warmth.

Their eyes meet.

Batbayar looks at them, and the moment passes.

Bolormaa's skin tingles. She ducks her head to hide her flushed face. She has been dreading the meeting all week. So why was she acting this way, blushing over a man who had barely spoken to her?

"I have *pashka*," her mother says to Ganbaatar. "Would you like some?"

"I'm afraid I've already eaten too much."

"I insist."

"If you insist." He smiles, setting the rag down, "I suppose I can't refuse."

The evening is saved by dessert. The *pashka* is creamy and luxurious as a custard should be—but not too heavy—brandished with dried cranberries and chopped walnuts. By the time plates are cleared, the accident has been forgotten. Even Batbayar cannot find anything to complain about and returns to his earlier interest in Ganbaatar's history of horse racing.

Bolormaa is the only one who cannot swallow more than a bite, overly aware of her soaked skirt and the fact that Ganbaatar hasn't bothered to converse with her, even once.

By the end of the night, her father declares Ganbaatar the best *khoral* player he's ever met, while Batbayar is fascinated that their guest won several horse races in the four, short years he competed. Her mother comments that he is the most gracious dinner guest she's ever had.

But Bolormaa can't make sense of how she feels. This man—who she has no interest in—has wormed his way into her mind. And yet. Aside from the moment with the rag, he barely glanced at her.

She scrubs dishes as Ganbaatar trades jokes with her youngest brother. She replays the evening over and over. Perhaps she should have spoken more. But jokes don't come easily to her, especially with someone she doesn't know. She doesn't have her brothers' charisma. She never has.

Because she lives too much in a dream world, her mother often says.

Bolormaa tries to shake those lingering feelings off. So what if he seems handsome, intelligent, even capable of joking?

She's too young to marry and too young to leave her parents. As much as she dreams of a different life, she's never truly known exactly what she wants. And no matter how much her family seems to admire Ganbaatar, she has no interest in marrying someone who won't even acknowledge her presence.

Bolormaa's mother appears at her side. "Come, our guest is leaving, I'll take care of the rest of these dishes."

Night has fallen, and sleet has started to fall from the bitter, cold sky. It's late. Riding at night can be treacherous, especially in the chill of winter.

Ganbaatar thanks them for the meal and slips into his fur coat. With his fine cap pulled down partially over his eyes, he appears even grander, almost ethereal.

"You can't go now!" Bolormaa's mother protests. "A storm is coming."

He laughs softly. "I have traveled in far worse conditions."

"Let him go, Sarnai." her father adds. He turns to Ganbaatar. "She's overly cautious. No offense meant to you."

"None taken, I assure you."

Outside, the wind howls louder.

"We hope to see you again soon." Bolormaa's mother glances at her daughter, but Bolormaa remains silent.

"I hope so, too. Good night." Ganbaatar looks back one last time, nodding before he steps into the chilly night.

After he leaves, no one speaks.

The dessert dishes need to be cleaned and the floor swept. Bolormaa is grateful for the work, to escape her swirling thoughts. Had she done something wrong?

The *ger* still smells of mutton meat and rich custard. Her brothers settle in the western half of their home. Batbayar's blankets have fallen off, and his slight frame shivers in his sleep. Their mother slips two more blankets onto her youngest son with a tenderness she has not shown her daughter for many years.

"Bolormaa," she says softly.

"Yes?"

"It's late. I will take care of the rest."

"Are you sure?"

Her mother looks more worn than Bolormaa has ever seen her. Wrinkles line her face like the lines of an old book. Her shoulders have become more stooped, and her hair glints with silver threads.

"Yes. But Bolormaa—" She catches her hand.

"What?"

"Did you like him?"

The question takes her by surprise. "He seems pleasant," she says carefully.

"Pleasant?" her mother repeats.

Bolormaa gazes at the rug beneath her feet, intrigued, as always, by the colors her mother has woven—blue for the Mongolian sky, yellow for the sun as it rises, orange for dusk. Each thread was woven by hand when Bolormaa was an infant and their family had just started. She wishes she could have woven the rug with her mother, although she has no skill and little patience for such things.

Though she cooks meals, cleans the house, and feeds the livestock by her mother's side, it has been a long time since they have discussed anything of substance, anything more than a passing, "Would you mind starting the tea kettle?" or "Make sure Batbayar isn't still sleeping."

Bolormaa knows that by asking this question, her mother is offering her something. A consideration. She can see that. The only thing is, Bolormaa has nothing to give back.

"He seems polite," she says.

"He is a handsome man."

Bolormaa bites her lip. She isn't about to admit the

    Erin Jamieson

churning in her stomach, or how her hand tingles. Besides, it's obvious he has no real interest in her. Not if he enjoys her brother's company more than hers.

"I suppose," she says finally.

"You aren't taken with him, are you?"

"We need more dung," Bolormaa mutters, gesturing toward the dying embers. "It's getting cold."

"Your father only wants what's best for you. He thinks Ganbaatar is an honest and decent man. He comes from a good family with a sizable herd and handsome horses. It would be a comfortable life."

"I'm going to get more dung for the fire."

"Bolormaa—"

"We can't let the fire die," she says, turning away. As she steps outside, the cold is deep. Sleet has transformed into blinding snow.

As she stumbles in the darkness, the wind howls in her ears and blocks out all thought. The white is a blanket, coating her eyes and entering her nostrils, freezing her shallow breaths. The pain is good.

It reminds her that she is alive.

TWO

ALL WEEK, BOLORMAA battles competing thoughts.

Ganbaatar hasn't returned, and, to her knowledge, hasn't said a word to her family. Either he's too busy, or he's trying to back out of the arrangement. She tells herself this is fine. Wasn't she—despite her mother's reassurances—dreading the meeting? If anything, it's a blessing. Maybe it's good she made a fool of herself.

Yet.

Sometimes, as Bolormaa cleans or feeds the goats, she thinks back to the moment their hands briefly touched. Or the warmth in his soft brown eyes when he laughed. Or how he bit his lip when he was trying to win a game.

But there's too much happening to dwell on Ganbaatar.

Three days are spent battling the aftermath of a blizzard. Two older, frail goats are lost. It's a big loss—they cannot easily replace the animals—but these losses are inevitable in the Gobi. The rest of the herd remains ravenous, so desperate for food they nibble on her sweater and gloves.

One day Bolormaa forgets about them, and the animals flee to the front of the *ger*, smelling the dried jerky set out for the midday meal. They butt the entrance, and she takes pity on them and slips a few sesame crackers into her pockets when her mother isn't looking. They greedily eat the little she has collected, the larger and stronger goats butting others out of the way and taking more than their share.

Her stomach is constantly empty, too, but having lived her whole life in the Gobi, she has come to expect this. They eat dried beef and cheese curds, washing it down with herbal teas and the occasional glass of *airag*. They are all in want of more, but only Batbayar complains. Everyone knows this is how things are, and will be, until the thaw in the spring.

Bolormaa's life dissolves into a pattern: feeding animals, fleeting thoughts of Ganbaatar, bundling up for the harsh winds. Sometimes, she envies Batbayar, who takes studying for granted. She used to attend one of the makeshift schools then resorted to studying at home between chores.

She's an adult now, with primary school completed. And though sometimes she wonders what it would be like to learn more, she also worries this would mean leaving the Gobi, the only home she's ever known. As much as she dreams of a larger life, the idea of living in the crowded and dirty city of Ulaanbaatar makes her skin crawl.

Today she gazes out the front of the *ger*, watching as delicate snowflakes fall on the frozen soil. It is still bitter, but the cold is bearable, and the wind that kisses her cheeks makes her feel alive. She has been cooking for hours, whittling the afternoon away by curing marmot to be dried and preparing a new batch of mare's milk curds.

The work is exhausting, and the *ger* feels too small, as it always has. There is something about living under a blue sky that expands to infinity, a sky that swallows you whole, that makes confinement even more unbearable. Bolormaa felt this when she was a student, sitting in the tent and dreaming of distant places in books, and she feels it now.

"Bolormaa? Did you finish the meat?" Her mother walks to the east side of the *ger*, where the cooking supplies are kept. Her cheeks are flushed with cold, and her hair is coated with a fine veneer of snow, making her strands appear to sparkle under the dim afternoon light.

"Almost." Bolormaa's hands are covered with blood and spices: turmeric, paprika, pepper. She knows from experience it will take time and effort to scrub her hands clean.

"Good. Batbayar should be home soon, and you know how crazy—" She stops, her eyebrows rising as she looks around.

"Is something wrong?" Bolormaa asks.

"Your father. Has he been in?"

"I don't think so."

Her mother bites her lip.

"Why?"

"Not even to have something to eat?"

"I wasn't paying attention." Bolormaa rubs the last of the meat and picks up the soiled pan. "He could have come in, but—"

"I'd better go check on him."

"But he always—"

"He's slowing down, Bolormaa."

It feels as if ice has been shoved down her throat. She longs to wash her hands, to rid them of the smell and the mess. She cannot imagine her father getting older. Mongolians living on the Gobi cannot "slow down." Their family's livelihood depends on the daily care of the livestock and the household. Without it, they would have nothing.

"It's nothing to worry about," her mother says, as if

Erin Jamieson

reading her thoughts. "It happens to all of us. Your brother can help take care of things."

Bolormaa nods. "I'll clean this up before Batbayar comes in and gets blood everywhere."

"I'll be right back," her mother promises, her face unreadable.

After she leaves, Bolormaa takes the pan out to the small tributary a quarter mile away. She shivers as the cold water cascades over her skin. It does not take long to wash the blood away, but afterwards, she can still smell the stench of meat on her hands.

When she returns, Batbayar is animatedly telling their mother how he scored top marks on his Tibetan lesson without studying. Cholbasen, the middle brother, has retired in his sleeping room, straddling a mat while he writes. Bolormaa's father and Altan are nowhere to be seen.

"What's for supper?" Batbayar asks without taking a breath.

"I don't know yet," Bolormaa's mother admits.

"I can help," he says, puffing his chest.

Bolormaa laughs. "You've never cooked a thing in your life."

"Doesn't mean I can't."

"Why the sudden interest?"

He makes a face. "None of your business."

"Enough, you two," their mother says. "Batbayar, don't you have studies?"

He wrinkles his nose. "I hate Russian history."

"That doesn't mean you can neglect your studies," she says. "Perhaps Bolormaa can help."

"I thought I was cooking dinner."

"I can handle it." She brushes a sweaty strand of hair from

her face. Bolormaa keeps quiet. She is tired of the humidity near the simmering pot but doesn't fancy the idea of poring over Russian history. No one likes Russian history. It's been an area of contention in the Mongolian education system for as long as she could remember. Students now spend a mere three weeks on Mongolian history compared to the three months they study Russian and Chinese history.

Her father rarely talks about it, but ever since the Five Races Under One Union Flag was erected in the capital, nothing has been the same. He once said it was like being squeezed between two powers—Russia and China—and all the Mongolian customs and traditions no longer mattered. This blending was more of an erasure.

Even though more women were advancing their education, Bolormaa didn't want to go to the city to study. Here, in the Gobi, it was easier to pretend that nothing had changed since the invasion. They could continue their nomadic ways as though her country is the same as it always has been.

But today, something isn't right. Bolormaa's father hasn't returned, and he's been out for hours.

"Batbayar, why don't you and your sister study on the dining mats?" Bolormaa's mother reaches for a cooking pot, taking her place beside her daughter. Helping, out of habit. Or perhaps because she doesn't completely trust Bolormaa with the meal.

Bolormaa opens her mouth, then shuts it. Her mother will tell them if something has happened. Won't she? A chill passes through her as Bolormaa realizes she is not sure. Father has always been healthy. Until—

"Are you going to help me or stand there?" Her younger brother tugs on her arm. "You've gotten lazy since you quit school."

     Erin Jamieson

Quit school. That last day, in autumn, when the leaves covered the ground like rotting carcasses, crumpled orange and red snapping under the weight of her new dress shoes. The wind was cool but pleasant, and the air tasted already of the coming winter. Skies blue and expansive as life itself seemed to stretch forever in the distance. Clouds wispy as a sigh were fading under the golden haze of the afternoon sun. Laughter and exclamations filled the dirt path as Bolormaa left the school tent in the heart of the Gobi, one final time, smiling along with her fellow graduating classmates although her chest felt filled with water. Smiling, because that was expected.

"I didn't quit," she says finally.

"Huh?"

"Let's start studying." Bolormaa sighs. "I want to get this over with."

"Like I don't."

They settle on the mats, and Batbayar groans as he retrieves notes from his satchel. The aroma of fleshy meat fat fills the air, along with the sounds of a sizzling pan. The smell of onion makes Bolormaa's mouth water. They haven't had an onion or any vegetables since Ganbaatar's visit, except for pickled beets.

"What do you have to do?" she asks, turning back to her brother. She tries to read his notes, but his cramped writing makes them impossible to decipher. "What does this say?"

He scowls. "I don't know. Aren't you supposed to tell me?"

"Not if I can't read them." She shakes her head. "How am I supposed to help you study?"

"Wasn't my idea."

Bolormaa rubs her temple. "All right. Read me what you

have, and I'll try to take some notes of my own. Then I can quiz you."

"Won't that take a long time?"

"Do you have a better way?"

He doesn't, so they follow Bolormaa's instructions. After nearly an hour, she has a sense of what he is studying.

"What caused the decline of the Kiev dynasty?" she asks.

He blinks. "Kiev?"

"In the twelfth to fourteenth century?"

When he stares back blankly, Bolormaa sighs. "How much have you studied?"

"Five minutes yesterday."

"When is the test?"

He squirms. "Tomorrow."

She lets the notes flutter to the ground. "I can't help you. Not if you don't know a thing."

"Who says I don't?"

"You didn't know the first thing I asked—"

Their mother enters the room, her small frame enveloped under a heavy dress, flour coating her hair, and tiny splashes of soy sauce speckling her stubborn chin.

"Bolormaa won't help me study," Batbayar whines, but their mother doesn't seem to hear.

She stares off indifferently. "Batbayar, why don't you put your books away for now?"

He is elated and unceremoniously wads his notes together. Springing from the mat, he asks if supper is ready.

"Not yet," their mother says. "Why don't you see what Cholbasen is up to?"

He hurries from the room, evidently enthralled with any excuse to abandon his history lesson.

"He's going to fail his test," Bolormaa says. "He didn't

          Erin Jamieson

even know—" But then she sees her mother: lips, bloodless, and hollow eyes like a fish that has been gutted.

"*Ta nadad tuslahgui yu,*" her mother says softly. "I need your help."

THREE

GANBAATAR DOES NOT remember the most important day of his life. He was two, three at most, and his parents had done the customary thing, inviting distant cousins donned in city garb and herding friends and peers from his father's school days.

His mother, ever the industrious woman, had labored nearly four hours, cooking until her scalp was dripping perspiration and ordering his father to clean the *ger* not once but twice. A handsome meal was spread, roasted horse meat nestled in candied carrots, covered in a honey ginger glaze. There was clotted cream, cabbage stew, and *süütei tsai,* his mother's acclaimed salted milk tea.

The food was not the most magnificent spectacle. Spring blossoms adorned the tent and were sprinkled on the mats and floors. The handsome forks and knives his mother had received as wedding gifts were set out.

Ganbaatar remembers none of this.

What he can recall comes in fragments, like images that have been spliced and presented in random order. He remembers the sharp sting of vodka hanging in the air like perfume.

Laughter, insidious, a clatter echoing in his tiny chest. And what felt like a hundred eyes trained on him.

His mother loves recalling the day.

How the scissors glinted in the sun, and he sat still as stone when she lifted a black, glossy lock and made the first cut. How he remained still as his father made a second cut, and their grandmother a third. And how, when Chulun, one of his father's childhood friends, approached, Ganbaatar began to shriek. "*Nadad buu khur!* Don't touch me!"

Whenever she tells the story, his mother always laughs. "That was the most we'd ever heard you speak. You seemed to think Chulun was going to hurt you."

Eventually, Ganbaatar calmed down enough for everyone else to snip a lock of hair, but only after his mother sang a lullaby and assured him over and over no one was going to hurt him. That was his first haircut, the moment a Mongolian boy becomes a man.

And Ganbaatar had entered this new world wailing, clinging to his mother's side, unable to accept the change.

Now, nearly twenty-five years later, Ganbaatar wonders if this was a sign he would never grow up to be the man his father was. Broad-shouldered and muscular, he is, physically, the spitting image of his father. Everyone says so, except for his eyes, which are the warm brown of his mother's. Although he may resemble his parents, he is nothing like them.

His father lives for their livestock, treating the goats, sheep, and horses as beloved children. His mother is nearly as enamored, spending copious time with the animals, even in the blistering heat or blinding cold. Ganbaatar is their only son; his mother miscarried twice, and they lost hope. After seven years, he came as a surprise. A miracle baby, his mother would say. A gift for the suffering they'd endured.

Ganbaatar is no miracle, and he never has been.

He is a mistake, and he feels it more and more the older he becomes.

When he was twelve, he was one of the best riders for miles and won numerous races. He learned to feed the animals long before he learned many words. He knows instantly when one of the livestock is ill.

But these are the things his parents see.

He has had to strive for all of it. What comes as naturally as breathing for his parents, he must earn, watching his father day in and day out, always terrified he will make a mistake and risk their livelihood.

He hates the flat, endless landscape with no vegetation and few neighbors. He hated attending a school in a makeshift tent, when he knew his cousins went to classes in an actual building. He hates the everyday labor that makes his muscles ache, hates knowing he will have to wake up and do the exact same thing the next day, and the day after that.

At twenty-eight, he is a profound disappointment to his parents. Handsome though he is, he has expressed no interest in marriage.

What point is there in carrying on the family name if it means nothing to him? He was born in the Gobi and would die in the Gobi. From the minute he first opened his eyes, he was expected to follow his father's lead. From that first haircut, he was preordained as the man to continue the family.

Several weeks earlier, Ganbaatar and his father had met another man taking his herd to the same pasture. Grazing grounds are scarce, made even more scarce by the current drought. Men and women try to share these lands; ultimately, there is only so much land and far too many animals. The less fortunate herds die from starvation.

The day they met Gantulga, Ganbaatar had twisted his ankle badly. He'd been leading an obstinate camel, who kept turning and spitting on the barren ground. Frustrated, he'd yanked harder on the rope, then stumbled over something sharp on the ground.

It was a carcass, the magnificent rib cage of what was once a horse. Remnants of rotting flesh peeled like pieces of salmon parchment. The stench was overpowering, putridly sweet as the sun baked the skin dry. Most of it had been eaten away by a predator, leaving odds and ends—glazed eyeballs and a stiff tongue, too brown. Hoofs, bleeding and broken. Fragments of the mane, billowing in the wind.

Ganbaatar's father worked the tongue out of the skull. "This will make an excellent stew." He looked up. "Are you hurt?"

"Twisted ankle. I'll be fine." He felt nauseous in the heat. "Mind if I graze here?"

Ganbaatar and his father turned their heads. A middle-aged man with leathery skin was surrounded by a pack of handsome, sturdy goats. His broad shoulders were slack, and he had the look of a man who'd lost a great deal of muscle in a brief period.

"You were here first," Ganbaatar's father grunted. The heat was oppressive, even with the heavy wind, and he wiped his perspiring brow with the back of his knobby hand.

"There's enough," the man insisted. "We can share."

There wasn't, but he nodded. "*Bayarlalaa*. Thank you."

"You from around here?"

It was an odd question for a nomad. Were they really from anywhere? They moved up to five times a year, and this year, they'd been forced to move six. There is no home, except the tent you sleep in. There is no risk of growing attached to a certain patch of land, because by the time you've become familiarized with the landmarks around you, it is time to move on.

"Around," Ganbaatar's father replied vaguely. "You?"

The man tilted his head to the east. "Half-mile, for a short time." His eyes rested on Ganbaatar. "Family?"

"My son."

Ganbaatar introduced himself, feeling childish as always. They didn't have time for pleasantries.

"I have a daughter," the man said. "Probably around your age."

Ganbaatar nodded, out of politeness.

"How old are you?"

"Twenty-eight."

"Ah, a little older. My daughter will be eighteen soon."

Ganbaatar nodded again. Eighteen. She was a child. He wandered over to a sheep that had strayed and guided it back to the green pasture.

"Have him over for a meal," the man was saying.

"Well, I don't know." Ganbaatar's father squinted into the sunlight.

"After all, we're grazing on the same land."

There was a pause before his father motioned to him. Ganbaatar

"Yes?" Ganbaatar said.

"He's invited us for supper."

"That's very generous."

"You'll go?" the man asked. "Tomorrow?"

"Tomorrow," Ganbaatar's father agreed, answering for both, like always.

The next day came, and they did not go. The man had

     Erin Jamieson

fallen ill and sent word. Ganbaatar was relieved. Maybe the whole thing would pass over.

And for a time, it seemed as if it would. Weeks went by without a dinner invitation or mention of the man's daughter. Ganbaatar's father and the man grew close, swapping stories the way one did in the pasture, sharing midday meals of dried beef and cold *airag*. And Ganbaatar worked harder than ever, not interested in joining their conversations, feeling as forgotten as the flat expanse of land without trees or vegetation.

One evening, as dusk was falling, his father informed Ganbaatar he'd have to bring the herd in.

"By myself?" he asked nervously.

"It's about time, don't you think?"

Ganbaatar fell silent. He was only a few years from his thirtieth birthday. It had been about time for nearly ten years.

"I'm going to Gantulga for the evening." His father paused. "I think he meant to invite you."

"Someone needs to take the herd back," Ganbaatar said. "Mother hasn't been feeling strong lately. She couldn't do it."

His father's eyes darkened. "Yes, I'm worried about her."

"It's the weather," Ganbaatar said. "She becomes weak with the heat."

"Yes, that must be it. Look after her. I won't stay long."

"We'll be fine," he said, as much to himself as anyone. He had no way of knowing that after his father's visit, his life would take a detour.

His mother's hands are lined like ancient writing, her skin sallow, her frame diminished under heavy sheets that seem to swallow her whole. When he enters the room, the sharp stench of liquor and fermented milk assaults his senses.

"Ganbaatar." She holds out her arms. "Come closer."

He does, careful not to look at her too closely. "Here," he says, tucking her into the sheets. "Better?"

She nods as a shiver runs through her body.

"Father says you wanted to see me. "

One of her eyebrows rises. "He told me you had news."

"News?"

"Oh, come now." His mother's gaunt cheeks stretch into what's intended to be a smile but looks more like a grimace. "Don't leave your old mother in suspense."

"You're not old," he says, but she is. Nearing her forty-fifth birthday, far older than most mothers with a son not yet thirty. And it shows.

"What news do you have?" she insists, patting the mat for him to sit.

"I don't—"

"A girl. Woman, I should say. Your father says she's lovely."

So overnight, his father had decided. Ganbaatar's mouth is dry. "Do you need anything? I could heat up the stew."

"I don't want stew."

"You haven't eaten since last night."

"I'm not hungry," his mother says, pushing the sheets away with her bird-like arms. "Tell me about her. Please."

Her eyes seem more hollowed. He has witnessed that look in old sheep as they near the end of their lives: the eyes of something that knows it's dying or perhaps is already in the process of dying. His mother's tan skin is papery and yellow, her lips chapped and blistering. The drought, the heat and intense cold, the weeks with little sustenance. She's too old for this, he realizes.

"I don't know anything," he says softly. "I've never met her."

Her face contorts. "But your father said—"

"I met her, but not formally," he lies. "She is a lovely girl."

His mother sits up, dullness passing from her eyes. "Pretty?"

"Beautiful. Not as beautiful as you."

She chuckles, which turns into a deep cough. He hands her a piece of cloth, and she coughs until her cheeks flush. Though her eyes water and her voice is unsteady, she looks better with some color.

"Intelligent?" she asks.

"Yes."

"Good. Pretty girls are nothing without a brain. Especially in the Gobi—" Her words catch on another cough. "Have to be smart to survive."

Survive. The word hangs in the air. And what of his mother? What good had surviving all these years done for her? Ganbaatar reaches over and pats her wrinkled hand, careful not to apply too much pressure as she continues to question him about the young woman he couldn't care less about.

FOUR

ONE DAY LATER, Ganbaatar's mother dies.

It is expected and quiet; she slips away during the night. She's given a sky burial, her body left to become one with the land, but little is said for her send off. Ganbaatar knew this day would come, and yet something breaks inside of him, something he believes will never mend. His father is stoic, the way he is when one of the herd dies, a silent acceptance that doesn't betray a hint of emotion.

"She's at peace now," Ganbaatar's father says. As if this alone is enough to say goodbye. He turns to his son, expressionless. "The good thing was, she was never alone. She had me, and then you. To die alone—that is the most terrible thing."

There will be no herding today, no chores. Ganbaatar sinks into the grass, shivering despite the brilliant sun. Dust catches in his throat.

Never alone.

His father chooses his words carefully. Ganbaatar despises the way he lets go so easily, stepping away from a woman he supposedly loved.

He would never treat someone as his father has. He

would love her intently, grieve her, let her memories linger on everything he did, like fine dust collecting on fabric, until she became as much a part of him as blue was part of the sky.

But his father was right about one thing.

Ganbaatar did not want to die alone.

He imagined having no one to spread his ashes. No wife, no children, not a single soul to miss him and safeguard memories.

Two days later, on a gray morning when the air tastes of rain, he agrees to be married. What does it matter if he has never met the girl who would become his wife?

He will not be alone.

He will love her in a way his father never loved his mother.

He will be away from his father's expectations, have his own household, and he'll be strong in ways his father is not.

His father is happy but explains that the wedding will not happen right away. "She's young, and though her father is agreeable to the marriage—pleased in fact—he thinks it would be best to wait a few years."

A few years is a blink of the eye. Now, after grieving his mother's death for months, Ganbaatar realizes nothing has changed. He still feels nothing. He still wakes often, his body cold as if it has been brushed with death itself, his throat and belly bloated with the memory of his mother's laughter. He still helps his father but feels as if he could disappear into the hard ground and become less than nothing, dissolve into rock or ash. No one would notice the difference.

There is nothing remarkable about the girl. She has a plain, pretty face, with classic Mongolian eyes, long, dark hair. She is short and dainty, like a child, reaching only to his shoulder in height. She could be anyone, and Ganbaatar knows if he met her elsewhere, he wouldn't have given her a second glance. As it is, this morning, he cannot recall her name. Starts with a B? But the name is lost on him.

Ganbaatar knows something is wrong.

Dirty dishes line the small counter, beside a kettle which is burnt on the bottom. The air is filled with the stench of rotting milk and over-brewed tea. These things are nothing new. Their home has not been clean since Ganbaatar's mother first fell ill.

What's different is that his father is nowhere to be found.

"Father?" Ganbaatar's voice echoes from the ceiling around the walls of the tent. "Father?"

He is not there.

The morning is cool, and Ganbaatar shivers and wanders to the mat where his mother took her last breath. The pillows hold her lingering scent. Her bed has not been made and is still covered with wrinkled and stained linens and the quilt woven in green and blue meant to capture the Gobi in summertime. A single tissue lies on the pillow, yellow and slightly bloodied.

"Father?" Ganbaatar calls again.

No answer.

He must leave. His heart is in his throat. He cannot remember a morning when he woke up alone.

His stomach is empty and aching. He forgets to eat often now. He reaches for the kettle and slams it back down. The handle is still hot, and his hand smarts from the contact.

His father must have recently left. Ganbaatar finds a stale cracker on the counter and crams it into his mouth. It is tasteless and dissolves quickly, but at least it is something. Without glancing back, he escapes.

     Erin Jamieson

Dawn is faint, pink fingertips caressing the open blue skies. A goat bleats, and Ganbaatar's heart jumps. The herd is still here.

The goats are bustling with nervous energy, heads bent to the ground. They butt each other, fighting for imaginary grass, and do not acknowledge Ganbaatar as he wades through. The horses are still here, too, raising their heads slowly and lazily blinking. Like all Mongolian horses, they are broad-shouldered and handsome, with sleek backs equipped to accommodate heavy loads. Ganbaatar's stallion nuzzles him as he walks past and snorts when Ganbaatar ignores him.

"Father?"

"Ganbaatar."

He turns around, nearly knocking into a man a good three inches taller. He has a stern, pitted face. He looks familiar, but—

"Your father said you'd be up soon."

"Who are you?"

"Never mind that. We don't have time." There is a gurgling sound, and Ganbaatar sees what he hadn't before: a camel, fine-boned, with filmy eyes.

"You can ride with me."

"Who are you?" Ganbaatar repeats.

"A friend of your father's."

"My father doesn't have many friends. And I know all of them."

The man shakes his head. "We don't have time. I'll explain later."

"You know where my father is?"

He nods impatiently. "Yes. Now hop on the camel—"

Ganbaatar has no choice but to trust this man. "I'll take my stallion."

"It would be easier—"

He is already mounting. The stallion jostles under his weight and sighs appreciatively.

"Now," Ganbaatar says, careful not to approach the camel too closely. "Show me where my father is. And if you're lying or a thief—" He reaches into his boot, retrieving the dagger his father gave him. "I swear, I'll cut your throat."

The man doesn't flinch. "No need to be hasty."

"I don't trust many people."

They ride several feet apart, but the camel keeps trying to steer the man towards Ganbaatar and his stallion.

"I can see that."

"Father taught me." Ganbaatar's breath is short. The day is mild, but the wind is cold and makes his throat ache.

"Good man."

"You do know him, then."

"I said I did."

They continue along a rocky, flat stretch; sparse, frail grass grows like a receding hairline. The sky is violently blue, as if pressed from wild blueberries, and the sun hides beneath a heavy blanket of voluminous, gray clouds. The air smells of dust, but odor wafts in the breeze and when Ganbaatar glances down he sees the source—what was once a small pond, nearly evaporated, with rotting fish skin peeling from spiky bones and fish eyes yellow and lifeless, staring at something no one else can see.

"Just a little further," the man says.

Ganbaatar lifts his head into the wind, longing for the clouds to release the desperately needed rain. Knowing they will not.

"And my father will be there?"

"Yes."

They reach a small camp of makeshift tents as the first roll of thunder sounds. The ground trembles in excitement, and Ganbaatar dismounts quickly, gazing up at the darkening skies.

"*Xeex*," the man says in a reverent whisper. "Looks like it'll rain after all."

"Wouldn't count on it," Ganbaatar murmurs.

"Your father is here."

A young woman, slight, with a pale complexion, approaches them. She has high cheekbones and is distinctly Chinese. Yet she greets them in Mongolian.

All his life, Ganbaatar has been told that Chinese people want to erase Mongolian culture. Is she an exception, or is this another lie he's been told by his father?

He does a double take. Not only is this female speaking in Mongolian, but she's the most stunning woman he's ever seen, with shapely hips, silky hair, and long eyelashes. Her full lips are complemented by an impish smile and a slightly crooked nose. Unlike Bolormaa, her gaze is unabashed, as if she's challenging him to say something. As if she's ready to argue against his assumptions about her. As if this land belongs to her as much as it belongs to him.

"Of course," the man says. "Where is your father?"

"Nearby. He's just returning now." She frowns at Ganbaatar. "But who is—"

"He's the son of the man who helped us."

Her smirk deepens, though her words are polite. "I am pleased to meet you. We all are."

"And you are?" Ganbaatar asks, forgetting his manners.

"Aisin." She arches her eyebrow.

So she really is Chinese.

They are not welcome around here, the Chinese. His

father has taught him from birth that they are all the same. "Cheap men," his father always said. "All they care about is making a profit. Never do business with a Chinese man—I don't care who he is or what he looks like."

When he asked how every Chinese man could be the same, his father shook his head. "Trust me, they are. They want to control how Mongolians live. They think they're better than us, know better than us." Just the week before, they'd heard rumors about a herding collective confiscated by a group of Chinese men. Mongolia had gained its independence nearly four years ago, but the Chinese were slow to respect this. And, if his father was right, perhaps they never would.

"My father helped you?" he asks.

"He helped my father," she says, crossing her arms. "Half his herd was dying."

Ganbaatar waits.

"He showed us good grazing grounds and allowed us to share them."

He holds his tongue. There isn't enough to share. Already, they are sharing. How will their herd survive now? He's supposed to hate her—she's supposed to be the enemy. Isn't she taking up their grazing grounds? Isn't she who his father has always warned him about?

But he can't.

"Where is my father?" he asks finally. Better to get away from her, stop the incessant fluttering in his stomach. Forget about her stubborn gaze, her confidence.

"Over in the first *ger*."

Ganbaatar has nearly forgotten the man, who has dismounted his camel. He hands the lead to Aisin. "Take care of him, will you?"

"Of course, Uncle."

               Erin Jamieson

As they reach the first tent, Ganbaatar cannot help but ask, "That's your niece?"

"Yes."

"But you're Mongolian and she's—"

"Here's your father," he interrupts, pointing.

Sure enough, Ganbaatar's father appears from the tent, looking drained and pale but otherwise well. He blinks when he sees his son. "What are you doing here?"

"That is my question for you."

The creases around his father's eyes soften. "I forgot to tell you. I was needed here today."

"I don't understand."

"Good to see you," the man says behind them. "I wanted to thank you personally."

"You already have, and then some, Baterdene."

"Still. You saved my brother's herd."

"Not all."

"Yes, but many wouldn't help, considering."

"It was nothing," he says quickly. "I assume you're responsible for my son's presence?"

"Ah. Surely, he would have worried about you?"

"Yes. I suppose." His father's tone is stiff, oddly guarded. He turns to Ganbaatar. "We should head back. Have you fed the horses?"

"Of course."

"Good. The goats?"

Ganbaatar hesitates. "Yes."

"You forgot," his father says. He sighs, rubbing his temple. "They aren't strong, son. We can't afford to lose even one. You should know that."

"Do come back," Aisin's uncle says. "My invitation still stands."

Ganbaatar glances at Aisin. She's still smirking, like he's part of a joke. And yet. It doesn't seem like she's making fun but rather, challenging him. Like she knows the conflicting thoughts he's fighting. Like she expected him to make assumptions about her.

No one has ever challenged him that way. He's used to being told what to think. With few words and a glance, Aisin is making Ganbaatar unnerved, but in a way that is…exciting? Overwhelming? Exhilarating?

"*Bayarlalaa*," Aisin's uncle calls.

"*Zuuger zugeer.* You're welcome."

They mount and leave, riding toward the afternoon sun with Ganbaatar's father leading the way.

Against his wishes, Ganbaatar turns his head in time to see Aisin retreating, her silky hair billowing in the wind. Something tugs at him. She seems so free. She rides like she is one with the horse. Her back is straight, her every move certain.

She's someone, he thinks, who never lets her emotions or dreams overpower her. Someone who knows what she wants.

Aisin. Her name lingers on his lips, and it's suddenly impossible to think that he could marry someone like Bolormaa, impossible to forget someone like Aisin exists in the same world he inhabits.

Forbidden as it is.

As his horse strides smoothly across the barren land, he waits for her to turn around and look back at him, to show him the connection he feels. But she never does.

     Erin Jamieson

FIVE

BOLORMAA'S FATHER LIES on his back like an over-turned tortoise, his skin mottled and bruised purple. Across his jawline, there is an angry eruption that will become a scar. Tiny rocks are embedded in the skin, and yellow pus seeps out. He is still unconscious, as he has been for the past three hours. His hands are clammy to the touch. Bolormaa stands back, watching her mother bring things he is not awake to care about: warm tea with lemon, biscuits hard as the earth, watery porridge with clotted cream.

"He'll wake soon," she mutters repeatedly. "Bolormaa, please stay with him."

"Where are you going?"

"I have to fix dinner for Batbayar."

"Can't he make something himself?"

"I don't trust him with a hot pot."

Bolormaa presses her lips together. She wants to be any-where but here, staring at her lifeless father, mind racing as she wonders if he will wake.

Altan has taken over the duty of tending the horses and other things she might be doing. She wants to escape this hot tent and its humidity, the sickly stench of her father's wounded jaw. Her mother had attempted to clean it when they found him, fallen beside his horse, hand clutching his chest. They believed him dead; her mother shook him, calling his name over and over.

Only Altan had been calm and sensible enough to check for a pulse.

But their father hasn't woken up, and now, hours later, the infection is spreading. Bolormaa watches as her mother slips into the next room and starts chopping turnips. How can she do something mundane now? Bolormaa's hands clench into fists at her sides. Why must she stay here and take this burden? Even if her father does wake, what can she do for him?

When she opens her eyes, the sun has faded into evening. The *ger* smells strongly of stewed cabbage and over-cooked turnips.

"Bolormaa," her mother calls. "Should I bring your supper?"

"I'm not hungry."

"I'll leave some for you. Does your father need anything?"

"He's still—"

"I'll leave some for him," she murmurs. Dishes clang as the meal is set. Her brothers are quiet. Silence fills the house and along with the stench of pus and dried blood and cabbage, it is too much. Bolormaa bends over and vomits on her father's feet.

There is a soft moan, and she jolts up.

"Father! Mother, come quickly!"

"What is it?" She appears instantly, cheeks flushed from cooking, a spatula in one hand.

"Father, he—"

There is another groan, and Bolormaa's mother pushes

     Erin Jamieson

past her. "*Khairt?*" She bends over, blocking his face from view. "How do you feel?"

Another soft moan.

"What was that? Don't talk if it's too painful."

Altan rushes in, the two brothers on his heels, all trying to catch a glimpse of their father. "He's awake?"

"Father?" Batbayar whines.

Their mother smooths the sheets covering him. "Hush. Give him a little space."

"What can I get you?" Altan asks.

"Horse," their father mutters.

"Horse?"

"What happened to my horse? My chest…tight…fell off…"

"Your horse is fine."

"Did you feed it?"

"Altan did," their mother answers.

"Water?"

"Yes, now we need to take care of—"

He throws the sheets aside and sits up. His eyes are beady and wide, his hair as disheveled as his soiled clothes. "Is Bolormaa here?"

Their mother blinks. "She's right here."

"Can I see her?"

"Why don't we get you something to drink—"

"I want to see her."

She glances worriedly over her shoulder. "Bolormaa, your father would like a word with you."

Bolormaa walks slowly to the bed, her nostrils filling with the pus, the blood, and the perspiration again. She is careful not to look her father in the eyes but lets her gaze fall instead on the hand-woven rugs under her feet.

"I have news," her father says.

She lifts her head. "News?"

"Yes." He nods at her brothers. "Leave us."

Her brothers file out. Batbayar asks if their father wants to play cards, but their mother hushes him, saying she has fresh bread in the next room.

Once they are alone, the room teems with humidity. There's the lingering scent of smoky *suutei tsai* tea in a pot next to her father.

"Come closer," he says.

Bolormaa is near enough to count the sunspots on his nose, and the creases and folds of his leathery skin. He is old, she realizes. He is old. Once, she believed her father would live forever. Or maybe she simply hadn't thought about it. But now he seems as old as the earth itself.

He grabs her hand and squeezes it tightly. His skin is papery and thin, and Bolormaa wishes he would let go.

"The other day, I saw Ganbaatar again."

Ganbaatar. The name is familiar, but Bolormaa has buried it, like a spice hidden in a dish of lamb.

"He is coming over again. Soon."

"Oh," she exhales. Ganbaatar. The man her father wants her to marry. "About that, father, the other night when he—"

"He's a striking young man, isn't he? Didn't I tell you he was?" He coughs, and his face reddens.

Bolormaa hands him a handkerchief. "Are you feeling any better?"

He grimaces. "My chest is heavy. No, don't get your mother. She'll fret."

"She has a right. We're all worried about you."

"You never answered me."

Of course. Bolormaa can't admit what she feels—but she

Erin Jamieson

can't fully deny it, either. As much as she's tried, she can't get Ganbaatar off her mind. The way his warm, brown eyes crinkle when he smiles. How patient and kind he is with her younger brother. The lazy way he stretches and the dreamy, soft look in his eyes when he's not trying too hard to be polite.

But.

She can't let herself feel these things, not when he hasn't shown any indication that he feels the same way. She doesn't want to make a fool of herself all over again.

"He seems nice enough," she says finally.

"You don't wish to see him?"

She looks away. "He doesn't like me, Father." Her words come out softer, more broken than she planned. So much for not making a fool of herself.

"Nonsense. Why wouldn't he like you?"

"He didn't look at me once!" she says, and the words come out with surprising force. Even her father seems taken aback.

"He was being polite!"

Bolormaa falls silent. Her father's face is flushed, his cheeks plump and pasty.

"You'll see," he says, "when he comes over." He's calmer now, but he's looking at Bolormaa like he doesn't recognize his own daughter.

Then his words register.

"He's…coming back? When?"

"Soon, I thought—" He coughs and swipes the back of his hand across his mouth. "Curse this cough."

"Not before you're well?" Bolormaa asks. Guilt bubbles in her stomach. Certainly, she is worried about her father, but she's also using his injury as an excuse.

She wants to see Ganbaatar, at the same time she never wishes to see him again.

But never seeing him again sounds worse than making a fool of herself. Bolormaa's thoughts and emotions are jumbled, more than they've ever been.

Her father laughs, and a bubble of spit dances on his blistered lips. "It may be a long time until I'm well, Bolormaa."

"Father, you'll be well before you know it."

"Whether I am or not doesn't matter. Promise me you'll give him another chance."

The pressure of his hand on hers is too hard, almost painful. Bolormaa can feel her resistance ebbing, for a chance to see Ganbaatar again. To hear his laugh, to touch his hand again—

No. It won't come to that. She'll see him and forget him. She'll see him, realize that he can never love her, and that will be that.

Bolormaa takes a deep breath, careful this time to keep her voice even. "He can come. But Father, I don't want to marry him."

Her father drops her hand and turns towards the wall. "What do you mean? I looked hard for you."

"I know you did."

"Men from good families are hard to come by."

"I'm sure they are." She lowers her eyes. What she hears instead: *Not just anyone will have you. He might be your only chance.*

And her only chance doesn't seem interested.

"Bolormaa, listen to me. Let me make myself clear. It was difficult to find someone as willing as Ganbaatar."

"What do you mean?"

He tilts his head. "They offered a handsome dowry. A well-bred camel, a sterling, two goats. And grazing lands to share for the season."

     Erin Jamieson

She freezes. So that's what this is about. Not love, or a happy life. Reality not daydreams. Of course.

"We already share," she manages.

He smiles, mistaking her panic for enthusiasm. "He wants to marry you. You needn't worry." He starts coughing again, and her mother rushes in.

"Let's get you something to drink. You shouldn't be sitting up like that! Bolormaa, grab a cup of tea for your father. Altan's calling for a *shaman*."

Her father protests, but all Bolormaa can think about are the words she did not say.

What if I don't want to marry him?

What if he can't love me?

She spills hot tea over her hands and scalds her fingers. She runs cool water over her skin, but the pain does not subside. In a few weeks, it will blister, and finally, scar. And the scar from that afternoon will remain with her, an imprint on her skin, until the day she dies.

SIX

GANBAATAR COMES FOR dinner three weeks later. Following the doctor's advice, Bolormaa's father has remained propped up in bed with pillows supporting his scabby arms and legs. Altan has assumed the responsibility of tending the horses, and although he does more than an adequate job, Bolormaa sees the longing in her father's eyes each time the younger man exits the *ger*.

He gets out of bed only to eat or dress, and, while the doctor assured them his heart needs the rest, Bolormaa's father seems to be lose himself a little more each day. He forgets to shave, and his beard grows long and gray. He wears the same shirt for days before he notices the stench, and he becomes a careless eater, letting vodka dribble down the front of his shirt and stain the sheets. Sometimes he reads and sometimes he writes, his script becoming tinier and cramped. Most of the time, he simply watches the rest of the family as they go about their normal activities.

The only thing that keeps him engaged, it seems, is the topic of Ganbaatar. Frequently, he reminds Bolormaa that the tent must be spotless for her suitor's visit. He tells them things he knows about their anticipated guest: how he will drink vodka straight from a flask but cannot stomach black tea sans honey, how he prefers his rice in broth and his dumplings slightly overcooked.

These are things Bolormaa should know or care about, but neither is the case.

The evening of the dinner, she doesn't help her mother. Instead, she slips outside and lets the cool, misty rain tickle her skin. Heaven has sent this rain, but the heavy clouds refuse to release any more. The ground is damp but still parched, even more after a sample of what it so desperately needs.

She is still outside, walking the perimeter of the *ger*, when she hears the snort of a camel.

"Bolormaa. Good to see you."

Ganbaatar is nearly beside her. Lost in her thoughts, she had not heard his approach. She recalls that he was once an excellent rider, and she peers at the camel, unable to stifle her curiosity. It is everything his horse was not. Old and worn, like an overused piece of fabric, the animal's fur is matted, patchy, and dull. When the camel spits, crooked, yellowed teeth are revealed, and its large eyes flicker at her.

"You came by camel," she says.

He laughs. "Observant."

He's sweaty, his cheeks red from the wind and rain, but he's as attractive as he was before—maybe more, as he looks directly at her. She wonders if he's laughing with or at her. He's much harder to read than her brothers.

He dismounts and hands her the lead. "Hold onto him for a moment, will you?"

Her fingers grip the rope until it digs into her flesh.

"You don't have to hold on so tightly. He's not going any-where." Ganbaatar takes a long drink from a leather-covered flask he pulls from a bag draped over the camel's hump.

"Our camels pull away if we don't show them who's boss," she says.

He takes the rope back from her and ties it to one of the poles holding up the *ger*.

"You're leaving it here?" she asks in disbelief, without thinking about the propriety of challenging him.

"Yes," he says, frowning.

"My father taught me never to tie an animal to a tent, even for a moment." Her words rush out, and she feels foolish at the same time she knows she's right. "Your father is a smart man," Ganbaatar says with an air of solemnity that seems sincere. He takes one more drink and twists his flask shut. "Show me where you'd like him."

At that moment, Altran walks out of the *ger*, and the smell of frying oil follows him. He smiles stiffly at Ganbaatar. "Didn't know you were here already."

Ganbaatar nods. "Bolormaa was helping me settle my camel."

"Is that so?" He looks at his sister. "Why don't you go in, Bolormaa? I'll help."

She looks back and forth between them as the rain coats both men in a slick, watery layer. As Altan leads the way, Ganbaatar glances back twice.

Bolormaa stifles a grin.

Ganbaatar may be handsome, but it feels good to see him challenged a little.

And… he looked back at her. Twice. He seems to have noticed her this time.

As hard as they've all been working throughout her father's convalescence, the remnants of his illness are everywhere for Ganbaatar to observe—the soiled linens and the state of his clothes, the floors no one has had the heart to sweep. There is a simple arrangement of *chartsargaans*, the last of the season, but their perfume cannot mask the odor of grease and sweat.

No one eats much, except for Ganbaatar. He manages two hearty helpings of salted milk stew with *banash* and two *boortsogs*, the delicate, lightly sweetened cookies made only for special company. As he drains his cup of milk tea, Bolormaa tries to hide her disgust, but her face burns. Not that he would notice. She wonders about the good manners and upbringing of someone who would feast during a family's time of trouble.

And then Ganbaatar does something unforgivable.

"I'm sorry to hear about your father," he says as Bolormaa's mother clears dishes. "This must be difficult for all of you."

Bolormaa stares at him, and Altan nearly knocks over his cup of tea. Even Batbayar stops chattering abruptly. Their father is a mere two feet away and able to hear every word.

Evidently, this doesn't concern Ganbaatar.

"When my mother fell ill, everything stopped for us. Father checked on her more frequently than he fed the animals. We hoped she'd improve."

The air is thick enough to choke on.

"More tea?" Bolormaa's mother offers.

"No thank you. I'm already quite flooded."

"If you change your mind, there's plenty left. Food, too."

"I appreciate your generosity. I know how much work must have gone into this dinner."

"Do you know?" The words rush from Bolormaa's mouth.

Silence fills the room, and heads turn toward her.

She exhales. "I didn't mean—"

But she did, and everyone knows it. Bolormaa's mother, ever the peacemaker, offers more cookies to Ganbaatar, and, when he refuses, to everyone else. She continues clearing dishes, and Altan jumps in to help. The other brothers slink away, leaving Ganbaatar and Bolormaa alone with the abandoned leftover meat and cookies.

Her father's snores punctate the silence. Good. Maybe he slept through everything, though she knows he could not have.

"I can help," Ganbaatar says.

"No need. Mother is almost finished now."

"About what I said—"

"I should go help her."

He tries to catch her eyes. "I didn't mean for it to sound—"

"After all, it's a lot of dishes. And Altan needs to finish up outside. Don't think the animals—"

"Bolormaa."

He says her name with such tenderness that she stops and falls silent. Unable to help herself, she looks into his soft, brown eyes.

He clears his throat. "I know what I said upset you. Perhaps it upset everyone."

"Don't worry." She looks away.

"That's the thing," he says, taking a step closer. "I can't not worry."

"Why not?"

One step closer. He is near enough to count the small sunspots on his nose, to smell the wind in his hair and notice the dash of green in his left eye. Bolormaa has never been this close to anyone in her life, except for occasional hugs from her mother.

"I never meant to upset you."

"Who says you upset me?" she whispers.

"Will you come with me? I want to show you something."

She blinks. "'What?"

                    Erin Jamieson

"It'll be quick. I promise."

Outside, the ground is still blanketed in sleet, the cold nearly unbearable. Night has fallen and a mere foot from the *ger*, Bolormaa and Ganbaatar are swallowed in darkness. She can hear the bleating of sheep, and her chest aches from the cold and from her heart, which beats loudly, strongly. She realizes they are utterly alone.

"We should go back inside," she says. "It's too dark."

"Just a minute."

She balls her hands into fists. "If you wanted to show me something—"

"This," he says. "This is what I wanted to show you."

"I can't see anything."

"Yes," he says, "I know." He takes her hand and squeezes it. She freezes, but he doesn't let go. It's a firm, deliberate touch, and it feels natural, as though she's known him much longer. He speaks to her as he's never spoken before, with a soft, almost tender voice. He tells her that he's always done what his father asks, but now he's realized his father is wrong about many things. Bolormaa squeezes his hand back, urging him to continue.

"I've always—well, it's silly."

"What?" she whispers. He's close enough that she spots a faint scar or birthmark on the side of his nose.

"I always had dreams, dreams that I could do something besides what my father does."

"Like what?"

"I'm not sure," he admits. "Maybe explore life somewhere else."

"Like a city?" Bolormaa doesn't want to ruin the moment. She tries to keep the fear—but also excitement—from her voice.

"I don't know." He locks eyes with her. "Haven't you ever had dreams of a bigger life?"

Her heartbeat is in her throat. "Yes."

He leans forward, his lips inches from hers.

Footsteps.

Ganbaatar pulls away, looking at Bolormaa with wide eyes as her father approaches.

The older man stands before them, his skin ashy in the scant moonlight. "Night walk?"

"To make sure your animals were tended to, sir. The cold will hit hard tonight."

Bolormaa peers at Ganbaatar in amazement. He lies so easily! It both fascinates and alarms her.

Her father appears amused. "And were they?"

"*Tiim*. Yes, sir."

"Tell me, Ganbaatar, are your animals well?"

He appears taken aback. "Yes, I believe so."

"Altan says he hasn't seen your father lately."

"My father has been involved with…other affairs."

Bolormaa's father tilts his head. "Affairs more important than tending his livestock?"

Ganbaatar smiles stiffly. "Yes, I'm afraid so."

"Father, we should go inside." She worries about his strength and whether he should be out in the frigid air.

Nothing is more important than tending to one's herd. In the Gobi, you are nothing without your camels, sheep, and horses. This is their way of life. A fool knows this.

"Do you require help with your herd?" her father asks.

This, from a man who can barely muster the strength to lift himself from bed every day to relieve himself.

"Thank you, but we are managing." He doesn't offer anything more, and Bolormaa's father nods slowly.

     Erin Jamieson

"If you say so."

"I'm sorry about your poor health, sir."

"Ah. *Bi uvchtei baina.* Sick one day, healthy the next. Such is life for someone my age."

"You aren't old, Father," Bolormaa protests.

He smiles. "See there, Ganbaatar. She'll make a faithful wife. Loyal to the end, even if it's not true."

"So I see, sir."

She glances at Ganbaatar, trying to catch a glimpse of the moment they just shared—it seemed he was about to kiss her, or did she imagine that? Now, his words are polite, distant.

"You'd better head home if a storm is coming, as you say it is." Bolormaa's father turns back towards the *ger.*

"Very true, sir. Hopefully, the next time we meet, you'll be back to tending your own herd. He glances sideways at Bolormaa, and his face is unreadable. "Goodnight, Bolormaa. It was wonderful to see you."

Was it? Is his heart pounding as hers is? Does he speak to others about his dreams and his family?

"Be careful," she says, and when he looks up, she adds, "The storm."

He mounts his camel and gives the command to start the journey back.

Back inside, Bolormaa stands close to the fire, but her bones still ache from the cold.

"He'll be fine," her father says. "He's accustomed to the cold and the dark."

"He shouldn't have left so late."

"No," he agrees. "Perhaps he lost track of time." He stares long and hard at his daughter.

She can't shake the feeling that he knows what happened between her and Ganbaatar. Or—almost happened.

"I don't think you should marry him," he says.

Her head jerks up. "What?"

"I don't want you to marry him. I'll tell his father when I'm well enough."

Bolormaa's stomach drops. Isn't this what she wanted? To not have to marry him, to find another path for herself? That was before tonight. Before he took her hand, told her his dreams, almost kissed her—

She shakes her head. "I don't understand."

"Do you trust me?"

He asked the same question when he proposed an arranged marriage.

She looks over and sees the resoluteness on his face. She knows it well and knows there's nothing to be done. She nods. But the memory lingers, Ganbaatar's warm hand on hers, his breath on her cheek. The words of a dream larger than this life, a dream that seemed like it might include her.

The feeling, for a few moments in the frigid night, that someone could feel for her, want her.

"I see," her father says, rising from his mat with a significant effort.

She crosses her arms over her chest. "There's nothing to see."

Then he does something he rarely does. He pats her fondly on the shoulder. She feels like one of his horses.

"Those feelings will pass," he says. "We'll find someone else. Someone better."

"Better how?"

Her father shakes his head. "Attraction, romance, those feelings don't make for a long marriage."

Her face flushes to hear him speak of such things, and she busies herself preparing for sleep. Outside, the snow has begun. If it becomes too heavy, they will have to provide more shelter for the animals. But Bolormaa cannot think or feel anything. Lead has settled in her abdomen, and she can only sense its undeniably metallic presence. She knows her father loves her and wants what's best, but she doesn't want to be married to Ganbaatar. But that was before. Before tonight.

Was she making the same mistake all over again? Daydreaming? Shoving aside what is practical?

"Bolormaa?" Back on his mat, her father watches her.

"Yes?"

"Everything will work out. Try to trust your old father."

Bolormaa walks over and kisses his forehead. "You're not old." She hesitates. "Did he say something to upset you?"

Something flickers in her father's eyes. "I don't want him to hurt you."

What did that mean? Tears well in her eyes, and she notices a thin parchment in her father's hands. "What's that?"

"Something I need to keep." He yawns, shoving the parchment under a blanket. "Would you fetch me some broth? I'm afraid my appetite is awakening again."

"Yes, Father."

He gazes at her. "And get some rest. You look exhausted."

Bolormaa wanders outside after her father is snoring faintly, and her mother's sleeping sighs fill the *ger*. Her wool jacket covers thick pants and a printed dress. An alpaca scarf circles her neck like a serpent, covering her cheeks and nose up to her eyes. Her hands are shielded by two layers of gloves. But it is an earth-shattering cold, thirty or forty below. She cannot stay out long; this cold is dangerous.

She thinks about what Ganbaatar said, in the dark, when he held her hand and traced a life greater than what they knew in the Gobi. He seemed to speak with care, with love, with excitement.

These are all the things she won't have because her father thinks the match isn't what is best. Because, maybe, Ganbaatar admitted something to her father that he couldn't say to her.

She should accept her father's decision. Instead, she gazes at the dark expanse of sky and thinks about disappearing. She imagines her bones becoming part of the soil the cattle feed on, her skin dissolving like snowflakes as they hit the ground. She sticks her tongue out, but the snow tastes ashy and hurts her throat because it is so cold.

The snow is fighting the darkness, creating trenches of light. Five minutes pass, then ten, and still she does not go back inside. Her eyelashes are freezing together. Her tears become tiny icicles on her cheeks, burning her skin.

And then her mother grabs her arm, shakes her until her teeth rattle. What was Bolormaa thinking, going out in this cold by herself?

The truth is, she wasn't thinking at all. For a few, blissful moments, she'd been light as air, free as the freshly fallen snow, unaware of the encapsulating darkness. Creating her own light in the void.

And as she often did, she'd been dreaming of a way to escape this life. A new question had formed as well, building like snow on flat ground. Was her father's word on Ganbaatar the final one?

SEVEN

GANBAATAR LEARNS TO hate his father three days after the last time he is invited to dinner with Bolormaa's family.

It is midday, and he and his father have come back to rest from the cold. Their cheeks are raw and threaten to blister despite the layers of scarves they wore. Inside their *ger*, a delicious, meaty smell emanates from the marmot that hangs and rotates slowly on thick rope, waiting to be butchered.

Ganbaatar's mother—although distinctly Mongolian—would have hated the sight. She'd butcher animals immediately to render them unrecognizable from their form in life. She was not sentimental about an animal's life—no one living in the Gobi could be—but she believed the best way to honor an animal was to end its life quickly, both literally and figuratively.

His father preferred to leave game out, roasting in its carcass to produce the strongest flavor. He'd shot the marmot with a single bullet to the forehead, almost perfectly centered between almond-shaped eyes. Then Ganbaatar had made a small incision in the lower abdomen, through which they dug out the organs and inserted stones heated by camel dung. They'd left it to roast all morning, while the animals grazed.

Now, the smell is overpowering and pungent. It whets Ganbaatar's appetite but also makes his stomach churn. The heart and kidneys were cooked long ago, and Ganbaatar's father suggests they eat those first.

"Let the rest cook longer," he says, fondly patting the desiccating hide. "We'll have it for supper. What we don't eat, we should dry."

Ganbaatar splits the heart with his father. It is fleshy and surprisingly sweet. But when his father offers to share the liver, he declines, saying he isn't hungry.

That isn't a lie.

His appetite had waned since his mother's passing, and even more after the day he met Aisin. He hadn't seen her again, although he often found excuses to return to her camp. But each time, he'd see her uncle from a distance and hurry away, not wishing to be discovered and having to explain to his father.

Because his father has made it perfectly clear they are not to communicate with anyone from that community again. Whenever Ganbaatar tries to ask what happened, his father pushes his questions aside and says something vague about finished business.

The truth is, Ganbaatar shouldn't want to see Aisin. Aisin—her stubborn jaw line, the playful smirk, her silky hair and curvy hips. The confident way she rides.

Never mind what his father would say about her being Chinese. Up until a day ago, he was engaged to another woman. A woman he'd shared a moment with—or thought he had—one night. A woman who, somehow, had inspired him to talk about his dreams.

His engagement to Bolormaa had ended more swiftly than it had begun; his father simply informed Ganbaatar he'd

Erin Jamieson

changed his mind. He wouldn't say why, only vague comments about "things that came to light."

Had Bolormaa rejected him? He tries to recall their last encounter, what might have gone wrong. He'd almost kissed her. He shouldn't have. Had he offended her? He thought there was a connection, but had he misread her?

Besides, he couldn't shake Aisin from his mind.

Even if he did feel a connection with Bolormaa, it had occurred once, a single, mystical night in a moment of vulnerability. Bolormaa was calm and quiet, everything Aisin was not. He wasn't afraid of Bolormaa's rejection.

But now, Ganbaatar can't determine how he feels.

A broken engagement, a single moment.

And lingering, forbidden feelings for Aisin, who probably would laugh in his face if he told her.

He looks at his father across the table. "Father, why did you stop going over to the camp?"

He abruptly sets down the marmot kidney. His face is mustached in dried blood. "You should be asking why I helped them in the first place."

Ganbaatar holds his breath.

"Most of them are good people, but the man I helped has a niece—"

"And so?" Ganbaatar blinks.

"Chinese." He pushes the remaining kidney around the plate. "You don't hide something like that. Well, perhaps you do, but not when someone is helping you."

"You stopped letting him share grazing land with you?"

He lifts his head. "What makes you think that?"

"I don't—"

"Course I didn't say he couldn't share." He pauses and takes a swig of camel's milk. "But I didn't tell him I've found a better place. If he can't find a decent grazing area, his herd deserves to perish."

"But you've led him to believe that's all there is. He's new here."

His father shrugs.

"He hasn't always lived as a herder," Ganbaatar says. "Someone told me he grew up in Erdenet, northwest of Ulaanbaatar."

"Yes, I know where Erdenet is. At least four hundred kilometers from the capital."

Far away from the heart of the Gobi, a journey of many weeks. A life so different from the nomadic life Ganbaatar had always known.

"I'm not surprised," his father says. "Seems fairly incompetent."

"You can't fault him for living a different sort of life until now."

The older man raises his eyebrows. "Perhaps not."

"At least he has a well."

"He does, but I'm afraid it's unusable."

"What do you mean?"

"It's old, foolishly placed. The soil is full of heavy metals."

"How do you know this?"

"I've heard rumors," he says grimly. "The water contains arsenic."

Ganbaatar's eyes widen. "You didn't tell him?"

"Too late. He's been using that water. Maybe that's why half his herd is dying."

"Father, you have to tell him."

"I told you. I can't have him grazing with me."

"Not about the grazing lands. About the well."

"It's not my responsibility, Ganbaatar."

     Erin Jamieson

"You're going to allow his people to use that water and die?" He thinks about Aisin, and his chest tightens. How carelessly his father speaks of this!

His father waves a hand. "Don't be dramatic. He'll notice the animals weakening and relocate, whether he discovers it was the well or not. Even a fool from the city would do that. I wouldn't want to offend his pride."

Ganbaatar pushes his plate away loudly. "This has nothing to do with respecting his dignity."

"It's none of your concern."

"You tricked them! You told them the land was good." Ganbaatar's hands ball into a fist. His father's lies could destroy lives.

Her life.

"There are things you don't understand, Ganbaatar. It is already too late for his herd. Besides, he stopped using the well when he found another one closer to the land where his animals graze."

"But he wasn't warned about the other one."

His father's hands are fists on the table. "As I said, it's not my responsibility."

Ganbaatar wipes his face clean. His lips are greasy, and his entire body feels as if it has been submerged in animal fat. He stands up and throws his scarf around his neck, not bothering to button his coat or find his gloves.

"What are you doing?"

"Something you should have done."

"Wait," his father grabs his hood. "You can't go out now. There's a storm coming."

"I'll survive. I need to tell them about the dangerous well."

"They aren't using it—"

"I'm not sure I believe you."

"Ganbaatar—"

But whatever his father's words are lost in the rush of wind as Ganbaatar slips out the front of the *ger*.

When he makes it to Aisin's camp, he searches the area for her. Each *ger* looks the same, and he doesn't see anyone outside the structures. He's shivering so hard his teeth are chattering inside his skull, and his hands are long since numb. His fingertips have a pale, bluish hue. He knows what this means. His feet are likely no better, soaked under the leather because he hadn't bothered to wear socks.

The afternoon sun is dipping in the sky; majestic, orange rays meet misty snowbanks that fold in the wind. He cannot take another step. He must.

He should have ridden a camel. A horse. His throat feels like a knife has been plunged into the flesh inside. His head pounds. The world exists in brilliant flashes: the earthy tone of each *ger* against the pale blankets of snow, the saturated gray blue of the cloudless, forever sky. The wind, tasting of fallen snow and perspiring animals.

He makes it a few feet into the camp before his body becomes heavier and heavier. So heavy he cannot propel himself forward. The shivering stops. He is a limp doll, all flesh, his bones dissolved fine as the snow.

Warmth radiates in his chest although his skin has grown cold as marble. His mind is blank as he collapses beside the well. His head slumps against the stone surface, and he closes his eyes. Snowflakes nip his eyelashes like tender kisses, and he imagines it is his mother, saying the words she did not have time to say on her final days on this earth.

　　　　　Erin Jamieson

Something wet and heavy covers his eyes. Even before he blinks them open, he can feel they are swollen as melons.

"I told Uncle you'd wake."

"Aisin." Slowly, he opens his eyes. He is inside a compact *ger*, a single room of close quarters. There are two cots, the one where he lies and another several feet away. A few pots hang from a wall. Nearby sits a handcrafted chair, the wood splintering like an animal shedding hair. Ganbaatar smells something putridly sweet, almost floral, and his stomach clenches. He glances down at his hands, remembering. They are wrapped tightly in bandages, but he can feel the blisters erupting underneath.

At least he can feel something.

"What were you doing?"

He forces his attention back to Aisin. Near her, it is difficult to concentrate. Her hair is swooped up in a tight bun on top of her head. There are soft creases around her eyes and dark shadows underneath, as if she has not slept well recently. An apron is tied around her waist and underneath, her dress and pants are dotted with flour, snow, or both.

"Out in the cold," she says, "without gloves or socks." She stoops down beside the bed, holding up a blanket. "Thought you knew better than that."

"So did I." He watches her. She seems angry and won't meet his eyes.

"Did you walk all the way over here?"

"Yes."

She shakes her head. "If I hadn't gone to the well for water—"

He stares at the teacup in her hand. "Is that from the well?"

"Yes, of course—"

"Don't drink it," he blurts.

"Why?"

"Trust me. Please."

"You're not making any sense. You're tired."

He slaps the cup out of her hands, sending it to the ground where it shatters into a hundred shards.

She shrieks.

He rises and begins to collect the shattered glass. His body aches but he can only focus on her. They are inches apart, her hair close enough to tickle his face. He counts five freckles on the nape of her neck and sees the exact place where she parts her hair.

They bump heads as they reach for the same shard at the same time. His hand brushes hers.

"Sorry," she murmurs.

"No," he says softly, "I am."

He is not thinking at all when he places his bandage-covered fingers on hers. Her hand is so small under his. Aisin's fingers are delicate and slender, her skin several shades paler than Bolormaa's.

When he thinks of Bolormaa, it is like thinking of a sister. But now, when his fingers are knotted with Aisin's, he feels as if their hands fit perfectly.

She meets his eyes with hers.

"The well," he says, moving his blistered lips as little as possible. His hand has begun to throb, but he doesn't want to let go.

"The well?"

"That's why I came. It's poisoned, old arsenic."

Her mouth opens wide. "That can't be. We've been using that water."

"For your livestock," he says sadly. "And a number of your animals have grown sick or perished."

"How did you—"

And then Ganbaatar makes one of the biggest mistakes in his life.

"My father," he says. The words drip from his lips like warm honey but sting.

Her hand flutters away from his and curls into a tiny fist. Her expression remains placid.

"You're not surprised?" he asks.

"About the well, yes. Not about your father."

Questions flood his mind What did she see in his father that Ganbaatar couldn't? Did his father poison the well? Is he capable of that?

"I want to help you," he says. "Whatever I can do. If that means coming up here for a while, giving you some of my animals or—"

She looks at him with innocent confusion. "Why?"

"Because I—"

At that moment, two shadowy figures enter the *ger*—his father and Bolormaa's. It makes no sense. He blinks, but the two men still stand next to each other, waiting.

"Ganbaatar, you fool," his father says. "You could have died."

"You have to be careful these days," Bolormaa's father adds in a raspy voice. He has more color in his cheeks than the last time Ganbaatar saw him, although his spine appears stooped under the weight of his fur coat and muffler. He sways like a drunkard, and Ganbaatar's father places a hand to steady him.

"How did you know I was here?"

Ganbaatar's father avoids his gaze. "I saw your canteen near the edge of camp."

He's lying.

"His hands have been wrapped," Bolormaa's father mutters.

"Yes. I did what I could," Aisin says, speaking for the first time. Her voice is forceful yet cool.

"Can you feel your fingers?" Ganbaatar's father asks, ignoring her.

Ganbaatar flexes his pinky and winces. "Yes."

"Was any other skin affected?" Bolormaa's father asks.

"His lips," Aisin says.

For the first time, the two men stare at her.

"His lips," she repeats. "But I've seen worse. I think they'll be fine."

Bolormaa's father nods. Ganbaatar's father takes a step towards his son. "But your hands—" He reaches over and starts unraveling the bandages. The material rubs against the skin, and Ganbaatar closes his eyes, biting his tongue so he will not cry out.

"Sir," Aisin says, "I think it should stay—"

"We have to see what we're dealing with."

The freezing air tickles, then sharply pounces on his hands. Ganbaatar tells himself not to look. He longs to be alone with Aisin, longs to nestle his head against hers.

"Oh my," Bolormaa's father says.

Ganbaatar's father says nothing, but his dropped jaw says everything.

Then Ganbaatar does it. He looks down.

Instantly, he feels a wave of nausea. It cannot be his hand; it cannot be a hand at all. The flesh is mottled a deep, purplish black. His fingers are swollen into pockets of inflamed skin, bubbles like the yeast rising in carelessly kneaded dough. A putridly sweet stench fills his nostrils.

    Erin Jamieson

"His hands," Ganbaatar's father says finally.

"Yes," Bolormaa's father echoes. If he appeared weak before, he is paler now, his face bloodless as the haunted night moon, eyes drained and vacant. He is sweating profusely.

Aisin shakes her head. "It isn't black."

"I should have come sooner," Ganbaatar's father says. His eyes lock with his son's.

A Mongolian man is nothing without his hands. And by the tragic expression crossing his hard eyes, Ganbaatar's father is making it clear that Ganbaatar has no future.

EIGHT

AISIN PICKS UP the discarded dressing and places it in a tidy pile. Stooping on the ground, she squirts something into the palm of her hand, then returns to Ganbaatar's side. "May I?"

The stench of the ointment competes with the odor of decaying flesh. He doesn't care what it is or what it will do—if anything at all. He needs something. Anything.

He has lost capacity for thought or reason. All he knows is Aisin's presence, the softness in her eyes, the furrow of concentration between her dark eyebrows. Even under her soiled clothing, with her perspiring neck and proud shoulders, she stuns him into silence.

She is here. For him. She is doing this, for him, when all his father can do is stare.

"Yes, go ahead."

At first, the ointment is cool and seems heaven-sent. But after a moment, it burns so intensely he begs her to put it away. She ignores him, rubbing it on his fingers, between his fingers, on his palm and the back of his hands.

He is nearly howling when at last she says, "Finished."

"What the devil are you're doing?" Ganbaatar's father

demands. His throat is inflating and deflating like the dying embers of a fire.

"Saving your son's hand."

"What is that stuff?" Bolormaa's father asks.

"Ointment. Herbal remedy. My grandmother—"

"If it's something from your family, we don't need it. Take it off. We didn't ask you to intervene."

"I found your son," Aisin snaps. "I brought him in. And this ointment could be the difference between him losing his hands and keeping them."

"What are you, mad?"

"Mad enough to believe there's a God," Aisin says, smiling stiffly. "Mad enough to not give up before I've tried everything."

The two men fall silent. Heat crawls into Ganbaatar's cheeks. For a minute he forgets about his hands.

Aisin moves about, speaking over her shoulder. "The dressing needs to be changed often, but the skin also needs to be exposed."

"And you know all of this—"

"What would you like to do, considering?"

Ganbaatar knows if he loses his fingers, his entire future is in question. He will not be able to lead the camel or cattle, easily feed and groom the horses, or set up a ger. He will be a burden. He can feel his father pulling away, even as he stands nearby. Pity radiates from Bolormaa's father who will not meet his eyes.

So much can change in one afternoon.

"Let me change the dressing," Aisin says. Locks of silk hair form a curtain over her eyes, and her skin is pale, almost anemic in the fading, afternoon light. He sees her glance longingly at a set of pillows not far from her feet.

"When was the last time you slept?" he asks quietly.

"Sorry?"

"I said, have you slept lately?'

"We're taking him home," Ganbaatar's father adds.

"But the storm is not over! Given his condition, he really should—"

A tall, bulky figure enters the *ger*. Aisin's uncle. His toffee-colored eyes are hardened and dark with intensity, and his fat lips protrude in mistrust. He glances back and forth between them until his eyes settle on Aisin.

"Listen to them," he says. "You've done all you can. More, perhaps. Let them leave."

"Do you really think that's wise?"

He nods.

Ganbaatar thinks she will protest, but the fight leaves her. She goes as limp as a dehydrated plant under the gaze of the sun.

"All right. But at least take bandages and here—" She hands Ganbaatar a full container of ointment. "Apply this twice a day."

"I can't take all of this—"

"Aisin. Don't be a fool. That is expensive," her uncle admonishes.

"Apply it liberally," she says, "but gently. You don't want to irritate the skin—"

"We don't need your fake remedies," Ganbaatar's father mutters. "Come along, son. I have a camel waiting."

"Please. Take it."

Ganbaatar stares at the ointment, then back at her. The air is so thick, it's like he's being buried alive.

"I'm sorry. I can't."

"You must—"

"Aisin, let him be." Her uncle steps toward her.

"I'm going outside to prepare," Ganbaatar's father announces. He does not glance at Aisin or her uncle as he slips out.

Bolormaa's father follows, his face as pale and pasty as dough.

Aisin's uncle snorts as soon as they leave. "Would've killed them to thank us, I suppose. But no matter—" He reaches for the spilled tea kettle. "What happened to the tea?"

Aisin glances at Ganbaatar. "It was bad."

"Then make a new pot. I'm dying of thirst."

"Yes, Uncle."

He circles the cramped quarters, muttering under his breath an impressively large vocabulary of curse words.

Aisin returns to where Ganbaatar is now sitting up. "Promise me you'll use the ointment?"

"Aisin," he says.

She leans over him, so close he can smell the fragrance of tea and wind in her hair. "Yes?"

"Thank you," he says.

She looks away. "Anyone would have done the same. Besides, you helped me." She gives him a slow grin.

He wishes he could be like her, not caring what others think, joking when faced with adversity. His thoughts are overwhelmed with what his father is thinking, what his father will say outside.

"The tea," her uncle says before stepping outside.

His brain fogs. He tries to think of something clever or funny or at least interesting to say. He can't bear the thought of leaving her side again.

"Do you have any siblings?" he asks. Not clever or funny, but it's what comes out.

"Yes. In the literal sense." She shrugs. "The last time I saw my brother and sisters, I was nine. And then I came here to live with Uncle after our parents were gone. I was the only one who wanted to, the only one who was willing."

He doesn't need to ask where she's from. He doesn't want to press her about her parents' death. Instead, he gazes at her in admiration. "That was brave of you, coming here."

"Not really. You see, Ganbaatar, It's the opposite. I came because I was a coward. I couldn't stand the thought of facing life in a house where shadows had taken the place of my parents. I didn't want to spend any more days setting the table for people who were no longer there or seeing a handmade comb and buying it for my mother, only to realize she could no longer enjoy it."

She presses her lips together. "I did that, you know. Saved up nearly three month's wages to buy her a comb she'd always wanted. Beautiful flowers embellished on the side, painted and crafted by hand. Two weeks after her death, I bought it. I meant to take it back but never had the heart, even though my brothers and sisters needed every bit of money we had."

"What happened to them?" Ganbaatar asks.

"Wrapped it away in tissue paper and—oh." Her eyes glisten. "My brothers and sisters. We had my uncle, but we'd never met him. But we also had an aunt, old as time itself. Kind but strict. She took them in, and they've been well. But my letters have been returned lately."

"Why?"

Aisin laughs. "It's obvious to me. But you'd have to live my life, being who I am, living here. I always knew I might be hated here. But I never considered that I might be hated back home, too."

Ganbaatar reaches with a bandaged hand and brushes

                    Erin Jamieson

hers. Slowly he intertwines their fingers, white bandage against the creamy skin. Although it's painful, it also feels like home.

"I could never hate you," he whispers.

Her eyes narrow and lock on his. "Don't make promises you can't keep. Your father's waiting for you."

He squeezes her fingers and grimaces. "Yes."

"Let me help you up." She is strong for her small frame and steadies him on his feet. Their fingers are still locked together, and Ganbaatar doesn't want to let go.

"Aisin," he whispers against her ear, wanting to tell her something, anything, to keep her hand in his. He pulls away as her uncle totters into the room, smelling heavily of spirits, his lips dripping with vodka. It's the image that stays with him during the long, uncomfortable ride home.

Daylight streams in, fine and misty; the taste of salty sleet is in the air. Ganbaatar raises his head as throbbing travels from his fingertips to his wrist, radiating in his arms and legs.

His father watches him across the room in silence, arms wrapped around his chest. "Bout time. It's nearly noon."

Ganbaatar hesitates, glancing down as waves of nausea pass through him. His hands are unwrapped, and they look like purple, shriveled prunes or figs. There is little sign of flesh at all on his left hand. It is a complete degeneration of what once was skin, blistered and blackened folds of nothing. On his right hand are patches of fleshy pink, flushed as though badly sunburnt but recognizable. The smell is intolerable, worse than the day before.

"I'll send for someone," his father says.

"Won't that be expensive?"

He looks away. "One time. That's all."

His father has called for a *shaman* twice in Ganbaatar's life—once, when he was five and nearly drowned in Lake Ulaan, and, the week before his mother breathed for the last time.

The *shaman* comes, traditionally clothed with a headdress draped over his long, angular neck. Animal skins cover his shoulders so seamlessly they appear to be extensions of his body. He smells of incense and smacks tobacco between his yellowed gums as he is led in.

Ganbaatar's mother was a rare breed, a Manchurian Christian, and once or twice she'd read passages from the Bible. Ganbaatar remembered that main points—Jesus was the son of God who was sent to make up for the fact that everyone was a sinner. Though Ganbaatar had listened politely, he'd never believed a word. The weight of that religion was too heavy and impractical. Truth be told, he'd always much preferred his father's disposition towards *Shamanism*, the favored religion of the Gobi. Finding one's spirit made much more sense. Here in the Gobi, one had to rely on himself, so why not focus on your own spirit rather than some all-powerful being who let dust storms and droughts occur. Ganbaatar believed in his own spirit, rising and falling with the sun.

But Ganbaatar has doubts, now that the *shaman* bends over him, reciting incantations. Is it so simple? Could he enter a trance to ascend his pain and the damage? He closes his eyes and feels nothing. He longs for his mother, for the honey of her words he often tuned out, for her smile he often missed because he was always looking at his father. He sought his father's love, while she had loved him dearly.

The *shaman* asks him to emerge from the trance he never entered. His eyes flutter open as salt is sprinkled over his hands.

"Good," the *shaman* smiles. "Be healed in yourself."

Ganbaatar curls up on one of the mats, letting the heat of the fire crawl over his worn-out body. His father thanks the *shaman*, and the holy man leaves.

"Things will look up soon," his father says.

The next morning, Ganbaatar awakens in worse pain.

His right hand has improved considerably, and sections of damaged skin has begun to shed. But his left hand is worse. The purple is darker, almost pearly black, spreading to his wrist.

All day long, he writhes in a feverish haze, refusing food and water. His lips are dry as the Gobi during a drought, but he barely notices. He plucks at the unraveling threads on the blankets his father gives him, sleeping fitfully, only to be woken by a bird's song outside, or the waxing and waning light of the sun.

It is night or evening when his father shakes him lightly. He must have fallen asleep though he cannot remember doing so; he cannot recall any dreams he might have had.

Bolormaa's father is there, with his pale, pointed face. Ganbaatar turns away, closing his eyes. He longs to be left alone and wants nothing to do with the perspiring man that reminds him of tepid, over-brewed tea leaves.

"Yes, I think so," the man says quietly.

"There's no other way?"

"Afraid not."

Ganbaatar slowly blinks his eyes open to face the two

men. What is Bolormaa's father doing here again? After he broke off the engagement, Ganbaatar had never expected to see him again. Now, if he were stronger, he would have the ardent desire to kick the man out. He has no business being here in their tent, sitting on their mats, drinking from his mother's teacups.

"Ganbaatar?" His father's voice is heavy as *airag*. "I need you to listen."

He struggles to sit up.

"Your right hand is improving."

"Yes," he manages.

"But your left hand."

Ganbaatar licks his lips, knowing he looks like a wounded animal. "I need more ointment. I couldn't find it."

"Couldn't find what?" Bolormaa's father asks.

"Ointment. The girl who saved me gave me ointment."

"I threw it away."

"You what?" He tries to lift his head, but the effort is too great.

"That's foreign rubbish."

Chills erupt on Ganbaatar's arms, breaking through the fever. "I need it. Give it back to me."

"I had to throw it away, son. But listen. The skin is too damaged. It can't be saved."

"What do you mean?"

His father glances away. "The hand."

Ganbaatar stares at him, uncomprehending.

"I have no choice," his father says, his knees buckling. His strong, muscular legs, conditioned from a lifetime in the Gobi, hardened by freezing temperatures and harsh wind. Buckling before his son, like the coward Ganbaatar suddenly sees he is, has always been.

"You can't be serious. I need my hand. How will I—"

Bolormaa's father grunts. "Listen to your father."

"Both of you are crazy—" He thrashes in his blankets, pushes them aside. "I need my ointment. Where is it?"

"Son, please." His father's voice breaks. "I need you to stay calm."

"You aren't going to chop my hand off!"

"I have no choice, son. The infection is spreading. You could die."

The air is choking Ganbaatar. The blankets are too saturated in color, stark shades of blue and orange. He can no longer smell his mother's scent, as if she had never slept with these blankets, had never been there at all. In the distance, the unattended kettle on the stove is whining, a high pitch whistle over the gurgles as the water boils over.

"Father."

"I have no choice. I've sent for a doctor, a real one. He'll be here later today to take care of you."

"What will happen to me?"

He is met with silence. And he knows: there is a good chance he will not only lose his hand. He gazes down at the blackened and rotting lump, the same hand that once held the reins for a racing champion, the same hand that held Aisin's hand. In a few, short hours, it would be gone. He would be gone.

He can taste the ashes of the dying fire. He wonders if his mother knew when she was going to die, whether she noticed everything in great detail as he does now: the stubborn dimple in his father's chin, the scent of wind and animal droppings clinging to nearly everything. He ponders if, when the time came, she looked around their *ger* and longed for something else.

Unbidden, the words of a lullaby come to him, an ancient one he believed he'd forgotten but must have been permanently etched in his memory:

Emzeg tsetseg, untaj yavna. Emzeg tsetseg. Ene ni ch serekh ni tony tsag hugatsaa bish yum. Fragile flower, go to sleep. Fragile flower, it is not yet your time to wake.

The beginning and the end, tied and bound fast together. The sun setting not long after it has risen. A mother's words soothing an ache no child could not possibly understand.

The doctor arrives an hour afterwards, or two days afterwards. Time no longer makes sense or has consequences. Ganbaatar lies listlessly, extending his damaged flesh, a dummy, nothing more, to play with. The doctor asks questions, questions he is hopeless to answer. How long has he noticed the stench? Is he in pain? Can he move his fingers? Does the pain travel up his arm?

The answers tumble from his lips, sometimes yes and sometimes no, always something, always hoping the doctor will leave.

A day or two later, the pain is so unbearable that Ganbaatar can no longer concentrate on producing answers. A knife twists inside the veins of his right arm. When fever licks his forehead and makes the world around him blotchy, he can smell his mother's perfume, the sun in Aisin's hair. He can feel them watching, while also knowing this is impossible.

He is told to close his eyes, which is easy. He lets himself drift into a strange fog, where pain pierces the outer edges but never quite penetrates, where the smells of blood and pus are faint, as if dabbed out. He feels loss without knowing what. He feels weightless as the clouds. He lets himself become

Erin Jamieson

more immersed with the fog of pain, dying but not yet dead. The solace of not having to feel or think so much fills him. He escapes the Gobi in a way his life has never permitted him.

He wakes reluctantly. Someone is calling his name, turning it over and over like a precious gem.

Instantly, he regrets opening his eyes. A sharp pain runs up his spine, so intense it nearly blinds him. The left hand is better than he remembers, most of the flesh raw as sunburn but otherwise intact, blisters the size of his thumbnail painful but shrinking.

And at the end of his right arm is what remains.

A stump, swaddled in bandages, where his hand once had been, wrapped by the gentle hands of Aisin.

NINE

Spring 1919

ON HER WEDDING day, Bolormaa wakes at half-past five, when the summer skies are still dark but will fade into a milky pink as the sun rises. For now she is helped by her mother, as they splash her face with cool water. An hour later, she takes a bath near the tributary.

The water is frigid, but Bolormaa manages not to cry out as her mother lathers her with goat's milk soap, expensive and perfumed, purchased on her trip to Ulaanbaatar two months before. She washes Bolormaa's hair with similar precision, then combs it gently, strand by strand, until it hangs sleek, shiny, and smooth over her shoulders.

By the time the bath is finished, the sun has fully risen, and the day has begun. It is the first time in Bolormaa's memory that her father does not start the day looking for grazing land; instead, he's inside the *ger*, sweeping, scrubbing their finest dishes, and shaking the dust from mats.

Bolormaa is allowed ten minutes to herself, and she

immediately drifts to the corner where she has slept for the past twenty years of her life. It is quiet and cool, and she lies down, resting her head on a pillow tattered from years of abuse by her brother, Batbayar. He is out gathering dung, enough for the grand bonfire they will have after the reception.

A few years earlier, Altan may have completed this task, but ever since he and Cholbasen left to marry, more and more duties have fallen on Batbayar. Bolormaa has watched him spring almost overnight from an impish boy to a young man, still unfocused but more deliberate, his face speckled with the shadow of his first beard.

"Bolormaa?" Her mother pokes her head in, her face care-worn and fine wrinkles under her eyes. After Bolormaa's father suffered a second stroke that rendered him unable to perform heavy labor, they took on many chores, helping Altan—and, after he left—Batbayar carry supplies and tend the animals, in addition to preserving the meat and making *airag* and cheese curds.

All of this has aged her mother considerably. With her wrinkled hands and feet and stooped back, it is no longer possible to tell how beautiful she once was. But there is pride in her gaze as she takes in her daughter. Her neck is adorned with the fine pearls Bolormaa's betrothed purchased as part of his dowry, a reward for years of labor.

"It's time to get ready," she says.

"I just want a few more minutes."

She squeezes Bolormaa's hand. "Don't we all?"

Dressing takes nearly an hour and a half. Bolormaa's hair is pinned haphazardly on top of her head so it will not be in the way while her mother buttons the simple undergarments. Next, her feet and shoulders are heavily perfumed, her slender wrists weighed down with her great-grandmother's bracelets of turquoise and brown beads. They have been passed from generation to generation.

One day, she is expected to bestow these bracelets on her own daughter. Her neck is left unfashionably bare; they haven't had the time or money to purchase a necklace. Besides, no one will be looking at her neck, at least this is what her mother insists.

The beautiful silk *deel* clings to her sculpted soldiers; the pale, gold hue highlights her sun-kissed skin. It is intricate in detail, with a pattern of white blossom vines gracing the capped long sleeves and hem. The train is short and simple, and the neckline is a soft v that drapes slightly, as if touched by the wind. Her mother buttons the dress from the back, then helps her with the soft, gold slippers. They are the same slippers her mother donned on her own wedding day. They are slightly small for Bolormaa's feet but comforting. She likes the thought of walking to meet her intended in the same shoes her mother wore—as if by doing so, they will remain close.

"Is the dress too tight?"

Bolormaa shakes her head. Even if it was, she wouldn't say so.

"Your hair!" Her mother's fingers flutter to her head. "I nearly forgot. Hold still. We haven't much time left!"

Bolormaa becomes a doll, letting herself be arranged by her mother—which, she supposes, is fitting. Her hair is curled in tiny, elaborate tendrils and woven into a bun that rests at the nape of her neck. She allows her skin to be adorned with creamy makeup and splotches of crimson for her cheeks. Her lips are painted in a nearly maroon hue, eyelashes with heavy black. Her mother hands her a mirror.

"Do you like it?"

For a moment, Bolormaa only stares. She has transformed

　　　　　Erin Jamieson

into someone she does not recognize, a young woman with high cheekbones and a small but durable frame, almost beautiful, certainly. Only her eyes betray her—watery and uncertain, flickering doubt under the mask of cosmetics.

"It looks beautiful," she murmurs.

Her mother smiles. "No," she says gently, "You look beautiful."

They turn their heads at the patter of footsteps.

"Batbayar must be back," Bolormaa says.

"Hope not. He can't be finished gathering dung already."

Bolormaa smiles. "Knowing him, he decided he was finished."

"That won't do at all! If we run out—"

"I was only joking."

"Well, I wasn't." She pecks Bolormaa's cheek. "Let me go see."

Bolormaa nods, wishing she wouldn't leave. She doesn't want to be alone right now with the thoughts solitude brings. She wants to treasure every moment with her mother, but it is like trying to contain sand in her hands. The moments slip away, minute by minute, and soon there will be nothing left at all.

Her mother returns shortly, face flushed and eyes bright. "Everything is in order. Are the pots and pans ready?"

Bolormaa nods woodenly.

"Where are they?"

She swallows. It is the bride's duty to purchase the dishware that will be used in the new couple's home, but she can't remember where she placed the kettle and stewing pot her father ordered with his hard-earned money.

"It's all right," her mother assures her, patting her shoulder. "I'm sure they're around here somewhere. Just take a deep breath and try to remember."

Bolormaa allows her eyelashes to flutter shut. Unseeing, she is aware of things she has never truly appreciated. The warm, yeasty smell that hangs ever-present. The oven mats her grandmother had made nearly fifteen years ago. The taste of ashy embers from a dying flame, slightly bitter, slightly sweet. The rustle of the wind against the sides of the painstakingly constructed *ger*.

She can only hope her next home will have such things. She has been told her husband-to-be is an excellent craftsman, gifted and sturdy-handed, and the *ger* he built with the help of their fathers is compact but strong.

"I envy you," Bolormaa's father had confided to her one recent afternoon, when he'd been forced, as usual, to retire early due to exhaustion. His words were labored as he lay down, his neck dappled with perspiration. Bolormaa pretended not to notice—for his sake and hers. "You have a new beginning," he had said. "Everything is starting for you."

She'd glanced away, feeling the weight of what had been left unsaid: her father did not have a chance for a new beginning. His attenuated body had left him pliant like a young sapling, always in need of support to stand erect. That support would be his youngest son, Batbayar.

Though it was not against tradition for the youngest son to stay with the family and help aging parents, Bolormaa knew her father never would have consented by choice to such a life for either of them. But each day he grew weaker, and it was harder and harder to keep pace with the young livestock or keep up the renewal needed on the *ger*.

Moving was out of the question. They'd avoided it as much as possible, migrating to a new pasture only when there was nothing left at all. Even then, they'd moved slowly, with everyone helping.

When she was a girl, Bolormaa spent hours outside in the dry cold, daydreaming as she gazed into cloudless skies so vivid blue, she thought it would swallow her whole. She'd scale the fences her father had built, pluck wild berries from bone dry shrubbery, chase jerboa with their beady rodent eyes until they scampered across the rocky plain, tails swinging back and forth so quickly that she'd burst out laughing.

But over time, Bolormaa has become both blind and deaf to such things. The empty years after schooling ended, the first engagement and the second, her father's stroke. Her brothers and parents are growing older and further apart. These things have made her blind to the eagles with their majestic wings, deaf to the laughter of the earth. Now all is buried in this rocky land, no vegetation to be seen for miles, and clouds like splatters of ash in the sky.

It is funny that now, of all times, her father should suggest a new beginning. Peering outside the *ger* and watching the sun climb higher, she can see nothing but the same trials, in different forms, a long life of toil and scarcity headed her way.

"Bolormaa?"

Her mother is waiting for an answer to a question she has not heard.

"Yes?"

Her mother clasps her hand firmly. "It's time."

It takes a lifetime to walk down the aisle formed with white spring blossoms. The day is cool, and Bolormaa's arms are covered with goosebumps when the wind picks up. She is aware of the eyes of family and friends who have gathered, of the heaviness of the bracelets and the way her slippers sink into the earth.

The birds pierce the air with a hopeful song that seems tinged with desperation and regret. The taste of manure and seedling grass lingers, the smell of rain that refuses to release from the same, ashy clouds.

All of this, and she barely sees him until she is at his feet.

Ganbaatar stares at her resolutely, face cleanly shaven, eyes reflecting the grayness of the day. He is dressed impeccably, in a cream-colored suit lined with tiny jewels across the collar. His hair is finely combed, and he smells not of pasture animals, but *airag* and strong cologne.

They exchange traditional vows before a Buddhist monk, who chants ancient clauses that have lost their meaning with time. Bolormaa's lips are stiff as she repeats each command, but Ganbaatar, appearing more confident, recites with ease. The entire time, his eyes are trained on his bride but misted over, as if a fog has rolled in and he can't see her at all.

A soft peck on her forehead. Bolormaa's eyes flutter open and everything is alive again: the clapping of relatives she knows and does not, her finger weighted with the cool metal of a ring, petals descending on her hair, her eyelashes. She takes off her slippers, and he does the same, so they can take their first steps as man and wife together on the rocky earth. They walk past those gathered, past the small but handsome *ger* that is theirs, the one Ganbaatar has been constructing with their fathers for the past several months.

Everyone begins to filter inside for refreshments, but Bolormaa lingers. Ganbaatar has already entered ahead of her. Somewhere a bird is singing, a lovely, soft tune that rattles in her chest. The melody is so full of longing and promise, she feels like a little girl again, swallowed by this day, this sky, this life. With her feet bare, she longs to change out of the gown and run free. She waited for this day for so long. She has loved Ganbaatar from the moment she first laid eyes on him; it took some time for her to realize this.

 Erin Jamieson

And yet. For a moment, watching the skies, she spots a golden eagle, navigating the air, proud wings soaring a straight course. The eagle of her youth she'd once dreamt of following. With wings, she could explore the world and become someone new.

She is a wife now. This is also from a dream, what every mother hopes for a daughter. But for a fraction of a minute, Bolormaa feels consumed with the knowledge that she will never again embrace her parents in full privacy. Never again will she sleep on the mats of her childhood or eat fried dough as she helps her mother cook supper. She will see her parents often, of course. Family means everything to Mongolians. But she will now be a guest in their *ger*.

There will be no more school. The brief dreams she'd had of studying literature at the university in Ulaanbaatar or traveling outside the Gobi are now forgotten. Her future had been securely mapped for her from the day she took her first breath in this world. She'd been foolish to dream otherwise.

Ultimately, it is her mother, as always, who finds her. "Coming in? The celebration can't start without you."

"Yes," she says. Squaring her shoulders, she swallows one, last breath of cool air before joining her old family and her new one in the *ger* that will become her home.

A *ger* made of wood and sheep felt, a white felt cover, a vibrant red door frame with a green mandala. Checkered purple and gold mats, flanked by a pot to boil water, with worn utensils hanging from a wall. The colors are more vibrant than those she grew up with, the space much tighter.

She wonders whether there's enough room for her. Will she wake one day and forget her old home, its colors and smells, the sound of her brothers complaining.

She tries to ignore the ache inside, telling herself this is the way things are meant to be.

The carpet rolled out to welcome the new bride is beautiful, with gorgeous interlacing vines and bird's nests. Bolormaa has never seen anything like it, and she finds herself staring and almost misses what is happening around her.

The *ger* consists of two rooms and in the main one, the new pots and pans already hang, glinting in the early afternoon sun. A small hearth of mare's dung provides a warm, welcoming glow. Everything has been constructed with precision and care, from the felt ceilings to the plain, beige walls.

There are no decorations except for those for the wedding celebration: blushing bouquets in tilted vases, petals lining the floor, incense dancing in smoky swirls. All of this will be gone tomorrow, and the *ger* might be anyone's home. An empty, unlived-in place she will fill with her own mark and character. The thought makes her shiver despite the weight of the voluminous *deel*.

The wedding dinner includes stewed cabbage, roasted figs, dishes of wild rice, crispy marmot with orange glaze, yogurt with lime, and camel meat. And the centerpiece: the head of a young sheep, its upward gazing eyes the same blue as the sky.

Its tongue, of course, has already been cut out and is now tossed to the group of children clustering in a corner to see who will be lucky enough to catch it and have ten years of good luck. Bolormaa smiles when Khulan, one of Ganbaatar's cousins, outdoes her competitors. She is thin and wispy but strong, and her eyes are full of heated determination.

Bolormaa never caught the tongue. Because she never wanted it badly enough. Because, she realizes, she's accepted things her whole life, never fighting for fear she'd fail anyway.

A few of the boys try to snatch the tongue away from

Khulan, but she forms a tight fist and refuses to budge until, disinterested, her adversaries begin to wander towards the food.

"Please, everyone, be seated," Bolormaa's father says.

Normally, a bride sits next to her new mother-in-law. Ganbaatar, as always, guides her by the hand, and she settles between him and his father. After they sit, the others take their places, and the meal begins.

Bolormaa is expected to sample everything although she has no appetite. Everything is wonderfully prepared, but it becomes clear quickly that Ganbaatar and his father do not season or salt their food. What might have been delicious meat and rice is bland and pasty in her mouth, yet she manages a polite bite from each dish.

"Anyone want sheepshead?" Ganbaatar asks, and there is a murmur of affirmation. He smiles and reaches past Bolormaa, brushing her hand without noticing as he brings the platter over.

His face strains as he tries to break the neck. Holding it down with his stump, he tries to manage with his one, good hand. Everyone grows silent. When a new husband breaks a sheep's neck, it is a testament to his strength, his faith in the marriage, and his ability to provide for his future family.

Minutes pass. Ganbaatar sets the sheep's head down, panting slightly, his cheeks flushed. His father stares at his uneaten plate. Across the way, Bolormaa's parents become interested in their steaming rice.

He tries again. And again. But the sheep's neck won't break. After a few moments Ganbaatar produces a laugh void of humor. "Stubborn one."

A light laughter travels the room, but none of the guests will meet his eyes.

This is him at his prime, Bolormaa realizes. Making jokes while others would worry about looking foolish. It almost excites him, the idea of not living up to their expectations.

It was like the night he first took her hand. He told her then that he dreamt of something larger, larger than what others thought he would have.

He takes both sheep's eyes and offers Bolormaa the ears, but she shakes her head.

"Not hungry?"

"My stomach is a little queasy." She is supposed to take the ears, as a new wife, the listener. He is supposed to take the eyes, as he will lead the household. But he doesn't seem upset at her refusal; if anything, something like relief passes over his strained face.

"That's fine. As long as you're comfortable."

It is the first thing he has said to her all day. She nods, wishing she could think of something to say. She's infinitely grateful when her brother, strikingly handsome in a pale ivory dress shirt, leans over the table, his lips stained with orange glaze.

"So," he says, grinning, "Will your son be a horse racer like you once were, Ganbaatar?"

     Erin Jamieson

TEN

BOLORMAA IS NOT entirely sure how she came to be betrothed to Ganbaatar for a second time. She remembers when the possibility appeared again—a blistering, winter day, with snow falling fine as ash, the skies gray and callous.

She'd been busy all morning, feeding the livestock, sweeping floors, and scrubbing mats. In the afternoon, she'd struggled to help her brother with his Tibetan lesson, bribing him with *khuushuur*, fat from a young mutton fried that morning. She'd rewarded him with a single fritter for every correct answer. It wasn't an exaggeration to say that the plate was still plenty full for dinner.

Before they sat for the meal, her father pulled her aside outside the *ger*.

She noticed his wind-burnt cheeks and grave expression. "You've been out."

He chuckled. "Is that a crime?"

"No, but Mother says—"

"Your mother worries too much," he interrupted. "I can take care of myself."

She swallowed. "I didn't mean any offense, Father."

He nodded. "I have some news you might find interesting."

"Good news, I hope."

"Good and bad. You remember Ganbaatar?"

"Of course I do," she said stiffly. "I hope he's well?"

He watched her. "I'm afraid he's not. Nearly froze to death and suffered serious frostbite on both hands."

Bolormaa stilled. Why didn't she know about this? "You should have told me."

The smell of string broth emanated from inside the *ger*. Bolormaa's stomach tumbled uneasily.

Her father shrugged. "I didn't want to worry you."

"But… he…he's going to be all right?"

"He'll live. He's a young, strong man, but he may lose a hand."

Handsome, confident Ganbaatar, with one of his hands removed!

Never able to touch her hand again.

A mere three weeks before, she thought she was falling in love. And then her father informed her she would not be marrying him, without explanation. She hadn't wanted to think about the strong line of Ganbaatar's jaw or the way he'd talked softly into the night, looking at the stars. It had felt as if they were the only two existing in the vast world. She'd tried to bury those feelings.

And now. What was a man without both hands? She'd seen how much the stroke had pained her father, how his shoulders slumped in shame every time one of her brothers performed the hard labor he was meant to do.

When her kind-hearted mother prepared dinner, he toyed with it. He'd lost twenty pounds, shedding his sturdy frame for a sickly one, letting his face go unshaven and his hair grow long. She'd watched her father lose himself day by day, and she could only imagine his shame.

     Erin Jamieson

"I think it would be good to invite him over," he said now. "After everything clears up."

"What?"

"Ganbaatar. His father, too."

"You feel sorry for him." She clears her throat. "Why was the engagement canceled?" When her father starts to turn away, she clasps his shoulder. "Tell me."

"I was mistaken. I saw him one day, with another woman." He paused. "But he and his father were helping her, sharing grazing lands."

She imagined Ganbaatar kissing a faceless woman, probably one more beautiful and braver than her.

"I was wrong," he said. "A foolish mistake. I wanted to protect you. I was wrong."

Bolormaa shakes her head. "Why didn't you tell me?"

"I'd made the mistake already." He bows his head.

"Two mistakes don't make things right."

For a moment, needling doubt flickered through her mind. But… she'd felt how Ganbaatar had touched her. She'd seen how he'd looked at her.

Her father had ended things.

"You really care for him, don't you?"

Bolormaa nodded.

"Then let me make this right."

Bolormaa nodded again, but she worried and doubted. Was there a way to fix all of this?

Within a week, the engagement was back on, but something had changed, and what it was wouldn't be completely clear for some time.

❧

After the guests have eaten until their bellies ache and the dishes are cleared, the true celebration begins. Two musicians strum mandolins and sing full-throated melodies passed down from ancient ancestors. Men and women dance, flinging their bodies as if they are free as air, or perhaps air itself. A game of *shanghai* is established outside the *ger*, and children race one another to collect the most ankle bones.

Batbayar watches longingly, but he is too old to join the children. Besides, their mother would be livid if he soiled his dress shirt. Instead, he watches, unable to bring himself to cheer for the greedy and brawny younger cousins who shove the little ones out of the way to collect as many bones as possible. A prize of twenty-five *tugriks* is awarded to the winner, a beefy second or third cousin with eyes like a wild camel. He seems disappointed but is careful to pocket his winnings quickly and securely.

And then the crowd parts. The moment for Bolormaa and Ganbaatar to walk past their guests has come. He takes her hand in his dry and leathery one; hers is clammy with sweat. His hand is nearly twice the size of hers but feels like a perfect fit to Bolormaa.

Everyone is smiling and she smiles, too, but the corners of her lips are carved like a statue. She cannot feel anything, not the low afternoon sun or the chilly breeze that ripples through her dress. Ganbaatar holds her hand not too tightly, not too loosely, and his posture does not change the slightest as they pass down the long line of well-wishers. He stares straight ahead, as if he is wandering the Gobi alone, intent only on survival. The stump is heavily bandaged and hidden under his long sleeves.

Both sets of parents await them at the end of the line. Bolormaa's father, pale as freshly fallen snow, pecks his daughter's forehead.

  Erin Jamieson

"*Amjilt husey*, my daughter. May both of you be blessed in your marriage."

"Thank you," Ganbaatar says.

Bolormaa bites her lip, knowing if she speaks, she'll cry. She was raised not to show fear and says nothing.

Her mother grasps Ganbaatar's good hand and both of Bolormaa's. "I am happy to see my daughter with such a handsome young man. Take care, both of you. Be kind to one another."

Bolormaa forces herself to smile back; it's her default response now. Perhaps it's better this way, expressing the happiness she is supposed to feel.

Ganbaatar's father is the last. He does not offer his hand, nor does he smile. He looks at them and says nothing for a minute. Even with children's laughter and the hum of the mandolin riding the wind, Bolormaa feels engulfed in silence, waiting. For the first time, her husband's grip on her hand slackens.

"Son, I knew you'd find a bride." He speaks as though Bolormaa is not present at all, and she shivers under the veneer of her *deel*, wishing she wore something more practical.

"Yes."

He peers at her. "You make a pretty wife. But you also will make a good wife." He pinches her cheekbones, the way one might a horse for purchase. "You are exactly what my son needs. Strong and healthy. You will make a good mother, yes? Bring me grandsons."

Bolormaa's shoulders slump. She has not considered children or being a mother. Today, she has only thought about being a daughter, and how that will change now. She still feels like a child herself.

"There's no need to worry, Father," Ganbaatar says.

No need to worry.

Ganbaatar's father breaks into a tight smile, as if his muscles have been forced to stretch and cannot remember how. With his gaunt cheeks and leathery skin, he reminds Bolormaa of currants left to roast in the sun.

She manages to smile back at her new father-in-law. When he waves them off, they walk away like herded cattle.

The new *ger* is much larger than Bolormaa had thought at first. Once they're alone, it feels almost too spacious, with its tall ceilings and sparse furnishings. After the party dies down and they bid their guests farewell, they begin to clean. She has heard that wealthier families leave the cleaning to their guests, and the couple departs on a journey almost immediately following the reception. But if she knows anything, it's how to work hard. She is grateful for the normalcy of scraping food from dishes, shaking out mats, and rinsing soiled linen. It takes nearly an hour and a half before the *ger* is tidy.

It is so empty. Bolormaa's chest swells, threatening to burst her rib cage. She aches for the familiarity of her mother's woven tapestries and mats, for her great-grandmother's clay pots and even the rusted tea kettle, older than she is.

This *ger*, clean, new, and smelling of animal hides, might be an enclosure. It feels as if she has stepped into some other world, clueless to the language and its customs. She peeks out the front, swallowing greedy gulps of crisp air.

"Bolormaa?" Her new husband's touch is gentle but firm, pulling her back inside. When she faces him, his lips form a tight line, and dark circles shadow his eyes.

"You look tired," he says.

"So do you."

 Erin Jamieson

He shrugs. "Never was much for celebrations, all the noise and people. Exhausting, isn't it?"

Normally, Bolormaa would agree; she preferred quiet to spectacle any day. But she hadn't felt that today—at least not entirely.

"Would you like something to eat?" Ganbaatar offers. "There's plenty of meat leftover."

"I'm still full," she says, suppressing a hiccup.

"I'm going to have some." He pauses. "Is that all right?"

Why wouldn't it be? She catches his eyes tracing the length of her *deel*, from her neck to her chest, legs, and coming to rest on her chest again. She flushes and nods.

"I'll be quick," he says, glancing away. She sits across from him, not knowing her place but assuming he'd like company while he eats. When she asks about his father's health, he sets down the piece of dumpling he is chewing and looks annoyed. "Can I eat in peace?"

Stung, Bolormaa nods and settles on one of the mats a few feet away. The dress is irritating her skin, rubbing it raw with its voluminous, tight layers. She watches as her husband eats like a horse, his jaw working powerfully and head hardly lifting until he has finished.

The stench of the meat and fried dough makes her stomach churn, but she says nothing until he comes over and sits beside her on a worn wooden bench by the hearth.

"I told you I'd be quick. Are you a good cook?"

"I suppose I am decent enough."

"Good. I can cook, but I tire of it.'

She nods. "One time, my mother and I—"

"I asked if you could cook. You don't have to tell me a story."

Bolormaa is stunned into silence. If only her mother were here—but no, Ganbaatar is her husband, and he is only trying to help. He is telling her what she needs to hear, that her chatter is unwelcome. She knows her mouth tends to fly freely when she's anxious, so she bites her lip, as if the pain will stop more words from tumbling out.

But Ganbaatar shakes his head. "I'm sorry. I don't know what got into me."

"No reason to apologize."

"The wedding," he says. "My father. All of it has been stressful."

Bolormaa takes his good hand. "It's no matter. It isn't your fault."

His strong shoulders deflate. He's vulnerable, in a way he was the night he confessed his dreams. It has little to do with his injury. It's the way he looks at her, the way he holds her hand. Like he needs her, as much as she needs him.

And in that moment, she realizes she loves him even more.

He releases her hand and cups her chin, whispering her name. He kisses her forehead then kisses her full on the mouth, his lips soft and heavy against hers. The kisses are warm but urgent, and she remains nearly motionless, letting him take the lead. She shivers as he skims her jawbone, her collarbone, her breasts. He begins to undo the layers of her *deel*, fumbling with the lacing.

He leans back on the soft woven mat beside the bench, leaving Bolormaa with her chest exposed in the damp heat. She longs to cover herself but stays where she is, waiting.

He turns his back to her, muttering something incomprehensible. The bandaging on his stump is more visible with his dress coat removed.

"Ganbaatar," she says quietly.

    Erin Jamieson

"I need something to drink," he says.

"I can warm tea for you."

He laughs coldly. "Something stronger than tea."

"We have *airag*."

"I'll find something else."

He rummages through the new pots and pans and finds a half-empty bottle of heavy liquor used for the sheep's head sauce. He brings the flask to his lips and takes a few big gulps.

Bolormaa is not concerned. Both her father and grandfather loved their drink. Many Mongolian men imbibe, but nothing bad ever comes of it. She's heard stories of men abusing their wives, but they are cautionary tales. No one can survive in the Gobi without spirits—especially when drinkable water is so hard to come by. Bolormaa hates the taste of alcohol, even *airag*, but she has learned to tolerate it.

"I haven't been able to taste anything all day," he says. "But I can taste this, even if I hate it."

"Are you sick?"

He shakes his head. "Exhausted. I'll try to rest now if you don't mind."

"No, of course."

She waits for him to come over but instead he tugs at one of the mats and drags it to the other side of the *ger*. "I won't disturb you. I know it's early."

"Oh, you wouldn't disturb me."

"I'd rather sleep here. It's cooler."

She looks at the rug beneath her. "Would you like me to join you?"

"I need some rest." He lies down and turns his head away. "Good night."

Good night," she whispers. It is nine o'clock at the latest, and the night is swallowing her. She remains standing for a

long time, breasts exposed, looking at her husband as he falls
into a fitful slumber. Eventually, she removes her *deel* and
shrugs into a night dress, completing what her husband had
been unable or unwilling to do.

Over the next few days, they settle into a routine of sorts.
Bolormaa is no stranger to preparing food, but she finds the
new home so distracting that she struggles to have supper
ready in a timely fashion.

On this day, in a desperate attempt to break through her
husband's apathy, she has prepared his favorite meal: young
horse meat, glazed in dill and bitter cherries. They are rare,
expensive ingredients, and to retrieve them, she has traveled
to the bordering city of Erdenet, several hours each way. Her
back aches from the bumpy ride on the obstinate camel. She
is exhausted. Visiting town makes her head spin, with all the
people, noise, and movement.

She misjudged everything: the length of her trip, how long
her husband would be gone, and the amount of time needed
to cook the meat properly. When she hears Ganbaatar's footsteps outside, she panics, realizing the meat is not nearly done.

When he enters, he barely glances at her. His face is ashen
and slick with sweat, his eyes dead.

"Would you like tea?" she asks.

He grunts, slips off his boots, letting soil fall on the carefully slept floors. "I found some new grazing land," he says.
"We need to move closer."

She looks up from the pink meat, rotating hopelessly on
a spit. "So soon?"

"My father and I have been here for some time, since our
first engagement."

    Erin Jamieson

Bolormaa's face grows warm, but she holds her tongue. She knows they will have to move, but it is so soon, like everything else, the many changes in her life. She believes memories are what ultimately constitute a life; each phase of life should be meaningful. Moving after only a week, with nothing but the wedding to remember in this place, makes her ache.

As if reading her thoughts, her husband adds, more gently, "But we don't have to move right away. We can wait if you want."

She doesn't want to be the sole reason they stay longer. Surely, he would eventually blame her.

He watches as she continues to turn the meat over the fire. "Is it almost ready?"

"Yes," she lies.

"I'm starved." He smiles faintly. "Thank you."

She looks at him over her shoulder.

"For cooking," he says.

She blinks, surprised. She has assumed cooking is her duty, just as it's his duty to lead the animals out every day. She pauses then turns fully toward him. "I'd like to help with the animals."

"What do you mean?"

"I miss being outside. I've helped to raise herds my whole life."

"But you've also helped keep a clean home?"

She looks around.

His eyes twinkle. "I was giving you a hard time. I'd be grateful for your help. I'm used to working with my father, and it's a lot of work for one." He reaches for the spot where her hand rests. "Let's check this meat."

"It's not—"

She stops as his hand brushes hers. It is faint, without purpose, but the contact makes her shiver. His fingers are warm and leathery as always, comforting in a strange way as if she has known his touch for years. And yet there's so much more she wants.

"It's not done yet," he says. "Is that horse meat?"

She nods nervously.

"How did you get all of this?"

She tells him about her trip, about the long ride and the stubborn camel.

He listens, gazing at her with wide eyes. "That wasn't necessary," he finally says.

She looks down, her face burning. "I thought you'd enjoy it."

"There's no need to go to this trouble."

"I wanted to."

"I think we need to let it cook a little longer." He rubs his temple. "I will need to think of some way to thank you."

She intertwines her fingers with his. "No need."

His expression softens, and he looks at her in a way he has only once before—with understanding, even longing.

In that moment, Bolormaa believes her husband may also be falling in love with her, however slowly. After the horse meat is finally cooked and they have eaten until they are both satisfied, Bolormaa steps outside to breathe in the fresh, night air. She stands outside the *ger*, holding herself and looking upward. The sky is a map of glittering stars, the moon wispy and ethereal. But it's the wind she notices. It feels different, forceful and carrying someone unknown fragrance, as if everything is about to change.

 Erin Jamieson

ELEVEN

March 1920

GANBAATAR IS PREPARING *khuushuur* when he senses
something is wrong.

His fingers are unsteady. He chops the meat to be folded
into pastry dough for the small meat pies. But the knife slips,
and he nicks his thumb. Blood stains the pale dough and his
curses echo in the empty *ger*. He has already spent nearly an
hour roasting the meat and rolling the dough. Now he'll have
to start over again.

Except.

He takes a cloth and wipes the board clean, discarding the
spotted portions flecked with blood.

There.

Bolormaa won't notice, and what would a little blood
hurt, anyway?

Guilt flutters in his stomach. At least he's preparing
supper! He has no intention of serving it late, not when his

sole purpose is to show her how to prepare a hot meal in a timely fashion.

As he scrubs the pans and board, feeling rather pleased with his efforts, a familiar smell wafts into his nostrils. At first, he ignores it; smoke has chased his dreams since that day when he was seven. But it is persistent, and he coughs.

And then he sees it: the tiniest flicker, so deep red it is nearly blue, by the horse dung. He forgot to close the hutch on the fire pit, and a small but powerful flame found its way onto the mats beside it. He hadn't put them away before lighting the fire to cook.

Don't panic. It's only one flame.

Except it isn't. More flames and more, thick with heat and aggression. They spread to the wedding quilt Bolormaa's mother made. The air is smoky and thick. Ganbaatar struggles to breathe. It's happening all over again. It's happening all over again.

His vision blurs, and dizziness overtakes him, but he has enough presence to reach for the bloodied cloth. Growing flames have sprouted around the perimeter, pinning him against the counter. He waves the fabric helplessly, until it, too, becomes engulfed. He releases it, and the fabric emits an angry hiss as it is consumed.

It's difficult to see. His hands shake as he desperately reaches out, only to grasp air. In his haste and fear, he forgets and extends his amputated limb, striking it smartly against a heavy kettle he did not see.

The pain is overwhelming.

He cannot see at all now.

His knees give in as he crumples to the floor.

     Erin Jamieson

Ganbaatar is no stranger to fire.

At the tender age of seven, his father brought him to learn archery. He'd attempted to mimic his father's stance and concentration as he pulled the bow back against the string, aiming for the target.

But his arms were thin and weak, his aim dismal at best. The men practicing in the next row laughed, and when his eyes filled with tears, his father yelled. "I thought you were ready for this!" he shouted. "Run along. You won't come with me again until you can handle a few drunk bastards!"

Ganbaatar fled as fast as his tiny strides would carry him, stumbling not once or twice, but three times on his way home. He needed his mother. She would gather him in her arms and tell him he'd done his best.

But his home wasn't there.

Giant orange flames licked the *ger's* felt top like a cat's tongue, angry and jubilant against the deep blue skies. The smoke spread quickly, passing like great clouds over the *ger*, their livestock, everything. And because he was only seven and smaller than everything around him, he did nothing. He didn't approach the flames or run away. He simply watched as the only home he'd ever known was engulfed in fire.

And then the smoke reached him, and his lungs strained and felt heavy.

As he coughed and cried, his entire body began to feel heavy. One thought echoed over and over: If my father sees me crying, he'll be angry.

With this singular fear, Ganbaatar didn't think about his mother, or that she might still be inside.

It is so hot, so hot. Another fire, but he's no longer a small boy of seven. He closes his eyes and feels a hand in his. Over the stench of smoke, he smells perfume. He feels smooth, cool skin.

"Aisin," he whispers.

She pulls him up, supporting him with an arm around his waist.

"Ganbaatar," she says, her voice breaking.

He leans into her. "How did you know?"

"I was coming home and saw the flames."

He looks down at her. She is more beautiful than the woman he has dreamt about, with her face flushed and eyes bright. Her body is soft against his, warm under his arm resting on her shoulder.

When she can tell he's steady, she breaks the embrace.

"Aisin," he begins, "if you hadn't come—"

"Don't talk."

The flames have stopped, but the floor is charred. The wedding quilt lies near his feet, ruined. They are standing on a pile of its ashes.

Aisin's silky black hair is wild and loose around her shoulders, her plain, brown *deel* caked with dirt and ash. She's not as composed as he usually sees her, but somehow, she's more beautiful, more familiar, like he's known her longer than Bolormaa. He notices, too, the alarmed look in her eyes. Was she more afraid for his life than he had been? His chest tightens as he tries not to think about the danger she could have been in.

As wrong as it is, he's glad about the fire, if that's why he's seeing her again. But he pushes those thoughts away, too.

"That's twice you've saved my life," he manages.

"Let's go outside. We can't stay in with the smoke."

He allows himself to be led out. The air is crisp, and thin trails of smoke seep from the *ger* and disperse above. Aisin follows his gaze and shakes her head.

     Erin Jamieson

"Don't worry. You didn't lose much."

"I'm a fool."

She squeezes his hand. "It could have happened to anyone."

Warmth floods his hand. It feels right, holding hands, and he doesn't let go when he should, and neither does she. It's so unlike when he touches Bolormaa. His wife, who is always trying to please him but is lost in a dream of what their marriage could be. They have that in common; they're both dreamers. Aisin's grip is firm, certain. Like she knows what they both are unwilling to say.

She glances at him. Ganbaatar leans closer. He imagines his lips brushing against hers.

Aisin seems to sense this, and a question lights her eyes.

He tucks a strand of loose hair behind her ear, a gesture that's somehow more intimate than anything he's shared with Bolormaa.

And then she pulls away. She's sensible in a way Ganbaatar isn't.

"When I saw the fire, I didn't realize it was your *ger*," she says. "I suppose you don't live with your father anymore?"

He can't bring himself to speak of Bolormaa, so he simply shakes his head.

"It's not worth fighting a fire," she says.

"It shouldn't have happened in the first place."

She releases his hand. "You can feel sorry for yourself, but that won't change what's happened."

He is stunned into silence. In the brief time he's been with Bolormaa, he has not been questioned, not once. But Aisin is right. He has spent many months feeling sorry for himself. Without realizing it, she is talking about everything after he lost his hand, not only the fire.

"We moved, my uncle and I." She smooths the front of her dress. "We settled a kilometer south of here."

He cannot help it: his heart leaps. She's nearby. This doesn't have to be the last time he will see her. It won't go beyond this, he knows it can't, but just being able to see her—

Or does he want it to go further?

Aisin's eyes settle on his ring. "I heard about your marriage. Congratulations. I should leave you to clean this up."

Of course she knows. Vast as their world is, those who graze together share news. He should have been the one to tell her.

Yet she rushed to save him. Held hands with him.

And she's not married. By choice?

He has a fleeting, irrational thought: what if she feels the same way about him?

Ganbaatar clears his throat. "Thank you. Now that you've settled nearby, maybe we'll see each other again."

Aisin smiles stiffly. "I hope it doesn't involve a fire or anything else life-threatening."

"Hopefully not," he says, unsure what he'd be willing to risk seeing her again.

Aisin glances over her shoulder, a look of alarm in her eyes. "I need to go."

She leaves mere minutes before his wife arrives.

Bolormaa's cheeks are flushed from the cold, but her eyes sparkle. She looks alive in a way that is dulled when she stays inside all day. More and more, Ganbaatar sends her to take the animals to graze, to sheer wool—things he knows he should be doing.

His wife halts at the entrance to their home; her eyes wide. "What happened?"

Ganbaatar hesitates. He can't tell her about Aisin. And

    Erin Jamieson

he doesn't want her to know he was cowering, afraid of the flames he carelessly ignited.

Aisin has seen him at his weakest—but doesn't judge him in a way he thinks Bolormaa would. No, his wife can't know about any of this. He clears his throat, still raw from the smoke. "Just a small fire, put it out quickly. Nothing to worry about."

Her gaze falls on the charred quilt, and her mouth opens.

"Bolormaa, I'm sorry. I couldn't save it."

She looks up, her eyes red and watery. "I'd choose you over a quilt any day."

It's not nearly as simple as that, and they both know it. But the loyalty of his wife warms him and for a moment, he forgets about the lick of the flames, the damage, even Aisin. "Thank you," he says. "I know the quilt was special."

And then she does something she has never done. She comes to him, wraps her arms around his neck, and buries her head against his chest.

The sun is setting, saturated orange pushing against the cold, gray skies, an undercooked egg yolk dripping into the night. It is nearly the same color as the flames, but infinitely more beautiful, casting long shadows and illuminating his wife's stiff but magnificent raven locks. She is impossibly small and beautiful in that moment, showing the vulnerability she's had all along, but he's never recognized. He notices other things: the softness of her skin, the calluses that have formed on her hands. Her hair smells of snow and dust and love. The tiny dimple on her left cheek when she exhales.

"*Ta büjiglej khüsch baina?*"

She pulls back. "What?"

"Asked if you'd like to dance."

She laughs. "Dance? Now?"

Ganbaatar's face floods with heat but he nods, unde-terred. "Why not?"

He knows there are hundreds of reasons why not. The floor needs to be swept and the mess cleaned. Their stomachs ache with emptiness. But they have never danced, not even at their wedding.

He has never cared for dancing, has told himself they weren't that sort of couple. And maybe they aren't, but now, he can feel her heart beating against his. His emotions flare. And he fails to realize that it is Aisin who has ignited this passion.

He takes his wife's hand, and they begin to dance, bare-foot, until their feet are coated with ashy residue, until his chest heaves and his head aches, and he tells himself he has never been more in love. He pulls Bolormaa close, whispering against the nape of her neck.

He is alive. He is alive. He kisses her passionately on the lips, on her collarbone and her breasts. He feels warm and heavy and confused, as if he's consumed too much *airag*. And later, when she lies beside him and he cradles her body against his, that warmth fades and that heaviness grows. He holds on tightly in the thick of the night, where the darkness is impen-etrable, and shadows call both of their names.

Speaking of the baby is bad luck, so they avoid the topic. Truth be told, Ganbaatar is afraid, more afraid of his wife's growing stomach and her flushed cheeks than he will ever admit. His father visits often now, asking after Bolormaa's health, bringing strange herbal remedies: salted tea for her aching back, fox's urine for mental clarity.

        Erin Jamieson

She takes everything dutifully, though she nearly vomits as she swallows the urine. And his father, encouraged, continues to come, bringing full dinners of *horhog*, finely roasted sheep meat, and *bantan* stew when his sharp breath reeks of *airag*.

Without asking, he sets a place for himself. Occasionally, he'll stay the night, insisting he is growing too old to venture alone in the dark, and won't his son take pity on his poor, old father?

One day, Ganbaatar returns home to find a *shaman* bent over Bolormaa's sleeping frame, chanting and rubbing oil over her expanding stomach.

Ganbaatar freezes. This is his father's doing.

"What is happening?"

The *shaman* continues to murmur with his eyes closed. His cloak strains against his generous girth.

"Get out," Ganbaatar says.

The *shaman* continues his ceremony.

"Damn you! If you don't get away from my wife, so help me—"

"Son, what's this?" Ganbaatar's father enters the room, his eyes heavy as if he's emerged from a long slumber.

"Father, did you send him here?"

He rubs his temple. "Yes, for your wife and the baby. He should be here any day now. I know it's a son, because—"

"Enough," Ganbaatar spits. "I can't do this anymore. We can't do this anymore. It's our child, Father. Not yours."

The *shaman* glances between them, mumbles something, nods to Bolormaa, and leaves. It's unclear if he finished as promised or dismissed himself early.

The older man's eyes widened. "I was trying to help."

"Do you think I can't take care of my own wife?"

His gaze rests on Ganbaatar's useless limb before returning to his face. It is only a half-second, but Ganbaatar doesn't miss it.

"I'm going to feed the horses," his father says.

"We can feed our own bloody horses. Go."

He looks at Bolormaa. "I think your wife needs help."

"Fine," Ganbaatar snaps before offering Bolormaa his good hand. As she is pulled up, she gasps and steadies herself.

"There," Ganbaatar says. "I did what you wanted."

But his father is nowhere to be found.

"I think he went outside," Bolormaa says.

"Damn him."

"Why does it matter?"

"Why does it matter?" he repeats in disbelief. "He's running our lives."

"He's trying to help."

Ganbaatar snorts, turning away. "Right."

"He's excited about the baby. A new life."

Ganbaatar walks to the front of the *ger* and peers into the dark. The wind howls, blowing heavy drifts of snow. The night is moonless and barren. In the distance, he can see snowbanks and the shadow of the herds. The air is salty and bitter, lonely and heavy.

"Ganbaatar?" Bolormaa calls.

"In a minute. Looking for my father." He slips outside. And although the wind is penetrating and the memory of what the cold has already taken from him sends a chill down his spine, he stays out in the blinding snow, waiting.

Some minutes later, his father emerges, his frail, bent form leaning into the vitriolic winds. Only then does Ganbaatar see how insignificant he is. His body is swallowed in the expanse of the storm, and he can barely keep himself afloat.

He was never strong or good enough to save Ganbaatar's mother.

His father stops before him, breathing heavily, and Ganbaatar turns away in disgust.

TWELVE

"WE DON'T NEED you here, Father. Go home."

"What?"

"I said, go home."

"It's awfully cold. Maybe we can discuss—"

"No."

His father swallows hard. His eyelashes are clumped together, and his unshaven face is speckled with snowflakes.

"Ganbaatar—"

But Ganbaatar is already leaving. He shivers as he makes his way into his *ger* with its fire and warmth and light. He should let his father back in, at least for the night. Instead, he stays by the entrance, half-willing the man to come, half-willing him to stay away.

When he enters the warm *ger*, there is a damp, yeasty smell. Bolormaa is crumpled on the floor, holding the sphere of her abdomen.

"Ganbaatar," she whispers.

He stares at her feet, bare against the woven rug.

"I think it's time," she says.

Bolormaa delivers their child ten hours later, on the same mats they shared on their first night together. The midwife is a wizened old woman of seventy-five, with ash gray hair and eyes sharp as her tongue, but she is careful and precise and the only one within fifty miles who can handle births. She cleans Bolormaa and the infant, gathering the soiled linens before calling Ganbaatar back in.

"Is she all right?" he asks anxiously. He listened to her moans for hours, unable to eat or sleep.

"Your wife and child are doing well."

"May I see them?"

She tilts her head, considering. "Your wife fell asleep. But you can see your child."

"Asleep? Is that normal?"

The midwife laughs, revealing yellowed teeth. "After giving birth for ten hours, I'd be worried if she wasn't tired."

He wants to see Bolormaa but doesn't press it. "Where is he?"

The midwife motions for him to follow. On the small, wooden frame Ganbaatar spent months constructing, the infant sleeps soundly, nestled under heavy layers of blankets.

"Now, be careful. Don't want your child to get too cold."

Ganbaatar lifts the baby tenderly. He marvels at the wrinkled toes and feet, at the impossibly small fingers. The soft sighs as the tiny body exhales.

He feels as if he will burst from happiness, shock, or both. He and Bolormaa have created something wonderful, this child, this new life with sweet, soft skin.

The midwife chuckles. "Your wife had the same expression."

Heat rises to Ganbaatar's face. "I'm trying to decide on a name." That's a lie, but he doesn't want to admit how overwhelmed he feels.

"That will come," she says.

Already, Ganbaatar cannot imagine having a naming ceremony. He has no desire to see his child passed from hand to hand, no wish to let strangers and distant relatives stare into his son's eyes.

The baby begins to cry softly, then the cries become louder as the tiny body thrashes in his arms.

"Let's see if your wife is awake," the midwife says.

She is. Bolormaa lies on the mat, her hair sweaty against her forehead and her kind, plain face strikingly pretty with a feverish glow in her cheeks.

She smiles weakly. "I wondered where my child went."

Ganbaatar stoops down and hands her the infant, who immediately nestles against her chest, rooting for her breast.

"Oh," she says.

"Let him have some milk," the midwife says. "He must be hungry."

Ganbaatar watches as Bolormaa peels open the top of her dress. Her breasts are heavy and sagging. Their son latches on, his jaw working powerfully.

"He's so hungry," Bolormaa whispers.

"Hungry and healthy. Strong boy." The midwife busily tidies the room. "I've delivered many infants in my time, and this boy is going to grow up to be strong." She lifts her head and reveals the first hint of a smile. "Perhaps even stronger than his father."

They watch the baby in silence for a while before she excuses herself. "If you need anything, send word," she says. "I'll stop by in a week to make sure everyone's well."

Ganbaatar thanks her then turns back to his wife. Their son is still on her chest, though he appears to have tired of the breast and sleeps against her tanned skin.

"A son," Ganbaatar says, gazing at them fondly. "A son."

     Erin Jamieson

Bolormaa's eyes are starting to droop. "He's perfect," she says.

"Want me to hold him?"

"I think he's asleep."

She's right, but he doesn't care. Already he longs for more time with his son.

"He'll be awake soon," she says. "Hungry again, I'm sure."

He leans over and brushes a lock of hair from his wife's eyes. "You heard what the midwife said. He's a healthy baby."

"She probably tells everyone the same."

"Maybe. Ganbaatar stretches down onto the floor beside her. "But in this case, it's true."

In the following days, he finds more and more excuses to stay inside, rising before daybreak to tend the herd, finishing outdoor duties carelessly. Each thought of his wife and new son makes his heart leap. Every morning upon waking, he rolls over to check on their sleeping forms, making certain he hasn't imagined them in his dreams.

He notices more things about his wife he never appreciated before. The sweet lilt of her voice when she's exhausted, the way her eyes light when he touches her hand.

While Ganbaatar holds their son as if he's made of glass, Bolormaa is a mother by nature, caressing, feeding, and cleaning the infant with a sure hand. At times, he is overcome with a strange mixture of jealousy and love.

The fact that Bolormaa is plain, soft-spoken, and dull at times has not changed. But now that she is the mother of his son, Ganbaatar is devoted to her the way he once was to his own mother.

For weeks following the birth, he is at her side whenever she gets a headache or is too exhausted to complete a chore. He becomes what he realizes she has been for him—loving and constant. He loves her for what she has given, continues to give.

He forgets about his father, about everything except for his son and this life. He forgets about Aisin. It feels like this has always been his life, cooking hot dumplings with clotted goat's cream in the mornings, holding the infant in the afternoon light, asking Bolormaa if she needs anything before they retire in the evening.

Ganbaatar is happier than he has ever imagined possible, but it's not the kind of happiness he once longed for. He forgets the heights of anticipation and yearning and settles in a pattern of comfortable routine. Every day, he has something to live for: to see his son growing bigger and stronger and his wife in this new way and focused on the same goal.

"Aren't you going to answer?" Bolormaa asks. It is evening, and their son, still unnamed, is strapped to her chest as she scrubs down pots. She's dressed in a crepe skirt and a wool jacket that covers the weight she still carries from the pregnancy. Her hair is pulled away from her face, and her cheeks glow in the heat from the fire Ganbaatar has built. "Maybe it's Odval," she suggests.

He grunts. Odval is his cousin and responsible for planning their son's naming ceremony. "This late? In this cold? I doubt it."

"Well, you can't just ignore them, whoever it is."

Ganbaatar bites his lip. He isn't sure he appreciates his wife telling him what to do, despite the months he resented her for timidness.

What if it's his father? They have not spoken since the day he sent the old man away. There is nothing either of them can say to make up for him missing the birth of his grandson, and now, the first month of his only grandchild's life. His father has, no doubt, heard of the birth in passing, by men he grazed with.

But it isn't his father.

It's Batbayar, Bolormaa's brother. They had not seen him since the wedding. He has grown several inches, and his shoulders have broadened. He doesn't smile when Ganbaatar welcomes him.

"Is my sister here?" he asks with a newly deepened voice. "I need to speak with her."

A shiver runs down Ganbaatar's spine. "Did something happen to her father?"

He shakes his head.

"Her mother?"

"Just let me in, and I'll explain." He passes Ganbaatar effortlessly, as one passes a patch of land, and Ganbaatar remembers with a pang the animated boy enamored with the thought of horseracing. The boy who pulled pranks and laughed at inopportune times. What had happened to him? Batbayar had grown into a formidably serious and stiff man. A man who didn't view Ganbaatar with friendship or respect.

"Bolormaa!" Batbayar calls.

Ganbaatar follows him to the east side of the *ger*, where she is still cleaning, her extended stomach pressing against the pot. She freezes when she sees her brother.

"Batbayar? I haven't—how are Mother and Father?"

"Mother is her usual self, running the household." He offers a toothy grin. "And father is just as you left him."

"You've finished school?" she asks.

"Yes," he says. "You didn't give me a choice, did you?"

"Good. I'm glad you came. I missed you."

"Miss the brother who spilled tea over your lap, the brother who broke things and blamed you?"

She laughs. "Yes, I do miss him."

"Well, I'm afraid that boy's gone." He straightens his shoulders and glances at Ganbaatar. "This is not a time for mistakes."

Her face falls with concern. "What's happened, Batbayar?"

"I came to warn you."

Ganbaatar steps next to his wife. "About what?"

"Things are changing quickly," Batbayar says, addressing his sister.

"What do you mean?"

He looks at Ganbaatar. "You own too many goats. Too many horses, probably. You obviously don't realize what's happening."

"Why don't you just tell us?" Ganbaatar

Batbayar's eyes darken. "The Mongolian People's Revolutionary Party is setting mandates on herds. They will control how many animals you can own, what crops you grow."

"They can't do that."

"Actually, they can."

He explains what's been happening, what so many have tried to ignore. Under Soviet rule, livestock would be considered publicly owned. Herders would be given production quotas, and all their activities would be subject to inspection. They would produce for the greater good. In return, they'd be awarded with support: supplies, a tighter sense of organization.

Some resented this ceding of control. Others—especially those who'd been struggling—embraced the change, hoping it would be easier to survive.

Batbayar crosses his arms. "I'm merely warning you. Officials have already been to our place."

Ganbaatar scoffs. "No one can tell me how to raise my animals." He does not care about the promised protection. He'd been raised to do this, hadn't he? Despite his dreams of having a different life than his father—dreams that faded day by day—he didn't see how these officials should know more than him or anyone else how to manage their herds. He knew he would not allow this without a fight. He was a stronger man than his father had ever given him credit for.

Batbayar looks at the infant then back at Ganbaatar. "I was afraid you wouldn't listen. You'll find out for yourselves, but it'll be more painful that way." He turns to head toward the entrance.

Bolormaa hurries to catch her brother, but Ganbaatar stops her.

"Let him go."

"I want him to stay for dinner."

"He's trying to tell us how to run our lives." He thinks of his estranged father trying to mold him. The rushed engagement to Bolormaa, the doctor who amputated his hand at his father's order. His entire life has been dictated by others.

"He's my brother," she says, her eyes welling with tears. "I haven't seen him for so long."

"I said, let him go."

And because she is an obedient wife, she does. They spend the rest of the evening in silence, and as Bolormaa puts their son to bed, Ganbaatar lies alone, shadows his only companion.

They come in the morning—two government officials with pointed faces, sallow cheeks, and yellowed teeth. The younger one is near Ganbaatar's age, smells heavily of hard liquor, and has eyes covered with film. His older companion—clearly, his superior—is clean in appearance and dressed in a handsome, navy-blue jacket.

Ganbaatar invites the officials in, but the older one gestures to the sheep.

"Yes," Ganbaatar says. "All the animals here are mine. The three horses and the camels as well."

"I see. May we have a look?"

He stills. The grass still smells sweet from morning dew, and the day is cold but not unbearably so. The light catches the manes of his horses, making their auburn necks glint as if made of precious metal.

Ganbaatar won't let himself believe what Batbayar said, that these men have come to take his animals away. Surely, they don't have the power to do that. But he never allows someone else, even a dear friend—let alone strange men, or slightly drunk men—handle his animals.

The older officer smiles grimly. "We'll only be a minute."

"Be careful around the horses," Ganbaatar says, "especially the mare. She doesn't like sudden movements and gets spooked easily."

"All right."

He stands at a distance, watching as the two men walk into the fog, skirting the scarce pastures where the goats graze, oblivious to their visitors. The heads of the animals lift slightly as the younger official reaches into his pocket for a rounded flask.

"Ganbaatar?"

Bolormaa peeks out of the *ger*, her hair wild around her shoulders and her eyes puffy with sleep. Even with the distance between them, she looks beautiful.

"Where's our son?'

     Erin Jamieson

"Sleeping." She steps outside. "What's going on?"

"Two men wanted to see our animals."

She freezes. "My brother—"

"They will only look. Don't make more out of it."

"But what if—"

Her words are punctuated by the sound of their son, wailing.

"You should go," Ganbaatar says.

"I will."

"I told you it's nothing," he says. "Are you going to check on our son?"

Bolormaa frowns. "Keep an eye on them."

"Don't worry," he assures her, "I am still the man here."

Her eyebrows rise slightly before she disappears inside.

The next morning, Ganbaatar is shearing the goat when he hears someone approaching.

"*Ugluunii mend.*"

"Good morning," he replies. The older man is nowhere to be seen, but the younger official appears steadier than the day before. "Where's your colleague?" he asks.

"Visiting another place."

"I see."

"I came back to talk to you about your herd."

"I trust you found them well cared for."

"Yes sir."

"Good." Ganbaatar sets down the shears, hoping the official hasn't noticed his bad left limb.

"You have many."

"Sorry?"

"I said, you have many animals."

"Have you ever lived in the Gobi?"

"No, I live in Ulaanbaatar."

Ganbaatar is unable to stifle a short laugh or what he says next. "Then you wouldn't understand our life."

The official frowns. "Our efforts will increase efficiency, prevent overgrazing, and spread resources more effectively. Are you aware that many struggle to survive? Some herders overgraze, without considering the consequences. By carefully distributing land and animal ownership, we can figure out what needs to be produced, and how to manage production using optimal timing."

"I don't understand."

The official spreads his hands. "It's quite simple, really. We measure the anticipated capacity and output of the land and decide how much a man or family can own. A man may have, say, three goats, when two would not only suffice for production needs but also prove more efficient. By owning two, the third can be used by his neighbor in a place where it is more needed."

"So the government thinks it knows best in these matters of…production?"

"The MPRP doesn't pretend to know everything. But the current policies implemented are meant to address economic disparities to make food and livestock production more efficient."

"More efficient for who, exactly? My family has been managing for generations, along with the others here. What gives you the right to take what we have earned?"

The official's eyes on Ganbaatar do not waver. "I understand your fears, and believe me, we sympathize. But surely you see the benefits? Don't you ever feel that surviving in the Gobi is loaded guesswork? Certainly with so many animals,

          Erin Jamieson

it must be difficult to know what you're producing, and for whom?"

Ganbaatar sees a mental image of his new family: Bolormaa, with her calm, beautiful face, and their chubby-cheeked son, with his inquisitive stare and melodious coos.

"No. I work for my family."

The man chuckles. "If only it were so simple."

"I'm afraid I'm going to ask you to get off my land."

That's the problem! "No one owns this land. You know that as well as or better than me."

Ganbaatar remembers his father's words: *Gazryn bükh khümüüst angid.* Land is free from all men. The Gobi, he would say, generates life for all. One could live fifty years, grow old, and never live on the same patch of land twice. There was magic in it. In other places, men were tied down and confined. Owning land handicapped them to dismal futures without hope for change. But here, a man traveled so he could seek what was right for him in the moment. Theirs was an uncertain future, his father would say, but the uncertainty made a future attainable.

"I'll be back tomorrow morning with information about your *negdel.*"

"I'm not interested."

"I'll be back in the morning," The official repeated, before mounting his horse and riding over the dusty earth.

Bolormaa keeps asking her husband what's wrong. The next morning, she is wearing a cream-colored nightdress while their son suckles. Every time Ganbaatar reaches for the child, she tells him to wait for the feeding to end. Through the mess with the officials, Ganbaatar realizes he has been paying little attention to his son. Moodily, he pokes at the hashed marmot Bolormaa has set on his plate.

"His naming ceremony will be soon," she says. "We should think about who's coming."

He doesn't mistake her meaning. "I don't care what you say. My father's not coming."

"But he's your father," she says gently.

"I said, he's not coming."

She stands and hands him their son.

"Where are you going?" he asks.

"I thought I heard something."

Ganbaatar tries to appease his son, but the baby fusses and squirms. Worse, it is hard to balance the weight of the child with only one good hand.

His son begins to cry, cocking his head in the direction of his mother while his face reddens. Ganbaatar stands and paces the room, patting his back and gently bouncing him as he has seen his wife do. When Bolormaa returns, the baby instantly stops crying and lets out a sigh.

Ganbaatar is relieved and annoyed. He knows he hasn't spent as much time lately as he should have with the child. But Bolormaa won't let him do more! Does she want their son to know his father? No, of course not.

"Someone's here to see you."

"Who?"

But he already knows, even before he steps outside into the cool air and sees both, waiting.

"Good morning, sir."

"What do you want?"

The older man blinks. "An agreement. A settlement for your animals." He hands Ganbaatar a piece of paper.

 Erin Jamieson

"I don't want to sell any of my animals," he says, looking up. "They're not for sale."

The younger man pinches his nostrils. "Let's not make this difficult. It's a handsome sum of money."

Ganbaatar looks back at the offer. It is. It is more than fair, more than he'd accrue selling the animals on his own. But his father taught him to never part with his animals. On the Gobi, they are a man's livelihood. He wouldn't sell for any amount of money.

"You are high on our list," the older official says. "You won't get this much if you wait."

Already the day is late, the sky deep blue, cloudless, infinite. Everything is infinite: the long stretches of flat, rock-infested land, the lines of grazing animals, the cool, crisp taste of late winter air.

This land and its resources were never meant to be parceled. Ganbaatar sees this, he lives it. This land dismisses demarcations, beautiful for its refusal to be bought or sold. It is one of the few places a man can work hard until he dies, indebted only to himself and the life he has made.

The truth is, Ganbaatar didn't send his father away for his controlling nature. He didn't send him away because he was forcing Bolormaa into a role, or because he tried to direct them every turn.

Ganbaatar sent his father away because he'd never been able to understand the older man.

He does now, yet he is even more relieved he has sent him away. His father, who would have fought to keep his animals, who would have done next to everything to defy these men.

For Ganbaatar, there is no choice. Slowly but surely, he has come to see this. He's watched as more and more around him capitulate. One man's animals were taken from him entirely when he refused to surrender.

He signs away the following: one camel, one horse, four goats, and his dignity. In return, he receives a heavy purse of *tugriks* that weigh down his pockets. For Bolormaa, he tells himself. For the boy. He has no choice.

He is careful not to watch as his horses and camels are led away. He stays inside when they come for the goats, and the soft bleating sends chills down his spine.

Erin Jamieson

THIRTEEN

May 1921

QUATAN GROWS DAY by day. A year after his birth, his cheeks have already lost some of their ruddiness, and his face is becoming more and more carved, with his father's strong jaw and his mother's soft eyes.

His naming ceremony, scheduled half a year into his life, was a somber, quiet affair, with Bolormaa's family and a few of Ganbaatar's cousins in attendance. They consumed fried dumplings and talked about nothing of substance, until one by one the guests left, leaving Bolormaa with her husband and son.

It's easier not to care about the outside world when she is tending to her son. Once she turned away for a minute and in the next—to her horror—she found him playing with a long-handled knife. She must have dropped it but couldn't recall doing so.

On a warm day, she carried Quatan outside to play in the tall grass, and he crawled past her to one of the goats, trying to pet it. Unafraid, he reached up, steady on his chubby legs. Luckily, the goat was more frightened of the inquisitive tyke than it was aggressive.

Bolormaa often wonders if she's a bad mother. She certainly wasn't ready to have a child, no more than she was to be a wife. Quatan is bright but already unruly; he cries to get anything he wants. He has mastered the art, clanging the pots Bolormaa has laid to dry, playing on the dirty floor, reaching up for attention as she cooks.

She watches him as much as she can, but he is always getting himself into some new mess. Some nights, she collapses on the mat and sleeps through his crying, only to be woken by her husband: "Can't you hear our son? He needs you."

Just once, she'd like Ganbaatar to get up and take care of Quatan. He used to help more, but now everything seems to fall on her. She is so, so tired, and Ganbaatar only jokes or changes the subject when she tells him how exhausted she is.

"Think that's hard? Try working in the pastures all day. And with the damn collectives, whatever progress I make gets sapped by greedy investors."

Bolormaa flinches. She misses working outside. She grew up tending herds. But along with the recent changes, everything has become more stringent, and Ganbaatar has pushed her away and back into the *ger*.

Her husband is bitter that the land is no longer free. He has been assigned to a *negdel*, a farming collective, and given a quota for how much and which crops to produce, and how many animals he can possess.

Though he won't admit it, he misses the horses, camels, and goats he sold. He visits them, bringing too much of their water and feed. He is happiest at home, but even then, he is distant and often stares at the sky as if imagining a different

 Erin Jamieson

world, a world that no longer exists. Often, she has watched the same sky, wondering about other places where it might look different.

The intrusion of the farming collective into their lives has made Bolormaa miserable, too. Required to work with other nomads, they must move when others wish to move. They relocate twice as much as before; or sometimes, they stay too long in one place. None of it is their sole choice.

On the evening of their son's second birthday, Ganbaatar comes home, smelling of sweat and looking frustrated. His hair is matted, his skin scorched with wind. There are lines underneath his eyes—whether from age or fatigue, it's hard to say.

"Everyone voted to stay again," he tells her. "There's nothing left here. Not for us, not for anyone. If we stay, our animals will perish."

Bolormaa hands him a cup of tea. He thanks her, taking a long sip before setting the cup down and looking at her. "I don't know what to do."

Her chest flutters. He is asking for her advice. In the other room, Quatan is sleeping peacefully, his soft inhales and exhales barely audible.

"Did you say anything?" she asks. "When they discussed—"

"Of course! They didn't listen."

She takes a deep breath. "Why do they want to stay? Perhaps it won't be for long?"

Ganbaatar studies her in a way he hasn't for a while. As if he wants to trust her, needs to trust her. His face softens, and Bolormaa thinks about everything they've been through, from that first meeting at her family's *ger*, to the life they share now. Can he ever learn to trust her?

She sets her teacup down, brushes back a strand of his hair, and kisses his forehead. "Do you know what my father used to say?"

"What?"

"*Nar margaash gegeerüüldeg.* The sun shines tomorrow."

Suddenly, a heavy roll of thunder shakes the *ger*.

Ganbaatar laughs. "If it's one thing I appreciate, it's your sense of humor."

Bolormaa frowns. "It wasn't a joke—"

But she never finishes the sentence because Ganbaatar is kissing her, kissing her as he has not for nearly a year. He kisses her forehead, eyelashes, and cheeks, brushes his lips against the nape of her neck.

He is kissing her deeply when Quatan begins to cry.

They become still, waiting.

Ganbaatar sighs. "Doesn't he ever sleep?"

"Every few days."

He smirks. "Bet I can reach our son faster than you."

"He's in the next room."

He kisses her again. "Race you."

"You can't be serious." She stares at him.

"Are you going to race me, or not?" He kisses her cheek. "On the count of three. One, two—"

She rushes around him. Ganbaatar protests, "You cheated!" Then they are neck and neck, leaping over floor mats, elbowing each other, and laughing. Ganbaatar trips on something Quatan has left on the floor, and as he falls, he brings Bolormaa with him.

"Are you all right?" he asks.

She takes his hand, and they rise. She tries to run again, but he grabs her by the waist and twirls her body. "Cheater."

     Erin Jamieson

"You never said we had to play fair." Out of breath, she grins.

"Funny," he says. "I never would have taken you for someone who relies on shortcuts."

"Funny," she murmurs with heat flooding her face. "I never would have taken you for someone who can't outrun his wife."

"I'm full of surprises," he says, kissing her again.

She kisses him back, as the warmth spreads through her body.

Ganbaatar could have stepped out of the collective at any time. The officials who came to visit were out of line, and the ordinances hadn't been made law yet. But news travels slowly; they realized this a year after Ganbaatar sold his animals. By 1925, the Mongolian People's Republic has been named the official political party.

"Just as well those bastards came when they did," Ganbaatar says. "I got a decent price, and it was only a matter of time before I'd have to sell. I'm already prepared, working in the collective for three years."

Bolormaa speaks softly. "But all along, you could have kept the livestock, decided what to grow—"

He holds up his hand to silence her. "I was a fool, but others will be fools soon. We are fine with the way things are. We have food to eat, and our son is growing strong."

For Quatan's fifth birthday, they are holding a feast. In true Mongolian custom, guests will wear traditional garb and attend the small *Naadam* festival Bolormaa and Ganbaatar have planned. With their modest but steady income, they can afford a true birthday celebration for their son, the event they'd ached to host when he turned one.

This time, they'll serve a feast of home-cooked dishes—
baaz, garlic roasted mutton, western-style onion cakes—and
plenty of *airag* and cultured mare's milk for the children. And
there will be a horse race, but Ganbaatar insists he isn't interested in participating. He'd be a laughingstock, he says, and
doesn't want to distract from their son's day.

Bolormaa has a sneaking suspicion there is much more
to it.

On the day of the feast, Ganbaatar helps her cook while
Quatan wanders, excited and always getting in the way.

"For me?" he keeps asking, pointing to every dish.
Bolormaa laughs.

"Yes, for you. But you must share. Emee and Övööe are
coming. Your cousins, too."

"Horsey?"

"Yes, there will be horses."

A grin spreads over his chubby cheeks. "Father, too?"

"Of course I'll be there." Ganbaatar ruffles his son's hair.
"Now, how old are you?"

He holds up four fingers.

"You were four last year," Bolormaa says. "How old are
you now?"

He frowns, then holds up one finger.

"That's right. You're one year older. So how old is that?"

"Let him think for himself," Ganbaatar says. "How old
are you, son?"

"Five," he answers timidly.

"How old?"

"Five."

"He already said five," Bolormaa says.

Ganbaatar glances at his wife. "He needs to learn to speak
up. He's a smart boy, but no one will ever know. At his age—"

"I know, at your age you might have been pushed more. But do we want to raise him the same way? Doesn't he get time to play and enjoy being a child?"

Ganbaatar bites his lip. Not because he disagrees, but because she's right. Bolormaa always worked hard; like him, she learned how to tend animals at an early age. But she also has memories he doesn't have, memories of chess and *khoral* games, and laughter shared with siblings. Bolormaa didn't bear the weight of a sick mother, with no siblings to help.

She hesitates, looking at him. A single strand of silver in his hair—just one strand—jolts her. He's still as handsome as the day they met, yet he's a different man. A man whose slightly dreamy look as sharpened, hardened with time. His lips are chapped, his face not cleanly shaved but speckled with an unkept beard.

They are changing, as quickly as everything else.

"You didn't invite your father, did you?" she asks.

"What do you think?"

Bolormaa falls silent. Quatan has met his other grandfather only twice. Once when he was an infant and two years ago, when Ganbaatar allowed his father to drop off a gift for the boy during winter festivities. But Quatan was far too young to remember either of these incidents. In his mind, he has only one set of grandparents, and he seems to believe this is the case for everyone.

Ganbaatar shrugs. "He can't come. You know that."

She nods, moving the tray aside. "I don't want you to regret it."

"He was running our lives, Bolormaa."

"It's been years. Is that the real reason?"

"What do you mean? He turns sharply, nearly spilling the wine Bolormaa will use to marinate the mutton.

But she is saved from answering because at that moment, their son begins to cry.

"What's wrong?" Ganbaatar asks irritably.

Bolormaa wipes her hands on the front of her dress. "Did you hurt yourself?'

Quatan's face turns blotchy and red as the tears stream. He has fallen and his knee is bleeding.

"Get up," Ganbaatar orders.

"He's injured," Bolormaa says. "Can you hand me a cloth?"

He grunts. "It's only a scrape."

"And he's only a child."

Ganbaatar watches as she dabs at the boy's knee. "He's our son, and he's getting older."

"He's only five!"

"I won't have him turning into a coward."

"He's five," Bolormaa says again.

He slams down the skillet of oil heating for the *baaz*. "If you want to pander to him, fine. But don't expect me to take part."

Bolormaa continues to soothe Quatan, paying no atten-tion to the oil crackling in the skillet behind her, or to Ganbaatar. "Feel any better?" she asks the boy.

He looks up at her with wide eyes. "It hurts."

"Yes, yes it does. But it won't always."

He gazes at her with innocent trust and admiration. "Really, Mama?"

Ganbaatar mutters something and leaves. His footsteps are fast and firm, but he will be back. Bolormaa knows that much.

"Yes, Quatan," she says. "It will heal with time. It will."

     Erin Jamieson

FOURTEEN

THE DAY OF Quatan's birthday celebration is bright and mild. The sun is out, and the ground is finally thawing in patches. Bolormaa shivers under her sweater, holding Quatan's hand on the sidelines. The race is about to begin, and riders mount their horses. A hum of anticipation is in the air.

The last rider is a woman, but Bolormaa can't tell from a distance who it is. She stares longingly at her graceful posture and confident handling of the reins. When Bolormaa used to ride, she was clumsy and awkward. It isn't uncommon for women to be accomplished riders, but Bolormaa can't handle a horse with such finesse.

Ganbaatar is nowhere to be seen and in his fascination with horses, Quatan doesn't seem to notice. He tugs at his mother's hand: "Mama, is that our horsey?"

"No, these aren't our horses."

He points to the nearest animal, a gray-spotted stallion with a coarse mane. "Can I ride that one?"

Their son isn't a coward. Bolormaa smiles. "When you're older."

"But I am older. Daddy said."

"A little older. When you're bigger and taller."

He straightens up, stretching. "I'm tall!"

She glances at her son. Five years ago, he was a newborn, with wrinkled skin and impossibly tiny toes. Five years ago, she had nursed him, and he had needed her infinitely. But already he is pulling away, holding her hand less often, wanting to make his own mistakes and discoveries.

She should be happy. He's healthy and growing. Instead, it makes her chest ache.

"Hush," she tells him. "The race is about to begin."

One of Ganbaatar's cousins stands in the open field, his boots kissed with traces of snow, wind flushing his cheeks red. "The race will begin on the count of ten. One, two, three…"

When he reaches ten, the riders tear off. The cousin steps aside as the leading rider reaches him. It's the gray-spotted stallion Quatan had admired. The horse and its rider have taken a generous lead.

The spectators scream as the horses turn, and a second rider pulls beside the first. From this distance, it is impossible to tell who is leading. Three horses fall far behind. The finish rests not far from the start. It is a short race, and Bolormaa doesn't want to miss a moment. She and Quatan run toward the finishing line as the horses make the last turn and begin the final straightaway.

There is a collective gasp as the first horse is overtaken by the second. The gray-spotted horse and its rider fall further and further behind. The leading rider throws up a hand, as if to signal victory.

"Mama, look. She is going fast."

And Bolormaa sees what her son does, what the crowd has yet to realize: the sole, female rider, trailing behind the leading pack for most of the race, is now vying for first place. Now, two horses are neck and neck, four hundred meters

     Erin Jamieson

from the finish. With two hundred remaining, they are still side-by-side.

And then the woman rider pulls ahead, and the crowd roars.

The race is over. The woman dismounts quickly, her hair still in place in a tight bun, her back facing Bolormaa. Other competitors rush to congratulate her. Most are stunned, lingering by their horses, waiting with the rest of the crowd.

Ganbaatar appears at Bolormaa's side. "Did you see that?"

The wind picks up her hair and blows it across her face. Quatan's hand is clammy in hers. "Where have you been? You missed the whole race."

"No, I saw."

"Why didn't you try to find us?"

"I did." He attempts to grab her hand, but she moves it. "Let's not argue right now."

Quatan pulls on Bolormaa's hand as he jumps up and down. "Daddy, did you see? Did you see how fast they went?"

Ganbaatar grins and swings Quatan to face him. "Did you enjoy the race?"

"I want to be a horse racer," the boy says. "I want to go fast, Daddy, like that lady."

"You will." Ganbaatar tussles his hair. "We can start practicing on—" He catches Bolormaa's frown. "What?"

"Isn't he young for riding?" she asks.

"He's the perfect age."

"But he's only five—"

"Which is only a year before I started. His chances are better if he starts younger."

Bolormaa scoffs. "His chances? He doesn't know what he wants."

"Make way for the winner!" someone calls out. The

crowd parts, and Bolormaa falls silent as the woman leads her tawny-colored, muscular horse across the glistening grass. The winner of the race walks with her head high, smiling boldly.

Bolormaa notices three things:

The woman is beautiful, with a creamy complexion and flowing hair that shines in the fading, afternoon sun; she is beautiful even in her disheveled riding gear.

When she gazes at Bolormaa, it seems as if they know each other.

Lastly, she isn't Mongolian. She is undeniably Chinese.

Bolormaa doesn't touch any of the feast. She hasn't eaten since morning, but her stomach is unsettled and queasy. Quatan piles his plate with dumplings, roasted mutton, and curried goat cheese curds, and smacks his lips after long swigs of cider, a rare treat. His cousins pass by, wishing him a happy birthday. He smiles, but his mouth is too full to answer.

They see Batbayar's children when they can, every few weeks. They live about a kilometer away. Bolormaa knows they should visit more often, but work dominates live for all of them.

Ganbaatar seems to be enjoying himself. He helps himself to generous portions of *airag*, sings with the talented throat singers, and dances as the day fades and the cold sets in. But he is oddly distant, so immersed in the festivities he doesn't seem to hear a word Bolormaa says.

Then she realizes that Ganbaatar is fully drunk. Quatan watches his father with a mix of amusement and fascination. The boy has witnessed adults drinking; it is an expected thing, grown men enjoying spirits in front of children and wives, with wives sometimes joining in.

But it is the first time Bolormaa has seen her husband like this, the bloodshot eyes and constant, ricocheting laughter,

        Erin Jamieson

his unsteady gait as he walks over to fill his plate again. A few others are drunk, but not like Ganbaatar, who flirts shamelessly with the women and dances with abandon, stamping his feet and clapping loudly.

Bolormaa pretends not to notice or care. Quatan tugs on her dress. "What's Daddy doing?"

"He's enjoying the party."

The boy's eyes are large and glassy, drooping slightly at the edges. "I want to race."

"We will rest after the celebration," she says.

"But Daddy promised."

"When you're older."

Quatan pouts, and it is uncanny how much he resembles his father, with prominent cheekbones and eyes as deep as charcoal. But on his young face, the features are softer, and Quatan's hair is wavy, unlike his father's stiff and waxy hair. Their boy is already handsome, and Bolormaa cannot help but wonder if someday he, too, will flirt with other women as his wife looks on.

Ganbaatar returns half an hour later, breathing sharply from the *airag* and smiling strangely.

"Enjoying yourself?" she asks.

He grabs her shoulders and guides her lips to his. "I am." His kiss is crushing and almost hurts. When he pulls away, their son is staring.

"I want to be a horse racer, like that lady," he says.

"Like that lady," Ganbaatar agrees amiably. Then his face changes. He takes a few steps away, leans over, and vomits.

"Daddy?" Quatan asks, pulling at his mother's hem.

"He's all right," Bolormaa mutters.

"Is he sick?"

She bites her lip. The air tastes of horses, manure, and grease from the cooked meat. She pulls a cloth from the pocket of her dress and hands it to Ganbaatar. "Your father will be fine."

It takes nearly two hours to clean up after the party, even with the help of some of Ganbaatar's cousins. Almost everyone has left, and there are still dishes to be gathered and washed. Bolormaa rubs her temple, wishing she were intoxicated as well so she could lie down and rest. Quatan and Ganbaatar are inside, dozing next to each other on mats.

As she gathers dishes, she feels a hand on her shoulder.

"Would you like some help?"

She straightens up. Behind her stands the Chinese woman, the one who won the race. Silky black hair, confident hazel eyes, a slightly crooked nose. Slender but strong, like she's worked hard most of her life.

Up close she is stunning, but not as young as Bolormaa had originally thought. They are likely around the same age.

"Oh, there's no need."

The woman smiles, and her face brightens. "Yes, but I'd like to."

"Be my guest." For a while, the two women work side by side. "Your Mongolian is very good," Bolormaa says.

The woman's smile falters. "I was raised here."

"I didn't mean— I haven't seen you before."

"Of course," she says coldly. "Did you want me to help bring in the dumplings and mutton?"

"I didn't mean to offend you," Bolormaa says quickly. "I know almost everyone around here."

"I understand." She doesn't raise her eyes as she helps strip the table.

"I'm Bolormaa."

The woman hesitates then smiles again. "Aisin."

"You're an excellent rider. You must have years of experience?"

"My uncle taught me. It's more of a pastime." Aisin gestures at the remaining tablecloth. "Taking this inside?"

"Yes, thanks. Here, you can give it to me."

"Do you need help with anything else?" Aisin crosses her arms over her chest, and Bolormaa sees the corded muscles in her arms. She's never met a woman like this.

"No, I think that's it."

Aisin nods. "I know what it's like to be left to clean everything up."

Bolormaa lingers. It feels like there's something else Aisin wants to say. Finally, she turns back to the *ger*. "It was nice to meet you," she says.

"Your son enjoyed the day?"

Bolormaa nods. "He wants to learn to race as fast as you."

Aisin chuckles. "In another year, he'll change his mind."

"Why do you say that?"

She shrugs. "When I was five, I dreamed of being a traveling doctor. Then when I was ten, I was convinced I'd see the world."

Bolormaa says nothing.

It feels like a lifetime ago when she gave up pursuing more education. Even longer since she dreamed of a different life, of finding love for herself instead of falling into it. She'd fallen into almost everything, rather than choosing for herself.

It is too late now, she thinks—perhaps for Aisin, but more so for her.

The afternoon is fading, the sky erupting into a flushed, pink sunset that strokes the saturated blue like a tender kiss. Under that show of color, Bolormaa finishes her tasks then goes inside.

When she tiptoes into her home, Ganbaatar is snoring faintly, but her son is awake, with bushy hair and bloodshot eyes.

He yawns when he sees her. "I'm hungry."

"You had so much at the celebration," she whispers.

"But I am."

She sighs. "There are dumplings left." She reaches for the dish and doubles over.

"Mama?"

She grimaces as another wave of nausea overtakes her. She vomits at her son's feet.

"Are you sick, too?"

"Go get your father."

He darts away. A moment later, Ganbaatar appears. "Couldn't you let me sleep for another hour?" He sees her face, notices the puddle at her feet. "What has happened?"

"Quatan, why don't you fetch Mama her green scarf?"

Eager to help, he disappears into the next room.

"You don't have a green scarf," Ganbaatar says.

Her eyes meet his. "I think I'm pregnant."

He blinks slowly. "Are you sure?'

"No, but this is how I felt with Quatan."

He takes a step back, rubbing his forehead. "We can't afford another child."

Bolormaa reaches for a bowl and vomits again. Ganbaatar puts his hand on her back, unsure what else to do.

She looks up at him. "You don't mean that."

He reaches for her hand. "We're barely surviving as it is.

Our collective isn't meeting production demands. My horses are aging."

"I thought you wanted another child."

"We have a healthy son." He pauses. "I doubt you're pregnant. You probably had too much rich food."

"Maybe," she says as Quatan returns. She fixes a plate of dumplings for him.

The *ger* is damp, dark, and cold; the last embers of the fire are dying. Ganbaatar pokes the embers but instead of reigniting, the little flame dies, and the pit is swallowed in darkness.

"We'll figure it out," he says finally. "A child is a blessing." He touches her shoulder. "I am happy, Bolormaa. I promise."

She exhales. "Is there anything I can get you? Tea?"

Quatan stops eating to stare at them. "Mommy?"

She ruffles his hair. "Yes?"

"Are you both better now?"

Bolormaa glances at Ganbaatar, who nods. "Yes," she says, "and you're going to be a big brother."

The boy's eyes widen. "Can I name her?"

Bolormaa frowns. "We don't know if you'll have a sister. It could be a brother."

"Wouldn't you like that?" Ganbaatar asks.

"I want a sister." The boy shoves a dumpling into his mouth.

"A brother will be good," Ganbaatar insists. "He can help your father with chores and become a horse racer like you."

Their son squints. "My sister can do that."

Ganbaatar's eyes darkened. "We'll see."

"You should go back to bed," Bolormaa says. "Let your father tuck you in."

"But I want to see my sister," Quatan whines, suppressing a yawn.

"Your brother's coming later. You won't miss him."

"Promise?"

"Promise."

"All right." He glances at his mother. "But I still want a sister."

Bolormaa watches as her husband guides her son back to bed. The darkness is climbing over her. When Ganbaatar returns, she reaches for him, but he doesn't notice.

"I should rest, too," he says.

Later that evening, after all the dishes are washed and put away, the rugs shaken out, and the place put in order, Bolormaa stands watching her husband's sleeping form until her eyes grow heavy. She lies down beside him, feeling weak as a newborn, her stomach still in knots. He seems to blame her for this coming child, although he certainly had something to do with it. She thinks about the added work and the ways their lives will change with another mouth to feed. Another child to love. She waits for him to turn towards her in his sleep, as he always does. But on this night, he stays folded into a ball, like a child himself.

FIFTEEN

Autumn 1926

THEIR DAUGHTER SPENDS her first moments gasping for air. Born too soon, she is impossibly small. Her skin has a bluish tint, and her initial breaths are ragged and rapid.

Bolormaa is nearly unconscious, babbling about Quatan seeing his new brother. Ganbaatar doesn't have the heart to tell her their second child is neither a boy nor healthy. Instead, he swaddles the infant and rocks her until her long eyelashes close and she sighs in her sleep.

If she survives, there will be no naming ceremony. Ganbaatar has no idea what he would call her. Despite her coloring, she is beautiful. Her limbs are frail and dainty, her cheeks gaunt but smooth as silk. It is obvious that, like her brother, she favors his side, with the same stubborn chin and intense espresso eyes. The little sprouts of hair are the same deep brown, slightly wavy and shiny. She looks nothing like her mother, though that may change.

While his wife and daughter sleep, Ganbaatar goes

outside to feed the livestock. The air is damp but kissed with the warmth of an early autumn morning. As the sun climbs the sky, he aches for his mother. She would have known what to do. She would already have a name picked out, would have been able to push past her disappointment and marvel at the miracle of another child. She would have prayed and thanked the eternal God for this girl's life.

But even more: she would make sure Ganbaatar's father was there to see his new granddaughter.

Ganbaatar has already had two tall glasses of *airag*, and his head is buzzing. The grass is too green, the sky too blue. His hands are shaking when he goes back in to pour himself a third glass.

"Daddy? Can I meet my sister?"

He sets his glass down abruptly and faces his son. "What are you doing here?"

"I wanted to see my sister."

"She's sleeping, like you should be."

"I'm not tired."

"Then work on your lesson. Your spelling last time was atrocious." Quatan has begun attending a nomad's tent school nearby, and already he is behind his peers. Still, Ganbaatar is not overly concerned. Book learning and literacy doesn't help prepare one for life as a nomad.

"You said you'd help," the boy says.

"I've been busy, helping your mother." He reaches for his glass and fills it.

"Can I have some, Father?"

"You can have milk tea."

"I want what you're having."

Ganbaatar shakes his head. "Milk tea, then bed or study. You'll see your mother later, but she needs her rest now."

"My sister?" he asks.

"I'm not sure," he says, drumming his fingers against the glass. "Quatan, there's a chance she might not stay with us."

He squints. "Doesn't she like us?"

"Yes, but she's very sick."

"But she's just a baby."

"Sometimes that happens."

"She's too sick to stay?"

"She may be."

The boy's lips form a thin line. "Tell her to stay. I want a sister."

His son is full of more goodness than Ganbaatar will ever possess. He may resemble his father, but his temperament has always been like Bolormaa's—sweet, gentle, compassionate.

"Go to sleep, and I'll let you know what she decides," Ganbaatar says finally.

"Mama or my sister?"

"Both. It's their decision together."

His wife's screams wake him mid-slumber. Ganbaatar pushes off the linens and rushes in. Bolormaa is thrashing on the mat, her face pale and bloodless, and her eyes wild with fever.

"What's wrong?"

She grabs his arms so hard he gasps. "Quatan. We need to warn him."

"Warn him?"

"He's not safe."

"What are you talking about?"

She rolls back and closes her eyes, mumbling until her breathing steadies and she falls into a feverish slumber. Her forehead is warm to the touch. Ganbaatar stands over her, his heart beating painfully inside his chest. Is she ill or merely exhausted? Should he be doing something? Their daughter is sleeping, too. Her skin appears blotchy, red, and raw.

He doesn't know what makes him do it. Maybe it is fear or desperation. Maybe he has been looking for an excuse. He gets dressed and leaves the *ger*. He heads south, in the exact direction where, years ago, before he married, he met a young woman who seemed to hold all the answers to his future.

The midwife is there, he tells himself. The midwife will make sure everything is fine until he returns.

He rides in a daze, not thinking. And then she's before him.

Her complexion is still creamy and smooth, her eyes still wide and intelligent, but her hair has been cut shoulder-length, and her eyes have hardened with either wisdom or disappointment. If she's surprised to see him, she doesn't show it. Instead, she smiles when she steps out from her uncle's *ger*.

"Ganbaatar. It's good to see you."

"Aisin," he says. "It's been too long."

"I thought you'd say hello at your son's birthday, but you never did."

Heat floods his face. "You were busy. I didn't know you raced."

"I don't often. But I heard you'd be a seasoned opponent."

"Not really."

Aisin shakes her head. "I think we're both lying. Uncle said you wanted to see me." She looks him squarely in the eye, with an expression he can't quite read.

"My wife," he says. "She's very ill."

"Bolormaa? She seemed so healthy and friendly at the party."

"You met her?"

　　　　Erin Jamieson

"Yes. We cleaned up together while you slept."

He looks down. At the celebration, he'd started drinking to fill the numbness of seeing Aisin again and the knowledge that when he returns his wife's smile, it would always be for someone else.

"What is wrong with Bolormaa?" she asks. "Did you call for a doctor?"

Ganbaatar blinks, feeling like a fool. "She gave birth to a baby. A girl."

"Why did you come to me?"

He hesitates. "I didn't know what else to do," he says finally.

Aisin steps into the *ger* and comes out wearing a heavy shawl. "She's alone?"

"No, we have a midwife. And my son is there. And our daughter." Guilt creeps into his voice anyway. Midwife or not, he knows he's being reckless, and he can't stop himself. All reason has left him.

"You have a daughter?" Aisin asks.

"Born today. Both she and my wife—"

"Who's also sick?"

Ganbaatar feels panic rising in his throat. "I don't—"

"We need to hurry," Aisin says before he can respond. "I'll take my camel."

"Ride with me on the horse. It'll be easier."

She hesitates for a fraction of a second before nodding.

Back at the *ger*, they are greeted by the pungent odor of dried blood and sweat. Quatan stands by the entrance, trembling, holding a bundle in his arms. "Father."

Ganbaatar brushes past his son. "Where's your mother?"

When Quatan doesn't answer, he shakes him gently. "Where is the midwife?"

"The infant," Aisin whispers. "Let go of your son."

"I don't see them anywhere." Forcing himself to ignore the swaddled bundle, Ganbaatar rifles through the bloody, damp blankets where his wife gave birth.

"Quatan, where did your mother go?" Aisin asks in a soft voice.

He shakes his head, clutching the baby.

"Answer her," Ganbaatar demands.

The boy wilts, and the bundle in his arms begins to drop.

Aisin rushes forward and catches the infant in her arms. The baby doesn't emit so much as a cry but stares blankly at Aisin.

"Here." She hands the baby to Ganbaatar.

The weight is surprisingly heavy and damp in his arms.

"Let me go find your wife," Aisin says.

Quatan watches silently. Ganbaatar doesn't want to be left alone with this new child whose birth he didn't witness, and his son, silent as stone. "Wait."

But Aisin shakes her head firmly. "Stay inside with the baby. I'll find her." She squeezes his hand. "I always find what I'm looking for."

She releases his hand and his phantom limb aches, remembering. He rocks the child back and forth, but she has already fallen asleep, all of them under Aisin's spell.

It's a girl. A daughter. The sister his son asked for. Ganbaatar sits down, holding her, waiting for her cries but she is eerily quiet and watchful. She blinks up at him, her mouth wrinkled into a tiny, thoughtful pout.

"What should we name you?" he whispers. It is the

     Erin Jamieson

furthest worry from his mind, but it has been some time since Aisin left. Quatan still has not spoken a word.

When Ganbaatar starts to relax his grip, the infant claws at him with her tiny fingernails. She stares at him steadily, her gaze over his left shoulder.

Aisin has returned. And, with her, his wife.

His first thought is that it isn't Bolormaa. It can't be. His wife is neat to a fault, her clothes crisp and her hair meticulously kept. This woman is disheveled and disoriented, hair bushy and knotted, her eyes bleary and bloodshot.

He rushes forward. "What happened?"

Aisin holds up a hand.

Ganbaatar sees that she is almost entirely supporting his wife's weight. Bolormaa mutters to herself, and her skirt is covered in dried blood.

"We need to get her to lie down," Aisin says.

He follows her commands, and together, they lead his wife onto the sleeping mat. Once they get her settled, her eyes flicker. For a moment, she seems to recognize him, but then she closes her eyes and falls into a quick, troubled sleep.

"What happened?"

Aisin presses a finger to her lips. "I'll brew a pot of tea. Stay here with the baby."

He is glad he is not alone. He wants to ask Aisin to stay but reaches for his wife's hand instead. Her fingers are waxy and warm with fever.

"She's burning up."

"She'll sweat the toxins out." When Ganbaatar glances at her doubtfully, she adds, "It's what my mother always used to do for me. Have a little faith."

Faith. Ganbaatar never has had faith. He's never believed

in his mother's god, or anyone else's. But he believes in Aisin. He waits for the tea to brew, then cool.

Aisin brings him a half-filled cup and he holds it to his wife's lips.

Bolormaa's eyes flutter open and she moans. She sips without speaking, then drinks more eagerly, until she is holding the cup herself.

Ganbaatar glances at Aisin, who nods and returns to fetch their tea. In his arms, their daughter wails softly, the first indication she is alive enough to care. She flails but settles when he soothes her with gentle rocking. He watches as her tiny eyes close. Perhaps there are still miracles left.

     Erin Jamieson

SIXTEEN

GANBAATAR SITS ACROSS from Batbayar, watching him drink honey milk. Time has passed, but their daughter still has no name. Although frail when she entered life, now she is strong and sturdy, able to walk on her own with few falls.

She follows Bolormaa wherever she goes and tries to sneak outside with Ganbaatar. She has a shrill cry, especially when Quatan picks her up. In fact, she squirms when she is held by anyone, even her mother. She'd rather be on her own, to explore and make her own way.

She has already discovered many ways to frustrate her family. She stands near her mother while she cooks, clawing her legs until she's given a scrap. She steals her brother's boots and attempts to put them on her own feet. She tears up his schoolbooks until someone pretends to read them. And all this Quatan bears, or even enjoys, as if there is no greater gift in the world than to have a sister threatening to claim everything for herself.

Batbayar wipes the milk from his mouth. "You must hold a naming ceremony before she's a year old. It's time."

The last thing Ganbaatar wants to discuss is his daughter—or anyone else, for that matter. He is bone tired after a day in misty, cold fields, forever behind the quotas he's given. The animals are worn and uncooperative, the air dense with despair.

Since their daughter's birth, Bolormaa has been weaker, more subdued. She is thought to have suffered a slight hemorrhage and, although much improved, her movements are slower and more cautious. She works exclusively inside, because the doctor fears her body is too weak for the extreme elements of cold and heat.

Sometimes Ganbaatar catches her gazing outside as she sends Quatan off to school or as he prepares to leave for the day. But it is the only time he recognizes any sense of longing.

She is a loving—if overprotective—mother. She frets when Quatan is late returning from school, and she encourages their daughter to stay by her side. She cooks plain but hearty meals, the same as she has since the start of their marriage: mutton stew, boiled onions, and *baaz*. The food is filling but utterly tasteless, and Ganbaatar doesn't have the heart to tell her so.

Batbayar visits often, today with his wife, whose midsection is swollen with their first child. Her name, Munkhtsetseg, means "eternal flower" and suits her well, with her classic Mongolian nose and mouth, straight teeth, and melodic and soothing voice. She is pretty and utterly forgettable, kind but in an overly sweet way.

It is she who has pushed the naming ceremony, who urges her husband to lodge at their *ger* to make sure Bolormaa is doing all right. As if they don't trust Ganbaatar to handle things himself.

"It could be a small affair," she says, pursing her lips.

"Just family," Batbayar adds.

Ganbaatar lowers his voice. "It's unneeded stress for Bolormaa."

"Think of it as a little celebration."

"Are we having a party?" Quatan asks as he walks in. At seven, he is strikingly handsome, tall and lanky, but his eyes are often lowered to the ground.

"For your sister," Batbayar explains.

"I want to have a party."

"Your father and I need to talk privately. Why don't you see if you can work on your Russian."

He wrinkles his nose, and Batbayar laughs. "I felt the same way when I was your age."

Ganbaatar feels a pang, remembering. Batbayar is still young, just shy of twenty, but in what seems like a lifetime ago, he was a petulant younger brother, unable to focus on his studies and dreaming of being a great horse racer. Unaware that soon, his father would become ill, and he'd never have the chance to pursue the sport.

"Fine." Quatan walks over to a far corner and plops open a sheet of the Russian alphabet.

"More obedient than I was," Batbayar murmurs.

"I should hope so."

He grins. "So, I'll have an astrologer stop by tomorrow, around noon?"

"We don't need an astrologer."

"It's tradition. Don't you want to give your daughter the best chance possible?"

Ganbaatar watches as his wife slowly rises and lifts their baby, already so independent, squirming furiously in her mother's arms. A baby that was predicted to be a boy by an astrologer. Lately he has lost faith in everything: in God, in predictions and traditions, and health.

"Bolormaa will feel better about it," Batbayar is saying.

And Ganbaatar, who has stopped listening, nods. "All right. If you say so."

The astrologer determines the best day for the naming ceremony will be the following Tuesday, so Ganbaatar informs the members of his collective he won't be able to make it, feeds the livestock as soon as he rises, and starts to help Bolormaa prepare.

Excused from school, Quatan is elated about missing a Russian alphabet test. He dances around the room, causing more trouble amidst the preparations, asking to hold his sister and trying to dance with her, only to have her storm away every time he takes her hand.

At precisely noon, Ganbaatar, Bolormaa, and Quatan head outside with the smallest member of their family. The sun is bright and the air damp as Batbayar, alongside his wife and parents, stands, waiting.

Wordlessly, Ganbaatar reaches for the canvas bag, writes down the name he has selected, and stuffs the slip inside. Everyone else follows suit, with Bolormaa ending the process with her daughter balanced in her arms.

Bolormaa's father steps forward, his gait heavily affected. He plucks out a single slip and unrolls it painstakingly. Under the sun his skin is a withered prune, pitted, lined, and nearly unrecognizable. It has been two years since they've seen him, a year since he suffered the stroke that partially debilitated him.

"Gerel," he reads. He slips the paper into Bolormaa's hand. She repeats the name to Batbayar and his wife, to her parents, and, finally, to Ganbaatar.

"Gerel." His daughter stares at him, wide eyed, her face tilted towards the sun. As if she understands the weight of her name, a bringer of light.

"Gerel," everyone echoes, and then the sun dips behind a blanket of clouds, and the moment is lost.

That night after Quatan and Gerel have fallen asleep, Bolormaa calls for Ganbaatar. She looks healthier than she has for a while. Her skin is flushed from the sun, and her eyes bright.

"Yes?"

"Just wanted to see you. Are they both asleep?"

"Yes."

"Good. Ganbaatar—" She hesitates. "Thank you for today."

"I suppose it's about time we named our daughter."

She smiles. "But still. It was meaningful to me—also, to see my father again. He seems well."

Ganbaatar stares at the rug below him, a wedding gift from his father, whom he has not seen since the days of Bolormaa's first pregnancy. He smells something sweet and citrusy. "Are you making something?"

"Cinnamon tea." She walks over to the kettle which has begun whistling. "Would you like a cup?"

"No, I'm headed to sleep. Long day."

"Oh."

He glances at her. "But I can help clean if you'd like." He starts to scrub away the charred oil but notices Bolormaa staring at him. He sets the pan back down. "What is it?"

She shakes her head. "Are you happy?"

The question catches him by surprise. He has never stopped worrying about whether he's happy. He's been taught the most important things are having a family and being able to provide for it. He isn't happy, no. Happiness is the flutter in his chest whenever he sees Aisin smile. Happiness was the days he spent with his mother, playing cards. The days when he raced in the fresh air and felt the intense need to win. All eyes on him, believing in him.

He is content. Stable. Safe.

"Are you sure you don't need any help?" he asks.

She doesn't answer. She's staring outside, peeking through the curtain. "It's raining. The cold will be here soon."

He glances out, then lightly brushes his lips against hers. "For now," he says, "Let's enjoy the warmth."

"You wish we had a son," she says, turning away. "I can tell."

"We do have a son."

"You know what I mean. A second one."

"Is that what this is about?" He cups her chin in his hand. "We have two beautiful children. Besides, we'll have more sons. We're still young."

"Promise?"

He's not sure what he's promising or what she's asking, but he nods and kisses her. "Promise."

It is a kiss, as always, without heat or passion. It is like coming home after a chilly day or bundling under sheets in the depth of winter. It is feeling comforted rather than exhilarated.

And it is all Ganbaatar will ever have. Is he happy? Is it enough?

"Let's go outside for a minute," he murmurs.

"Now?"

"Yes. Now."

They step into the night air, letting the misty rain brush their cheeks like thousands of caresses. They listen as it covers the earth, and they taste the air as it becomes cleaner, pure.

They stand side by side in the darkness for some time, listening to the rain, watching the earth become flooded, and praying for the growth it might bring.

     Erin Jamieson

SEVENTEEN

April 1931
Khövsgöl Province

FIVE DAYS AFTER they settle in their new location and two days after Gerel turns five, the air fills with smoke. Gerel is the first to spot it, pointing a chubby finger. "There's a giant in the sky!"

Bolormaa steps outside and stares. At some distance, a thick chain of billowing smoke rises like a phantom, covering the clouds with ashy residue. The air is thick and tickles her throat.

"What is it, Mama?"

She turns the girl away from the fire. "I don't know. Go inside."

"I want to see," she whines.

"I said, go inside. We'll wait until your father and brother come home."

Gerel crosses her arms and stalks back in. At five years old, she is obstinate and persistent.

Bolormaa stays outside, watching. She has never seen smoke rise so high. Fear spreads in her chest. How far away is it? What if it reaches their *ger*? They can't afford to lose anything.

One thing is certain: the smoke is spreading. She can feel the heat from the fire. It's getting stronger and closer. She tears back inside, where Gerel stands by the entrance, her eyes wide.

"I need you to help me," she says. "It's a game. Let's see who can find things the fastest. Your favorite things, your father's favorite things, your brother's favorite things."

"A game?" Gerel repeats, her eyes lighting up. "Do I get a prize if I win?"

"A prize? Yes, if you win. Better hurry." Bolormaa gathers a few colorful quilts. "I've already started."

"No fair!" Gerel shrieks, and she runs around and plops items at Bolormaa's feet: her pale pink dress, a corn husk doll, photos of Paris Ganbaatar bought. Bolormaa adds her own choices to the pile: the scarf her mother stitched by hand for her sixteenth birthday, Quatan's baby shoes, the beautiful pot that cost a fortune. She is rooting through her husband's jackets when she discovers a heavy stack of papers, bound together, with his slanted writing on each precisely dated page. It looks like some sort of diary. When did he write all of this? How had she never seen these pages? How odd to share someone's bed for so many years and not know something like that.

She glances at the first page, dated a day before their wedding.

The horses still need to be fed but I'm exhausted, a slave to cleaning and preparing for tomorrow. Tomorrow. I don't know—

"Mother!" Gerel shrieks.

The pages flutter to the ground, and she rushes over. "What is it?"

"There's a woman."

Bolormaa peers outside and sees no one. The smoke is growing dense in the air. And then she sees her, with ashy white cheeks and hair ragged and wild around her shoulders. The woman is dressed in a pale mustard morning robe, wrapped several times and knotted around a whisper thin waist.

"Aisin," she says, incredulously. "What are you doing here?"

She shakes her head, her eyes hard and lifeless. "You need to get out of here."

"The fire—"

"There's an uprising at the monastery. An armed group is burning down collective centers and killing any officials they can find."

"Armed? You can›t be—"

"They're determined the Communist regime is killing their livestock. They're executing anyone they can find."

Bolormaa lifts Gerel on her hip. "But they wouldn't–"

"The fires are spreading. People are being shot. Please. Listen to me, Bolormaa. You must leave."

She is stunned silent. She can hear distant screams, cries of triumph, the roar of flames. She wants to tell Aisin that she is not brave or strong like her. That she was never expected to be.

"I can help you pack."

"Why?"

Aisin turns to her in surprise. "Because I don't want anything bad to happen to you."

Bolormaa hasn't had a friend since she was a child, attending school. She nods.

"How much time do you think we have?"

Aisin looks over her shoulder. "Pack quickly."

Bolormaa was raised in a family who prided themselves on traditional values. They decorated during seasons of festivities and built a shrine and altar each time they moved. Her father prayed every morning facing the sun, bowing so low his chin nearly touched the ground. She was never asked to do the same; it was simply expected she'd follow her father's good example.

But as she grew older, she also grew disinterested and confused. Was she supposed to be praying to the east? How long, and for what? More importantly, to whom? Her father hadn't explained anything, and her heart felt empty as she copied his actions, until one day she stopped altogether. She realized she'd been praying to someone or something she didn't know.

Bolormaa never discussed spiritual matters with her family. Her parents believed religion was essential to living a worthy life but had never found the time to teach their children anything beyond rituals. So when she was married to Ganbaatar, she was relieved to learn he was not any more religious than she was.

Shortly after their wedding, she broached the subject one night. "Do you believe in anything? I mean, bigger than us? Life after this?"

He moaned and rolled over to face her. He looked majestic under the moonlight, his face unlined and his hair a vivid, shiny black. She could see the shadowed contours of his muscles.

"I have to be up in a few hours," he said.

She turned away, hurt. "Yes, of course."

But then he pulled her back to face him and kissed her cheek. "Why do you ask?"

"We've never discussed it."

He looked beyond her; his eyes were bright in the dark. "My mother was very religious."

He talked about his mother so infrequently, and with so much pain, that Bolormaa regretted her question. "It's not important to me," she said.

He studied her for a long moment. "I thought you were the devout type."

"Me? Devout?"

He shrugged. "Your father is a devout man."

Jutting her chin, Bolormaa said, "I'm not the same as my father."

He hesitated. "I'm sorry if I—"

"Assumed," she finished.

She couldn't say why, but it felt like something had shifted between them, and he noticed. His voice was quiet when he answered.

"I don't believe in anything, no. Believing in something else gives men and women an excuse to look away from what's happening in their lives. My father wasted time on rituals and praying, and my mother died anyway. What good came of that?"

Bolormaa was silent for a long moment. She hadn't had a loss of faith, as it seemed her husband had. It had been more of a gradual fade, not unlike how she might wear a *deel* time after time, only to realize one day how worn the fabric had become.

"I don't think it makes people care about life less," she said.

"But you said you don't believe anything," he argued.

"It's not as simple as that. I'm not sure what to believe."

Years later, when rumors of the closing of monasteries and the confiscation of religious books reached them, Ganbaatar didn't react.

But Bolormaa would come back to that first conversation and wonder if this had been the seedlings of a new faith, however tenuous. Not her father's faith.

Certainly, though she did not know it yet, that faith could endanger her family.

The screaming is growing louder. Bolormaa covers Gerel's ears, but she pushes her hands away.

Aisin is waiting for them, her face pale and panicked. "Hurry."

"What about Ganbaatar? My son?"

"You must leave. What if the fire spreads?"

"I'm staying until they come home."

Aisin shakes her head. "I'll wait. You go."

Bolormaa glances at her. For some reason, her stomach bubbles. There's something strange about this offer. "Why you? Why would you do that?"

Aisin hesitates, long enough for Bolormaa to suspect this isn't merely neighborly goodwill. Aisin, always showing up when someone is needed. Aisin, always ready to help, even though she has no obligation.

The light and laughter in her eyes whenever she looks at Ganbaatar.

"I'm not leaving, and you're not staying," Bolormaa says. She doesn't know if her suspicions are anything but that. But the longer Aisin is here, the more they grow, like weeds that one day may be too tall to prune.

Aisin's eyes harden. "Stay and wait, then. What happens if the fire does spread, and you're trapped? Ganbaatar has enough sense. He'll find a way around."

"And my son?"

"I'll make sure he's safe."

Bolormaa looks at Gerel's terrified face.

"That's a promise," Aisin says firmly.

"Why?" Bolormaa insists. "Why would you risk your life?"

The two women stare at each other. And in that moment, Bolormaa's doubts multiply. She pictures, again, how Aisin came running—not once, but many times. She is polite and friendly with Bolormaa, but light on her feet, exhibiting a different energy entirely when Ganbaatar is around.

But Aisin's answer is careful and measured. "Because you and Ganbaatar accepted me when no one else would. And because I have a lot less to lose than you do."

That last line.

Maybe something is going on between Aisin and her husband. Maybe it's all in her mind. But Aisin, like always, is one step ahead. She understands what Bolormaa understands.

Bolormaa cares about her husband, but Gerel's safety comes first. And right now, there isn't time.

"Please," Aisin says.

There's no time left.

Bolormaa grabs Gerel's hand, swallows hard, and then does the only brave thing in her life—something brave and cowardly at the same time.

She and her daughter run, leaving Aisin behind in the *ger* where the heat is building from the encroaching flames.

Gerel. Light. Her daughter's hand in hers is like holding a piece of the sun: a ray of hope, direction through cacophony, comfort.

Bolormaa repeats her daughter's name over and over, an encouragement for herself to keep going.

They run until their feet ache. Night has fallen, and the temperature drops steadily. They brought what they could carry on their backs: a few blankets and quilts, a bag of cherished items, some leftover dumplings which Bolormaa divides to eat cold. She'd like to believe the fires have stopped, but she has no idea. She thinks of the goats and horses, praying they escaped. She does not allow herself to think of Aisin, or her husband, or her son.

Gerel asks several times about her brother and father before she nods to sleep, her exhausted body wrapped like a present in a quilt. Bolormaa watches her daughter until her own eyes grow heavy and she begins to drift off, praying to a god she doesn't know that when she wakes, her husband and son will be there.

The air smells of ashes. When Bolormaa wakes, Gerel is watching, her face dirty from soil and sweat, her hair knotted. They traveled for hours in the direction of the capital city, far enough away from their *ger* that Bolormaa felt safe stopping. Closer to the outpost city, they might be able to find help if they need it.

Luckily, the weather has lifted, and the blankets—as well as the fire Bolormaa made—were enough to keep them warm under the night sky.

   Erin Jamieson

Not that she has slept much. Her one and only concern is to figure out what to do now.

"Are we going home?" the girl asks.

"After we eat some breakfast."

But then she remembers there's nothing to eat. She tells her daughter to pack up the blankets. "Today, we have an adventure," she says.

Gerel brightens. "An adventure?"

"Hurry," Bolormaa says. "We have to start soon."

They head back towards the *ger*, painstakingly slow on their tired feet. Bolormaa sniffs the air and searches the sky but sees no sign of smoke. The blue is penetrated, ashy gray, as if scarred with the memory of fire. The grass is spotted with residue.

They are nearly there and from a distance, it's obvious the small outpost town has changed. *Gers* are torn down, stripped bare. Charred remnants of past fires. Utter silence.

"What happened? Is that where we're going?" Gerel asks, sucking on her left thumb.

"No. We were just looking. Seems the fire didn't spread that far."

"Let's go home," she says.

"Will father be there?"

She remembers Aisin's promise. "Yes."

"*Akh ch gesen?*"

"Yes. Your brother, too."

Bolormaa and Gerel ascend the slight hill, the only one for miles, overlooking a series of tributaries in the vast, rocky red terrain. Their home for the last three months no longer stands there.

Instead, a heap of ashes stands where the *ger* once stood, and Bolormaa recognizes fragments of their belongings: the cherry wood dresser, blackened and splintered, curled corners of once-colorful mats. The air tastes of smoke, ash, and rot.

She sees part of a button-down shirt and picks it up. The sleeves are burnt away, and only the buttons are fully intact. She sinks to her knees. It smells like fire, and it still smells like Ganbaatar. When was the last time he'd held her as they slept together? When was the last time she let him?

"Are you crying?"

Bolormaa lifts her head. "Yes."

"You told me we shouldn't cry."

She holds Gerel close. "Sometimes it's all right."

"Now? Now we can cry?" As the girl watches her mother, her bottom lip quivers.

Bolormaa's throat is tight, her chest heavy. The air is too thick; the smoke and this shirt in her arms weigh more than she can bear.

"You can cry," Gerel says.

That breaks her. How will she tell Gerel if the rest of their small family is gone?

 Erin Jamieson

EIGHTEEN

"MOTHER." GEREL SHAKES her lightly.

Bolormaa can't see anything at first, only her daughter, standing over her, waiting. She blinks as her surroundings shift into focus.

"Mother."

"Hush."

Gerel breaks free and sprints away, down the incline. Bolormaa rises so fast, the blood rushes to her head. 'Gerel! Come back here!"

Her daughter is running away. Bolormaa follows, running as fast as she ever has. Her breathing is shallow, and Gerel is still far ahead. She'll never catch her. She'll never catch her.

But then the girl stops. Someone is running towards them, a small figure with a slight frame and his father's jaw—

"Gerel!"

"Quatan?"

Bolormaa stumbles at her son's feet, trying to catch her breath. "Quatan," she whispers.

He doesn't seem to notice her, wrapped in his little sister's arms, which barely reach around him.

"What's that for?" he asks, shaking her off.

"I missed you. Mother said you and Father went on a trip."

"We did. We moved the *ger*. That woman, Aisin, helped us. She said we had to move fast." He looks over her shoulder as their mother arrives.

"Bet you didn't help that much," Gerel giggles.

"Did so."

"Hush, both of you," Bolormaa wheezes, holding her chest. "Where's your father?"

"At our *ger*, with Aisin. He sent me to get water. He told me to look for you on the way."

Bolormaa nearly falls again, this time in relief. She lowers her voice. "How did you escape?"

"What do you mean?"

"The fire."

"Fire?" Gerel repeats, sucking on her thumb.

"Bolormaa, is that you?"

She turns. Her husband walks laboriously, his scalp drenched with sweat, his face unshaven and his clothes soiled and disheveled. His eyes have a crazed look. "Quatan," he says, "why don't you take Gerel back? She's probably hungry."

The boy grabs his sister's hand and leads her away.

Bolormaa watches as they descend the hill.

"I didn't think we should talk in front of our children." Ganbaatar's voice is cool and distant.

"I thought you were dead," she says. "Both of you."

He tilts his head. "Why?"

"Our *ger* is mostly gone—"

"Oh, Bolormaa. Didn't you think I knew? Didn't you think I had the sense to leave? The tension has been building. When the monasteries were shut down, people reached a boiling point."

 Erin Jamieson

"They are angry. Everyone is struggling. We are struggling. But to lay claim over our religious institutions? People need religion, a sense of autonomy."

"I moved the *ger*," he says.

"But we lost some things."

He doesn't meet her eye. "A few things. Nothing important."

She looks over at the ruins. "Nothing important?"

"Wedding gifts, things we don't really use. I saved what I could, but we had to move quickly—" He looks at her and shakes his head. "What the hell did you expect?"

She doesn't answer. Voluminous, ashy clouds shift in the sky, and the air is humid and tastes of rain.

"I lost a horse," he says. "Spooked by the fire."

They can't afford to lose an animal, even one. So much has already been taken from them. For the first time in her life, Bolormaa begins to hate this land: barren and unyielding, obstinate and harsh, despite their effort and pain. She hates the rocky terrain and the miles of nothing but makeshift tents and the scent of animal manure. She hates the startling blue skies against the dry grasslands, a blue so vivid it seems to hold promises but never delivers.

Ganbaatar straightens his back. "There might be more riots."

"You will join them?" she asks.

"I stand with our people. But I'm not sure right now what we need."

"Life used to be so much simpler."

His eyes darken. "Life was never simple for me."

"We could have been killed. The children—"

Ganbaatar stares quietly into the distance, silent for a long while. Slowly, he nods and faces her.

"These men, they're doing what they think they must. Everyone is trying to survive."

"By setting things on fire?" Although her mind is cloudy, she understands. Something she learned long ago from her father. Burning fields to prepare for new crops when the soil is depleted.

A need to destroy so that one day something new can grow.

In the sun's fading light, silver hairs glint on his head. He offers a sad smile and his face creases, showing fully their ten years together. He seems to have aged overnight.

"You'd be surprised," he says softly. "Sometimes there is a fine line between building a life and burning it down."

❧

It takes a week before they settle in again. Bolormaa wants to keep Quatan at home with Gerel, but Ganbaatar says she's being ridiculous.

"He's no less safe learning something at that school than he is sitting around at home."

She doesn't respond. They never have the leisure to "sit around." One horse and a few possessions poorer, everyone works harder. Bolormaa spreads their food supply as far as it will go, and Ganbaatar works long hours. Gerel slips out one day and Bolormaa, panicked, runs out to find her daughter feeding the goats, laughing as they nuzzle against her, attempting to nibble on her skirt.

"Gerel," she laughs, "What are you doing?"

She shrugs, nonplussed. "They're always hungry."

"It isn't your job to do that."

The girl turns to her mother with a serious gaze. "It will

be one day. Besides, I like being with the animals. Ask if I can help."

Bolormaa, stunned by Gerel's maturity and willfulness, only manages to pry her away after she agrees to talk to Ganbaatar. "I can't promise he'll say yes," she says.

The truth is, since the fire, her relationship with her husband has become tenuous, flimsy at best, liable to tear from the smallest stresses. Quatan is falling behind in school because he is too timid and ashamed to ask for help. Still slight for his age, he walks with his gaze to the ground, eating meals in silence. Bolormaa doesn't think he has any friends. He never asks to go outside in the afternoons as her brothers did at that age. She never sees any boys around their age.

Their son's demeanor is something Ganbaatar is bound and determined to change, even if he himself must change it.

One evening in late September as they prepare food, he tells Bolormaa, "You're soft on him. We need to force him to be more assertive."

"Assertive?"

"He needs to confront the boys who make fun of him. Defend himself."

"But that isn't like him." Bolormaa lowers her voice and lifts the stew pot from the fire. Steam coats her face in a shiny layer, and the air fills with the bittersweet scent of orange rinds and meat.

"That is exactly the problem," Ganbaatar answers.

Bolormaa sighs. She knows their son is quiet, in the same way she was. She knows she's done nothing to make him feel more confident. How can she, when she knows what it's like to feel everyone is trying to shape or change you?

Ganbaatar mistakes the silence and turns to see what she's preparing. "Beef again?"

"Lamb. Braised."

He nods, but his eyes flicker something close to disappointment. Like he wants to argue but is holding himself back. "Where is Quatan now?"

Of course. He wants to talk to their son alone.

"Studying," she says tersely, stirring the stew with a ladle. As he turns to leave, she places a hand on his shoulder. To her surprise, he stops. "I wanted to talk to you about Gerel."

"What has she done?"

"Nothing." Bolormaa sets the pot on the table. She focuses on keeping her voice strong. This is for her daughter. A daughter, she already knows, who will grow up to be stronger and bolder than all of them. "She wants to help you."

"What do you mean, help me?" He dips his finger into the stew, winces, licks it clean. "This is good, better than I thought."

"Meaning?"

"Nothing. It's very good."

"I found Gerel with the goats today."

He looks at her sharply. "And? You told her she wasn't allowed?"

"Yes, but she looked so happy—"

"She won't be when her arm gets chewed off."

Bolormaa wills herself not to look at her husband's stump. "Could she help you? She's a natural, so gentle, and she loves animals. She was feeding them—"

"You let her?"

"No, I found her. Please. Just for a day."

"I can't watch her while I'm working." He shakes his head. "Quatan's help is all I need. Gerel can help you."

"Quatan isn't interested. Gerel is."

     Erin Jamieson

"That," he says, "Is what worries me. Is our son ever going to be interested in the work he's meant to do?"

Bolormaa bites her lip. "Why does it matter what they do, so long as they both help? I helped my father with the animals."

"It's not Gerel I'm worried about," Ganbaatar says, lowering his voice.

She reaches for his hand. "Let's just let them be as they are. They're young. They have time to grow. Did we know everything about ourselves at that age?"

"I suppose not," Ganbaatar says. To her surprise, he laughs. "I mean, look at us now. We still don't know."

That, Bolormaa thinks, is one of the most truthful things he's ever said to her.

When October arrives, with short days and harsh winds, Quatan wraps his face with scarves, so it does not blister on his walks to and from school. Gerel continues to feed the goats and brush the horse's mane. After finally accepting his daughter's enthusiasm, Bolormaa believes her husband has come to enjoy Gerel's company, and the help. Their daughter is unabashedly fearless, feeding the animals at their worst tempers, and she's undeterred when the wind kicks the first snowfall into her face. Though her hands are chubby and her steps still infantile, she is good with the animals. Occasionally, Ganbaatar praises her, and she shines under his approval.

Meanwhile, Quatan improves in his studies but grows quieter and more distant as he approaches his eleventh birthday. When Bolormaa asks about a celebration, Ganbaatar suggests a feast. Surprised, she says, "We haven't done anything like that for years. Can we afford the expense?"

"We'll manage," he says, before he buttons his coat and leaves for the day.

So Bolormaa begins preparations, feeling lighter on her feet than she has for a long time. Finally, something to look forward to, after the fire and the demanding work that followed, a string of similar days. Even Ganbaatar's mood lifts, and Gerel is ecstatic to help her mother.

The feast takes days to prepare. Dishes are planned: *huushuur* meat pies, mutton served with a full head, stir fried rice, *boortsog* cookies for something sweet. They invite Batbayar and his family, cousins on both sides. Bolormaa worries about the time and expense but tells herself they need this day. A flicker of happiness, a time of celebration.

It's been too long.

On the day of the feast, Gerel scrubs down the counter where her mother has butchered the sheep's head.

"I'll miss you when you go to school next year," Bolormaa says.

The girl's forehead creases. "I won't be at school all the time. I'll come back home every day."

"I hope so." Bolormaa folds her daughter into a hug, the kind she used to give Quatan. "But still."

"Are we having sheep's head?" Gerel squeals.

"The eyes are for me," Quatan calls from the other room. He walks in, clothed in western-style clothes purchased from Ulaanbaatar: black slacks slightly too long and a cream-colored dress shirt. His hair is neatly combed. Today he will be allowed his first glass of *airag*, and Bolormaa remembers with a pang the tiny infant she once held in her arms. How terrified she'd been! Her son is still slight, but taller and more mature by the day. He's filled out a bit and while he's still quiet, he has a calm composure, always.

The more he grows, the less he resembles Ganbaatar. His inky, black hair has softened to charcoal; his nose has

     Erin Jamieson

become more curved, his jawline and cheekbones slightly less defined; every day he looks, sounds, and acts a little more like Bolormaa. While Gerel's features are becoming sharper and more defined, just like her father.

Quatan walks to where Bolormaa stands, knife in one hand, blood splattered on her apron. "Why are you looking at me like that?"

"You are so grown up," she says.

Gerel makes a face. "A year older, a year uglier."

"Gerel!"

But Quatan comes over to his sister and swoops her up. "You're getting heavy."

She is nearing his height, a sturdy build at five years old. Although they are young, it's already clear how differently they are built. Quatan is timid, with fine, almost delicate features.

The more she grows, Gerel exhibits a bravery that Bolormaa and Ganbaatar may never have.

NINETEEN

BOLORMAA GREW UP watching her siblings take turns plucking out the sheep's eyes for guests. Eyeballs are a delicacy, a gift. And thus, being the one to serve them is considered an honor. It was always a shift of momentum in the middle of a feast, with everyone watching to see who might be selected. Once Bolormaa was meant to be the honored server, but she fell ill.

Now, she watches, misty-eyed, as her son approaches the sheep's head.

Quatan has just plucked out the eyes when the thunder begins.

"We should go inside," Bolormaa murmurs, but it's impossible without abandoning everything altogether: family and friends are lined up on mats outside, bundled but comfortable under an unusually sunny and mild autumn afternoon.

Sunny.

"What was that?" Gerel asks.

"Maybe it isn't thunder," Batbayar's wife says.

Ganbaatar stands and looks toward the horizon.

Everyone turns to stare.

A woman in a magnificent crimson *deel* approaches, hair

tied behind her back, looking at them directly as she leads a camel. An older man walks beside her, leading another.

"Who is—" Batbayar rises, instantly tense.

"Aisin?" Bolormaa says. She tastes bitterness in her mouth, a bitterness that swells as Aisin approaches with her annoying, straight teeth, and not at all with the demeanor of someone who is intruding.

She pulls her camel to a halt. "Sorry to bother your party." Her eyes flicker over the group.

"Aisin and her uncle are in my collective," Ganbaatar offers by way of explanation.

The others stare at him blankly.

Bolormaa looks back and forth between her husband and Aisin. He told her, finally, the truth about what happened the fateful day he lost his limb. He would have died if not for Aisin. She knows Aisin is the reason he's alive, and that she should be grateful.

But why did he hide it for so long?

Was it because of Aisin's ethnicity? Did he really think Bolormaa would care?

And now this. Ganbaatar could have told her, many times, that Aisin was part of his collective. Not once did he mention her. Jealousy bubbles in Bolormaa's stomach. No matter the reason, her husband should have told her. And should have asked if he's invited her to the celebration. Aisin continues to appear in their lives, and Bolormaa has no say.

Aisin dismounts the camel in a flurry of colorful skirts. "There was another uprising. Tanks were brought in to take down the remaining insurgents. Others surrendered. We escaped during the final confrontation."

Everyone has stopped eating. Aisin is looking at Quatan and Gerel, both frozen, terrified, entranced.

Remembering herself, Bolormaa lowers her voice. "Enough," she says. "Children, finish your meal. We are safe here."

"I'm not hungry anymore," Batbayar mutters, shoving away his plate and grabbing his wife's arm. "We have to go."

"You can't leave," Gerel shrieks. "Brother hasn't eaten his eyes yet!"

"We should get back before dark." He doesn't meet Bolormaa or Ganbaatar's eyes as he leads his wife and children away.

Ganbaatar stares down at his bad hand, opening and flexing the other, over and over. He looks up after a long moment. "Party's over," he says. When they don't move, he raises his voice. "Did you hear me? The party's over."

Over the next half-hour, the guests leave. A few family members offer to stay and help clean up, but most of the cousins are gone within minutes.

Aisin stands at the edge of their gathering, still holding her camel in a tight grip, when her uncle nudges her. "We should move on, too."

She says something to him in a faint voice.

He grunts. "Remember, night falls fast." He mounts his camel and leaves, glancing back several times before disappearing.

"I didn't mean to disrupt your party—" Aisin begins.

"Nonsense," Bolormaa says at the same time Ganbaatar murmurs, "Not your fault."

"I'm the reason they left."

"You were telling the truth. There could be danger."

"I don't think your guests appreciated the messenger, either."

Nearby, Gerel laughs with delight. She has stolen her

     Erin Jamieson

brother's gift, a new pair of bows, and throws them haphaz-ardly, outrunning her brother every time he tries to catch her.

Aisin chuckles. "Your daughter is fast like her father."

"More like a little windstorm," Ganbaatar says, grinning.

"And a son who wants to be a racer, I remember that."

He frowns. "He's given that up. I didn't exactly foster his interest when he was younger."

"He's still young," Bolormaa says. She suspects Ganbaatar dropped racing for other reasons, after hoping his son would have the strength he never had.

Ganbaatar doesn't answer as he watches their sturdy daughter, their lanky son.

"Let me at least help clean up," Aisin insists.

"I can't have you cleaning for us again," Bolormaa says.

"You shouldn't travel alone in the dark," Ganbaatar adds.

Aisin scowls. "You're just as bad as Uncle. Here I am, a grown woman—"

"Fair enough," Bolormaa says quickly. "But it wasn't your fault." She says it more like a question, trying to see if Aisin will react or say more about why she chose to warn them.

In the distance, a faint roar can be heard, isolated shout-ing. Bolormaa shivers as she clears the tables and tries to coerce the children into helping. Aisin cleans twice as fast as Bolormaa and convinces Gerel and Quatan to make it a game, to see who can help the most. Aisin is a natural leader, effortlessly guiding without smothering them. Mongolian children and a Chinese woman, harmoniously working under the fading, afternoon sun and pressing blue skies. As if it has been this way all along.

Ganbaatar places a hand on Bolormaa's shoulder.

She rests her head against him.

"Worried about the tanks?" he asks.

"Are you?"

He hesitates. "Not if Aisin isn't. She knows more than we do."

They hear another shriek of laughter and watch Gerel stumble and pull her brother down with her. Aisin stands beside them, laughing so hard, her cheeks are flushed.

"I suppose we can trust her," Bolormaa says, but Ganbaatar has separated already and is no longer listening.

Erin Jamieson

TWENTY

October 1933

"*SHINE HURGELTIIN GOGLOGO.* Policy of the New Turn," Ganbaatar explains to Quatan the day before his thirteenth birthday.

"I know what it is. I'm not an idiot."

"Then you'll understand why it's so important to take good care of the horse."

"Because it's ours, and only ours now."

"It will be," Ganbaatar corrects. He pats the woven mat he's seated on, one of the few wedding gifts that survived the fire. It's decorated with blue half-moons and bursting sunsets, symbolizing hope and new life. Now, the edges are frayed and have begun to unravel, one thread at a time. Bolormaa insists it can be fixed, but he quietly believes the damage is irreparable.

"Can I go now?" Quatan asks. Over the past year, everything has become a chore to him, from finishing Russian exercises to feeding the goats.

"Not yet."

"Look, I promise I'll take better care of the horse."

Ganbaatar eyes his son, still slight for his age, with soft features and a complexion quite paler than the rest of the family. Ganbaatar only sees himself in his son when he is acting selfish. Most days, Quatan is a mystery, almost a stranger.

"Do you want to tell me about your day?"

Quatan hesitates, surprised. Then he nods. "I think I did well on my translation exam."

"The one you were so worried about?"

"Yes."

"That's good. How did your friends do?"

Quatan ducks his head. "I told you. I don't have any."

"Don't be ridiculous."

"I'm not. You asked."

"Everything seems bleak at your age, but you will realize how much you have."

He shrugs.

Ganbaatar stands up, brushing off dust. "If you tried to make friends— What do the other boys like to do? Play cards? Race?"

"You know I'm too old to race."

"You're in your prime years! When I was your age—"

"You'd already been practicing for half your life." He turns away. "I'm sorry to disappoint you, but I'm not like you. I don't like playing cards and watching people get drunk and betting—"

"I didn't say anything about getting drunk." Ganbaatar's cheeks flush.

Quatan stares at his father's shaking hands. "No," he says quietly. "You didn't."

Ganbaatar sips on milk tea, letting the warmth seep through his chest as Gerel helps herself to a hearty portion of stewed cabbage and beef jerky. She eats like a boy, with her hands, while her brother politely asks for more and takes small bites. Bolormaa looks worn, her eyes heavily lined and hair splitting at the ends. Her clothes are faded and stretched. Ganbaatar runs a finger through his graying hair, wondering how they have aged so quickly.

Midway through the meal, Gerel asks for a horse. She's old enough to ride now and has been asking for a while.

"Absolutely not," Ganbaatar says.

"Why not?"

"For one, we can't afford it."

"But I need one. You said with collectives shut down—"

"I didn't say that. I said they might be, but it won't happen overnight."

Gerel chews her food and swallows. "I need to learn to ride before I'm too old."

"You know how to ride," Quatan says. "You're a natural."

"I want to race."

"No," her parents say simultaneously.

"Aisin does."

Ganbaatar looks down. "Aisin's different."

"How?"

"Gerel," Bolormaa says. "Eat your food before it gets cold."

She pushes the plate aside. "You'd let Quatan do it."

"He's older."

"No," she corrected. "He's a boy."

Ganbaatar stops eating. The food tastes too salty and greasy, and his stomach is burning. "I don't want you racing, and that's final. Now eat your supper and hush."

Gerel stops eating, as do Bolormaa and Quatan. Outside, it has begun to rain, the first in weeks, flooding the parched ground. It's a comforting sound amidst the overpowering darkness. After they clear the dishes, Ganbaatar stands outside, letting the misty rain wash over his face.

He feels a hand on his shoulder. "It wouldn't hurt to let her try."

"You know how I feel about it."

His wife nods, a shadow crossing her face. "But you can't force your children to like the things you think they should."

"That's not what this is about. She could get hurt."

She sighs. "Other women race—"

"Yes, but—"

"Let her try. You know Quatan couldn't care less about racing."

"Once, he did."

"Things change." Her voice softens. "People change. And you need to let Gerel be her own person. In case you haven't noticed, they're quite different."

"I didn't mean to upset you," Ganbaatar says.

She is plain as ever, her hair slightly matted and sweaty, her skin lined and starting to sag. She is not beautiful, and she never was—although there was a time, in the glow of early motherhood, he found her so. He can hardly remember that now. Aisin, in comparison, has the same milky complexion and shiny hair she had a decade earlier. The same effect on him, although he has learned to keep it buried.

He turns away, unwilling to look at her. "Gerel shouldn't race. And Quatan should be doing something, so he isn't always an outcast."

"You'd make him try racing?"

"I'd have him try anything that would help."

"But what about Gerel?"

Ganbaatar shivers. "That's the problem. You're always changing the subject. Come on, let's go in before we get sick."

Inside, her skin is pasty under the thin stream of moonlight. Inside, she always looks tired and worried.

"Are you coming to bed?" she asks.

"Soon," he says.

He listens until he hears her soft snores. His body feels clammy and empty, and he reaches for the *airag* brewed earlier in the week. He drinks a glass and finds it utterly tasteless, so he reaches for the straight liquor and pours himself a shot. He drains it and pours another. He loses track after the third. His body is warm, his chest full to bursting. His skin feels as if lightning has been embedded inside. Flammable, combustible, full of light and heat.

"Father?"

He wipes his lips clean. "Quatan? Is that you? Why are you awake?"

"I got thirsty." He stills. "What are you drinking?"

"Just some *airag*."

His son lifts the empty vodka bottle. "This isn't *airag*. Did you drink all this by yourself?"

Ganbaatar falls silent.

"Does Mom know?"

"There's nothing to tell her. He grabs the bottle. "I am your father, and I wanted something a little stronger tonight. Your mother and I have been worried lately and I—"

"Decided you needed to drink."

"You don't understand."

Quatan stands at his full height, his narrow shoulders squared. "Who else knows?"

Ganbaatar shakes his head. "There's nothing to tell, nothing to tell your mother."

"No," Quatan says quietly. "Not if you promise to stop."

"Fine. I promise."

"I don't believe you."

It's the first time his son's voice has hinged on accusation, and Ganbaatar feels as if he's been stabbed in the chest. His head is throbbing. "I wouldn't lie to you," he says. "Tomorrow, I'll get rid of the rest of the liquor. We've had enough *airag* lately."

"You've already gotten rid of it," Quatan says darkly. But in a moment, they both laugh–broken, muted, comical, like the undeveloped wings of a bird who has yet to learn how to fly. Tragic and hopeful laughter.

Ganbaatar cleans up evidence of his drinking as soon as Quatan heads back to bed. He turns too quickly and drops the glass. As he scrambles to pick up the shards, he cuts himself twice.

He wraps his hand in bandages, he repeats a mummified lie, telling himself what he told his son: this would not happen again.

Men start missing the following week. First, several suppliers, grown and raised in Ulaanbaatar, the men who bring goods from the city such as superior feed, and blankets for sick animals. There are five that come through regularly, then three, then one. Cursing their inconsistency, Ganbaatar asks the lone supplier—a thin man with a bushy salt and pepper beard—if he knows of anyone else to contact.

"Unfortunately, no. There aren't many men coming to and from the city these days."

 Erin Jamieson

"Suddenly, they stopped," Ganbaatar says.

The man hangs his head. "I am sorry to hear it."

"People are so bloody irresponsible."

The supplier winces. "I am afraid there's more to it."

"I don't know what you mean."

A heavy breeze sends dust into their faces, and Ganbaatar's camel begins to snort. From a distance, he hears Aisin calling.

"If you think of anyone else—"

The man nods. "I'll let you know."

"Who was that?"

Ganbaatar turns to face Aisin, who leads her own camel through the blowing dust. Her hair is tied into a sweaty knot at the nape of her neck.

"Supplier."

"Which one?"

"The only one left."

She bites her lip.

"What is it?"

She shakes her head. "I must go. Uncle's waiting for me."

"You still answer to him, after all these years?"

Her face softens. "He's getting old. He needs me. For all those years, he helped me when no one else would."

In the afternoon sun, her skin is glowing, unblemished by time or hard labor, as if she has been preserved in the moment of time they first met. After some restrictions were lifted and Ganbaatar was able to choose his own collective, he proposed that Aisin and her uncle join him.

They see each other almost daily. Ganbaatar forces himself to leave her earlier than he wants to, making sure he comes and goes only as duties require. The few times Aisin has offered to help him directly, he accepts only if others are present. When she braids her hair, he pretends not to notice.

When she smells like clover honey and ginger, he steps away to taste instead the earthiness of the wind, the amber warmth of the sun, or the bland food Bolormaa has packed for him.

Today, Aisin is forlorn. Her cheeks are flushed raspberry with cold, her eyes drained and empty. Her uncle is all she has, and they both know it. Brave and intelligent though she is, she is still not Mongolian and never will be. In wake of the regulation and then deregulation of *negdels*, foreigners are still distrusted, maybe even more so. The only worse offense than being Chinese would be if she were Russian. He wonders what will happen to her after her uncle is gone, and his heart clenches at the thought.

"Is there anything I can do?" he asks.

She laughs softly. "You know there isn't."

"I wish there was."

A breeze sends a flutter of leaves—dead, flattened corpses at their feet. "You've been a good friend," she says.

He reaches to squeeze her hand, but she moves, and he ends up stroking her cheek instead. She stills, her body stiff but flooded with heat, strands of hair falling into her eyes.

"Ganbaatar," someone calls.

They step away from each other, as if magnetically separated.

Hexa, a middle-aged man with a small frame and salt and pepper hair, runs toward them. "Tell…what—"

"Did something happen?" he asks.

Hexa gasps, looking back and forth between them.

"Is one of the horses hurt?" Aisin asks.

The older man wipes his brow. "Eiji—"

"Where is he?"

He looks at Aisin. "In the field."

"Is he hurt?"

But Hexa is either unwilling or unable to answer.

"Come on." Aisin slips her hand in Ganbaatar's good one. Together, they run.

They find Hexa's son not far from where the sheep graze, lying face down in the soil, his small neck broken at an angle, swollen and mottled purple. His back is open and exposed, his tanned skin profuse with dried blood. Angry welts run down his sides. The closer they get, the stronger the stench becomes: nauseatingly sweet and rank.

"Eiji? What happened?"

There is no reply. Aisin gingerly places her hands on the young man's shoulders. "Help me."

"What are you doing?"

"Flipping him over. He'll breathe better that way."

They manage to turn him over, so his face is upward, under the fading, afternoon sky. His lips are bruised the same purple, his face pale and bloodless against his tan, sculpted shoulders. His mouth is a thin line, and his eyes are wide open, witnesses to something they can no longer see.

"Eiji?" Ganbaatar asks again.

Aisin presses his hand to his throat, then his chest.

There is no pulse. There is no breath.

TWENTY-ONE

THEY STARE AT Eiji's crumpled body. After the regulations were lifted, officials started purging anyone they considered leftist. People had gone missing; others had been found dead.

Ganbaatar wills the young man to raise his head and speak, but he is motionless, his skin cool to the touch.

"Aisin, did you find him?"

Before they can answer, Hexa is already there, stooped beside them, panting like a wild dog. "What? Is he drunk? Eiji, get up." He bends over his son and slaps him hard on the face.

Tears stream down Aisin's face as he slaps his son again. "Stop," she erupts. "Can't you see he's dead?"

Hexa freezes, one hand raised, his face tomato red.

"He's been beat up."

"Who would do this?" Hexa asks.

"We have an idea," Aisin says gently. "But that doesn't matter right now."

"To hell it doesn't," he says. "What bastard hurt my son?"

"We can help you move him," Aisin says.

"Listen, you bitch." He snatches her, shakes her like a doll. "I asked you who did this to my son, you filthy Chinese."

Aisin bites her lip hard, her eyes watering. "Someone,"

she manages, "who was an enemy of his and didn't support what he did."

"What do you mean?"

"Let her go," Ganbaatar snarls, shoving Hexa.

The older man falls beside his son's corpse.

Her eyes blaze. "You don't think I could have shoved him if I wanted? I've spent my whole life racing horses, lugging loads, and working." She stoops beside the older man, offering her hand. "Let me help you."

He takes it, his face ashen. "I don't know what got into me," he whispers.

Aisin shakes her head. "It doesn't matter."

It does, but Ganbaatar swallows his words. Hexa is shaking from head to toe, murmuring his son's name. Begging him to get up.

Eiji is Hexa's only son, his only child. His wife died suddenly two years earlier, and his relatives live in Ulaanbaatar. Ganbaatar feels a twinge of pity, but he cannot unsee the man shaking Aisin.

"Let's get him out of here," she says, "both of them."

"Where to?"

"It doesn't matter," she hisses. "Help me."

It takes all their combined strength to guide Hexa away from his son, and he fights every step of the way, sobbing and shouting.

When they are close to his *ger*, Aisin settles him down on a patch of grass. "Rest here, and we'll be right back."

"My son."

"We'll take care of him."

"Eiji. He's alone."

"We'll take care of him," Ganbaatar repeats with less conviction. "Stay here."

"My son," Hexa groans, barely moving his chapped lips.

"We need to get him inside."

Ganbaatar grimaces. "What if they come back, whoever killed Eiji?"

"Do you think that's likely?"

"If they did," Aisin says, "they wouldn't kill Hexa."

"They didn't hesitate to kill his son."

"That was different."

"I don't see how."

Aisin draws a shallow breath. "He was part of the league. I thought you knew."

"What?"

"The National Youth League started by the Russians. Their members favor collectivization and government ownership. People are frightened it will be like before. They'll be limited again, or this little freedom won't last. Now we have riots and protests again. If you are accused of associating with the league, you're in danger."

Ganbaatar nods, processing. He knows, deep down, things aren't simple. A group of children, these youth who supported the Mongolian People's Revolutionary Party. Some might support this communist party because they'd been raised seeing how education had improved. These were children who hadn't seen the changes on the Gobi, who were not bitter like Ganbaatar was.

They didn't realize what a dangerous game was being played, no matter which side you were on.

"But they wouldn't come for his father," Ganbaatar says. He thinks about Quatan or Gerel joining this league.

"I don't know."

"Let's get him inside," he says.

They guide Hexa into the *ger* and give him water, which

he refuses. Aisin is patient, holding his hand and whispering soothing words that mean nothing. Finally, he reclines and lolls into a troubled sleep.

"We should get Eiji," Aisin whispers.

"Why?"

She stares, her eyes blazing. "It's his son. We can't leave him out there." She gestures to the entrance, and they step outside.

The day is ashen gray, the cusp of late autumn. The cool air smells of frost and decay, and the blue skies are nearly slate gray, with heavy clouds building like rolling hills.

Ganbaatar speaks softly. "Why did Eiji die?"

Aisin turns. "Why did he die?"

He steps closer until their faces are inches apart. He can smell her skin, the sweet salty scent of perspiration in her hair. He can count the tiny imperfections and little moles, can see the birthmark beneath her jaw and a faint scar between her eyebrows from running into a tree during a race.

"Just because he believed in something different," she says, "doesn't change the fact he is Hexa's son."

"But what he believed—"

She takes a step back. "You don't have to help me. But we should move him, so he won't—" She shakes her head, unwilling to continue.

"Fine, I'll help."

Her eyes are fiery. "I'm not saying I agree with what he believed, but I don't know what's right anymore. We have more freedom, yes? But then we kill each other, abandon people we knew because they don't fit our mold or share our ideas. I've spent my life alone because this is what happens. No one accepts. No one considers that sometimes good and evil aren't clear. Eiji was trying to survive. He didn't deserve to die, and he doesn't deserve to be left alone."

"Aisin."

"Go home," she says.

"I want to help."

"You want to help me. Not him."

He hesitates. "Does it matter?"

"Yes."

"You can't do this alone."

"I've spent most of my life doing things alone."

He stares at her, seeing the haunted hollow to her eyes. The wind brushes her hair across her face like a veil, and he notices what he never has been willing to see before—a portion of her beauty is the sorrow she carries, how her eyes never quite warm with her smiles. He is surprised to find that—after many years—maybe he doesn't know her at all.

He could say the same about his wife, his children. The day he turned his father away, Ganbaatar shut everyone out to some degree.

"I'd like to help you," he calls after her, but Aisin is already putting distance between them.

"I know," she says over her shoulder. "But you can't."

Bolormaa's hands are stained with blood. Ganbaatar rushes to his wife's side, shouting for Quatan to run for help. He looks at the palms of her hands, waving and covered with red creases. Then he sees: beets. His wife is cutting beets. He closes his eyes and takes shallow breaths, but he can only see Hexa's son, bloody and beaten and glistening in the fields.

"Ganbaatar?"

He avoids her eyes. "I'm tired."

"Bad day?"

     Erin Jamieson

He nods. She cups his chin like she would a child. "Why don't you get some rest? I can take care of everything tonight."

It's a lie, but it feels like honey. Ganbaatar swallows its comfort, lies down on the sleeping mat, and pulls the blankets to his chin. His head is pounding, and his chest aches. He tosses for a while until he falls into an uneasy sleep. In his dreams, Aisin calls for him, screaming his name. But he can't find her. He's lost in a dust storm, and the grit coats his lips, his eyes, his ears, choking him, lodging in his throat. He calls and calls to her, but when he finds her, Aisin is no longer listening.

In his sleep, he pulls his wife close, presses against her warm shoulders. She nuzzles closer and when he wakes, he finds her asleep in his arms. He remembers dreaming of Aisin and along with a rush of guilt, he can't help but feel a twinge of disappointment.

TWENTY-TWO

Autumn 1941
Ulaanbaatar

ON HER FIFTEENTH birthday, Gerel eats a bowl of cool porridge, steps into her wool pants and dress, and shrugs into the colorful coat made of yak's wool. Around her neck she winds the scarves her mother knitted by hand last Christmas, and once outside the building, she turns in the opposite direction of school. Her teeth chatter as the sharp wind finds openings. No amount of wool or covering can fully protect from the bone-chilling cold. That much is the same here as the Gobi.

The sky is ashy gray, always covered with smog and the residue of factory smoke. By now, a familiar if not comforting scene, one that seemed oppressive when her family first left the Gobi unexpectedly five years ago. She has nearly forgotten the endless expanse of blue skies, the silence of a new day, and the scent of wet dew on grassland. These have been replaced by the slate canvas of sky, with strokes of exhaust and smoke at every sunset and sunrise. The milky, sweet scent of perspiring bodies juxtaposed with metallic odors, the hum and grind of machines day in and day out. The fields of grazing animals are street sweepers, middle-aged women with bent backs and scorched skin. The birthday feasts have been replaced with congregations of school children traversing the streets during lunch hour, factory men crouched over a spoonful of rice in front of gray buildings. It is a crowded, lonely place, where thousands of lives connect superficially, where you sit next to a man on the bus and never see him again, where a kind mother who offered an extra piece of bread might be struck dead by a wandering vagabond.

Gerel doesn't love Ulaanbaatar; she never will. But she has learned to live in it. She knows the proper change for taking the bus into the shopping district, which darkened streets to avoid, and which vendors sell poor cuts of meat. She has learned to select marmot over camel, because it is more affordable but also tends to be fresher. She has learned that, in the city, nothing comes nearly as easily—or as hard.

Soviet Union rule has made school mandatory, and children trek to institutions housed in old monasteries or chapels. In rows of identical desks, they read lessons in Russian and study Russian history. Unlike tent school in the Gobi, here rooms are divided by age, sometimes by gender as well. Students take breaks at different times, and over the past several years, only once has Gerel shared a lunch period with her brother.

Now, at fifteen years old, she worries this life isn't enough for her.

She and Quatan never have conversations beyond the scope of pure politeness: Please pass the salt. How was your day? Did Mother ask for potatoes today, or turnips? Quatan is twenty-one and engaged to a Mongolian woman with long, butterfly eyelashes and a forced smile that doesn't match her serious, toffee-colored eyes.

They are not in love, that much is obvious. Gerel has heard of parents who arrange marriages for their children, even today. Her brother had the freedom to choose, and he chose a marriage based on status and convenience. No matter what their mother says, Arban is a connection to her father and the banking business. With his intended father-in-law's recommendation, Quatan will study at the University of Ulaanbaatar in the fall. Arban's beauty—glossy, black hair, high cheekbones, and shapely figure—is a bonus, nothing more, nothing less.

If Quatan knew what Gerel was doing, he'd have a fit. Just thinking about it makes her smile, and the cold seems more bearable. Bell chimes echo in the distance, announcing the hour. At this time, she is usually settled in her first class of the day.

Instead, she's wandering the open-air market, which teems with the scents of drying carcasses, day-old bread, and earthy vegetables. It is difficult to move through the crowd. The vendor to Gerel's left is selling sheep's head; the vendor on her right is a seedy man of seventy selling root vegetables as wrinkled as his skin. Women shove past one another, bartering to purchase the eyes and ears of animals at the best price. An infant cries in her mother's arms as they navigate past a vendor selling fresh cabbage heads; this time of the year, it's quite a treat, and people shove past for a chance to bargain for one.

And then Gerel sees her—wispy, reedy, hair loose down her back, dressed modestly in a wool coat that is worn bone thin and a single scarf wrapped around her neck.

She knows what to do. But her heart is hammering in

     Erin Jamieson

her chest, and the street is too congested. The moment of hesitation costs her, and the woman disappears back into the crowd. She won't return until next week, at the same time. Gerel knows this, and she also knows that she has missed a day of school for nothing.

"Are you in line?"

She glances up and realizes she's blocking the cabbage stand.

"No."

"Can I squeeze past?" the woman asks. Already, she is shoving her way through.

"Sorry," Gerel mutters.

For a moment, she stands there, feeling the rise and fall of voices, the pulse of the undulating tide of men, women and children, all exclaiming over the food, admiring the plump melons and the fatty cuts of marmot.

Gerel pretends to be interested in a vendor selling camel's tongues—soft and fleshy pink on the mat before him.

"May I help you?"

Her eyes lock with the woman's. She is wizened, stoop-backed, with the same lost look in her eyes Gerel's mother has now, the same heavy sprinkling of silver hairs. A woman beaten down by life, who hates this city just as much as everyone else but will not admit it to herself.

Gerel's brows furrow. As much as she longs for help, there's no one left. She can't wait for help. She must do it herself.

"No," she says finally, "There's nothing you can do for me."

Gerel has raced exactly twice in her life. The first time, she was ten, nearly eleven. She mounted her father's stallion in the morning dew, rode past the tent school to an open field where a rumored race would take place. There, she lined up, side-by-side with the young boys. They scoffed at her, and at the other female, a wispy, nervous-looking girl about a year older. It was more than Gerel had expected: the exhilaration of the wind on her face, the dust in her eyes, the pounding in her chest as she urged the horse to run faster and faster. She felt fearless, in control and out of control at once, with the blueness overhead her only guide, and distant cheers urging her forward. She came in second place to the other girl. When she dismounted, her vision was so blurred she nearly fell over. And when she looked up, her father glowered down, hands on his hips.

After that, she was careful to practice in secret, in the dusky, summer evenings when her father would be occupied with the animals, or the few times her father and mother traveled to see relatives and left them at home. But it was never the same as that first time, and when she had finally mustered the courage to join another race, her father had informed them they would be leaving for Ulaanbaatar.

When asked for a reason, he would only say, "Everything changes."

Quatan swore it was because of the return of restrictions; after the time of blessed freedom, their father didn't have the heart to go back to counting his flock and deciding what he'd produce and how. "Gerel, a man shouldn't be told what to do with his animals," he'd explained in a contemptuous, all-knowing way reserved for adolescent boys. "Besides," he'd added, "it keeps changing back and forth. The rules, the government."

But Gerel didn't believe the restrictions were the only reason. Her father wouldn't leave suddenly unless something had happened. He loved the Gobi. He'd never known any-thing outside of the nomadic life and had never mentioned transitioning to the city. Gerel knew something else was to blame.

And now, all this time later, what she'd seen the morning before they left was confirmed. Standing in the marketplace after the stoop-backed women disappeared, Gerel was forced to admit what she'd known all along. Tomorrow, she promised herself, the same way her father had once promised she'd learn to ride. She would find her tomorrow, come hell or high water, even if it meant missing more lessons.

When Gerel comes in, her mother glances up from the chopping board, her silver hair forming a halo around her worn cheeks.

"How was school?" Bolormaa asks.

"Fine," Gerel lies. "What are you making?"

She grimaces. "Turnip stew. But I ran out of turnips, so mostly cabbage stew."

"Quatan will like that."

"He won't be home for supper."

Gerel strips off her coat, scarf, and gloves, leaving them in a tidy pile. "Why not?"

"Oh, he's visiting. They're getting married soon, and he hasn't spent much time with her family."

Gerel bites her lip. "Seems like more than enough time to me. We hardly see him."

Her mother looks up, barely missing her finger with the knife. "My hearing is going. What did you say?"

"Never mind," she mutters, turning away. "I have homework."

Gerel plops down on the slate gray carpeting in the adjacent room. It is unraveling and smells like dead moths, but they can't afford to have it replaced. The walls are the same muted gray, with paint peeling like dead skin and two high windows as the only source of natural light. The apartment on the third floor is either stuffy and humid, or, as it is now, clammy and damp. Gerel shivers as she glances out at the slushy streets below. Men and women are beginning to return home for the evening, mostly by foot, their cheeks glistening red under the veneer of falling snow.

The scent of roasted beets wafts in. The stove is warming the room, and Gerel rolls up her sleeves, feeling chilled and overheated at the same time. She begins working on her lesson, but each time she tries to read about the significance of Russian intervention or the effect of *negdels* on the Mongolian economy, she becomes distracted with questions of her own. Has the woman seen her? Is that why she ran away? Or maybe it wasn't her at all! Maybe she doesn't even exist. Gerel shoves these thoughts down forcefully, but they resurface again and again. After half an hour, she surrenders, puts away her lesson, and paces back and forth, from the worn, wooden table and chairs to the beige curtains her mother placed for a sense of privacy. Who could peer into a third-story window? They live in Ulaanbaatar, where privacy is a seven-letter word. In the Gobi, one slept and ate among animals; here, the land is crowded with people, people on the way to and from school and work, endless bodies pressed against each other, a sea of faceless men and women navigating through their days, often unaware of one another.

A soft thud sounds as the front door is opened and shut.

"Quatan," her mother exclaims. "I didn't expect you home so early."

   Erin Jamieson

He mutters something Gerel can't hear.

"Oh, my."

"Nothing to worry about." His voice is flat, defeated.

"Why don't you sit down? Supper is nearly ready, and your father will be home soon."

Quatan grunts and enters the room Gerel is in. As he peels off his winter coat, his eyes are watery and his face more pale than usual.

Has he been crying? "What happened?" Gerel asks.

"Nothing."

"Something happened."

He sighs. "I saw you today."

"At school?"

He narrows his eyes. "I saw you today," he repeats. A longer pause. "I told Mother I broke off my engagement."

She stares at him, stunned.

"But that isn't what's upsetting me," he says.

"I don't—"

"Listen, you don't say anything, and I won't say anything."

"What would I say?" she hisses.

Their mother calls for them to set the table. Neither moves.

"Why did you break off the engagement?" Gerel asks.

"Why did you skip school? For the second time in a month, to hang out at the meat market?"

She opens her mouth, closes it. "All right," she says finally. "If that's how it is."

Their mother enters the room, carrying a steaming dish that smells of garlic and crushed cloves. Beets and cabbage when they are all longing for meat.

"Yes," he says quietly, "That's how it is."

Their father is pleased and doesn't try to hide it. He

shovels forkful after forkful of beets, telling Quatan that he's made the best possible decision.

"You'll find a better connection, son," he says. "Besides, you're already in."

"What?"

"In the program at school."

"Oh, yes."

Mother frowns, setting down her fork. "I don't think that's what's concerning him."

"Women come and go. Careers don't. Education doesn't."

Quatan catches Gerel's eye, like he used to when they were younger. But then he lowers his eyes, and she isn't sure whether she imagined the moment.

"A family is something to be proud of," Bolormaa says.

Ganbaatar nods. "Of course. I only mean that he has made the best decision, for now." He squints at Quatan. "Didn't you?"

"Yes."

But he doesn't meet their father's eyes.

They finish dinner in silence, and Gerel is unable to taste anything.

The next morning when she wakes, Gerel feels something is different. The air is bitter and dry, and she drinks two large glasses of water. Water still feels like a luxury. She doesn't have to drink milk tea, endure the sting of *airag*, or force down rich camel's milk to quench her thirst. Here in the city, water is, at best, chalky and salty, but at least it is safe. Or so their father insists. Today she is too thirsty to care or know the difference.

It is quite early, and the skies are deep and saturated; the outlines of buildings are barely visible below as Ulaanbaatar slowly stirs to life. The first wave of street sweepers proceeds

   Erin Jamieson

through the blinding cold, heads bent against the wind. As horrible as her mother's job at the factory is, feeding fabric into metallic machines for hours, at least she is safe from the bitter temperatures. Not all have this, another luxury. Gerel wants to continue her education so she will never know the pains of an empty stomach, or the fatigue of waking before the rest of the city to sweep until her skin becomes raw with blisters and her head throbs from the cold. Some women, she has heard, lose fingers and toes to frostbite, if they aren't careful, or don't have enough coverings, or are too industrious and refuse to take breaks, to earn overtime. Employers never insist on breaks or warmer clothes because employees assume responsibility; in other words, as her father had explained many times, if someone lost a toe, it was her fault. They would avoid looking at his stump when he said this. Their mother would leave the room.

Mother had talked to them about her work at the factory. The squalor, the few windows. She said the air slowly suffocated you from the minute you walked in. In the summer, the rooms were unbearably humid, and the winters were cold and drafty. The lighting was inadequate and after many years, some workers developed eye strain. Mother had been working a few months, since Quatan's engagement. Father hadn't been happy about it, but she had insisted it was time for her to earn some money.

Father makes enough. They are never rich, but they always have food on the table and new clothes when they need them. They can make their rental payments on the apartment and host an occasional celebration. Not that there is much cause for celebration. Besides, they see their relatives so infrequently.

Their father agreed to let her try working for one month. "But don't complain to me when your feet hurt," he'd said.

Her mother had merely smiled. "I'm used to working hard," she'd said. "Why should this be any different than working with the animals?"

But it is, and now, two-and-a-half weeks later, her mother is already feeling the strain. Her shoulders slump with the weight of the hours and duties. She pokes at her food, and her clothes hang from her shoulders like they would on a hanger. Her cheeks have become sunken, her eyes dark and sallow, her hair split. Or she has been like this for a while, and Gerel is only now noticing. That is more likely, she decides.

Gerel waits until her mother has left, and then, glancing to make sure her father and Quatan aren't up, she snatches up a folded piece of paper, one she's kept hidden in her room. A document that has weighed on her for years.

Erin Jamieson

TWENTY-THREE

THE WOMAN ISN'T in the market today. Gerel shivers in the bitter wind and waits by the sheep heads stand. If she leaves now, she will make it in time for the lecture on Russian history. They'll have an examination next week. If she leaves now, nobody—not even Quatan—will notice her absence.

As she makes her way through the crowd, she sees a monk.

Tall, thin, agile, wispy as a willow tree, his face is severely cracked and lined, as if carved from wood. He is dressed in a brown robe and wears long, golden chains and a cross. A cross. He is a Christian monk, and she cannot help but stop and stare. It is rare to see any monks at all, after so many monasteries were shut down in favor of new schools and public spaces. It is still illegal to openly profess one's faith, but to see a monk that is Christian, not Buddhist, is rarer. Gerel has grown up her life without religion, but the cross glinting in the sunlight is so captivating that she cannot tear her eyes away.

He has a single tuft of hair, shocking white, on an otherwise balding head, but his eyes are electric blue. He meets her gaze and smiles.

Gerel continues staring.

And then she hears a scream, then the sound of heavy, echoing footsteps. The usual voices of bartering, exclaiming, and haggling flicker like a candle that has been snuffed.

No one moves, except for a lone officer, whose considerable girth seems to swallow the street. He pauses at the first turnip stand, as if considering a purchase. Everyone holds a collective breath. And then he looks at Gerel and begins walking towards her.

Panic seizes her throat. She has always been brave, braver than Quatan, who quit horse racing because he was terrified of falling. Braver than her mother, who would not go out if the skies looked strange. Braver sometimes than her father, who quit his life as a nomad instead of staying to face his problems. But Gerel, for better or worse, has always done what she wanted. She raced horses despite the danger and her parents' protests. Once, she visited a sick child who was coughing blood because she couldn't imagine being lonely. She had stripped down the *ger* almost completely by herself, knowing her father and mother lacked the heart when they moved.

But now, she is frozen in place. She has heard about the purges, and who hasn't? The people missing for endless weeks. The monasteries and churches burnt to the ground. Anything can happen. School is mandatory, one of the supposedly essential tenants of Mongolian society. A child caught skipping school not once, but several times, is disregarding the law.

What a fool she's been. Not brave at all, but a fool. Even finding the woman wouldn't have been worth this. Nothing is.

The officer stops before her and reaches into his pocket. She closes her eyes. Should she plead? Will he listen?

But when she opens her eyes, he has passed her. He was not looking at her at all, but at the monk standing directly behind her.

     Erin Jamieson

"Sir," he begins.

The monk barely blinks. "Yes, officer?"

"I need to ask you to change out of your clerical attire."

The monk raises his brows. "Change?"

"Yes," the officer says impatiently, gesturing at the robe and crucifix necklace.

"*Uuchlaarai*, I'm sorry. I can't."

"Can't? Or won't?"

Gerel spies a young man squeezing his lover's hand. She longs for someone to hold onto and is aware of how alone she is.

"Is there a difference?"

Someone gasps. Gerel has never seen someone outright disobey an officer, and a Russian one at that.

"I asked you to remove your garments," the officer repeats.

"Why?"

"Don't play me for a fool. You know the law."

"No law prohibits my attire."

"No public displays of religion," the officer snarls. "Are you belligerent, an idiot, or both?" His eyes lock onto the golden chain. "Both, I guess."

"You're asking me to remove my robes," the monk repeats slowly.

"Yes," the officer says mockingly.

The monk shakes his head.

"You won't?'

The holy man's face is placid. "It would seem I have two judges, God and you. I'm bound to disappoint one of them."

"You fool. It is against the law."

"Your laws," the monk says.

"What did you say?"

"Your laws. Not God's."

The officer throws back his head and laughs until his face flushes beet red. A second officer appears by his side. "Problem, sir?"

"This man," he says, shaking his finger doggedly at the priest, "thinks he's above the law."

The second officer, Gerel realizes with a start, is Chinese. Stoop-backed and slight, with a sinister face. The two make an odious pair.

"I see."

"I asked him to remove his robes."

"Not here? In the middle of the street?"

"No, when he gets home and no one's looking."

The Chinese officer sighs. "Please remove your robe, sir."

The monk stares.

"I said, remove them. Or we will do it for you."

Still, he doesn't move. The officers whisper to each other before the Russian one nods. "We'll give you to the count of three to change your mind."

"One, two," On three, they spring on the monk. One grabs him as the other pulls his hands behind his back. The monk doesn't struggle. Silent as stone, he is calm as his robes are lifted over his head and thrown into a heap at his feet. He is left shivering in his undergarments. Disregarding the circumstances, it is an oddly humorous sight: the mismatched pair of officers and the elderly, Mongolian man, disrobed, his veins milky blue, half-naked, with the golden crucifix still glinting in the sun as it rests on his cavernous chest.

No one laughs. No one moves.

"Your cross."

"I let you remove my robes, as you asked."

"You forced us. Now let us remove your cross."

     Erin Jamieson

Silence fills the air. A baby begins to cry and her mother, desperate, clutches her tightly.

Gerel inches away, but the officers are too fixated on the monk to notice.

The monk raises his chin. "You've publicly stripped a poor, old man. Isn't that enough?"

It is one thing to disobey, another to insult. Rage and admiration rise in Gerel's chest. She has never felt this passionate about anything, not even her will to race. This monk has something to live for, something she has never felt.

And because of it, the officers humiliate him. Officers charged with keeping the streets safe and the citizens content.

The Russian reaches into his pocket. "Remove the necklace and be done with it."

"I can't."

"Look here, we don't have time for this."

"I won't."

The Russian shakes his head, nods to the Chinese man. "Maybe this will persuade you." The pistol is dark, sleek, and tiny.

"You're going to shoot me? For wearing a cross?"

"For blatant disregard. We don't want it to come to this—"

"Then don't let it," the monk says hoarsely but steadily.

"Remove it. Now." The Russian raises his gun.

The monk smiles and shakes his head. The sun bursts from the covering of clouds.

"I said, remove it." The officer lifts his gun slightly, and then two things happen at once: the monk clutches the necklace at his chest, and the officer's grip on the trigger slips, and it fires.

The monk crumples into a heap on the ground, blood

bursting from his chest. His hand still holds the crucifix. There are screams, infants crying, someone sobbing.

The officer is shaking from head to toe but tries to keep the crowd at bay. "Stand back, stand back."

It doesn't work. Men and women shove to the front. The noise grows louder, an angry, buzzing sound. Vendors hurry to pack up. A sheep's head lobs to the ground. Turnips are squashed underfoot. Gerel steps back as a group of men lunge forward, their faces bestial and leathery, teeth bared.

The two officers gather, blocking her view of the monk. She feels sick and lightheaded as she struggles to break free from the crowd. Twice she is knocked to the ground, and panic wells inside her. She is not brave, not at all. Not like the monk or the officers who now face the crowd. She cannot get up the second time. She tastes blood in her mouth, and it is harder and harder to breathe…

Hands reach for her, pull her up. She clutches them, not knowing or caring who they belong to.

"Gerel, what are you doing here?"

She collects herself, taking in a deep gulp of air. And then she nearly falls back over. "Aisin?" she whispers.

"It's me." She sees Gerel's hesitation and pulls her. "We need to get out of here. Now."

Gerel is too numb to disobey. The smell of perspiring bodies, blood, dirt, and raw meat is nauseating. The streets are a blur of scarves and coats, worn boots and wool gloves, and frost glinting off half-swept walks. As they push through the crowd, Gerel clutches Aisin's hand as if it's a lifeline—which it is. They are forced to pass the spot where the monk lies.

The two officers point their guns, urging people to stay back. The Chinese officer sports a bloody nose; the Russian officer appears to have been hit on the side of the head.

                    Erin Jamieson

But it's the monk Gerel notices. His face is serene, mouth closed in a straight line, brow smooth and calm, as if he has expected this. His hand still clutches the cross, and his body is bent at a painful angle, his legs and arms forming a broken V. His chest doesn't move. He is utterly still, motionless amidst all the tumult.

Gerel has never seen anything so strangely peaceful in her life. His grip, so certain, his body exposed to the cold and his undergarments flapping in the wind.

Aisin releases Gerel's hand, takes off her wool coat, and throws it over the monk's body. It covers half his torso. She turns away, reaching for Gerel's hand again.

When Gerel glances back, the monk is still half-naked, half-covered, and the crowd presses in like angry vultures. The two officers are frightened and angry but hold their ground. The streets are lined with ashy blood.

It is a sight she will remember for the rest of her life.

TWENTY-FOUR

1941
Ulaanbaatar

AISIN IS FAMILIAR and unfamiliar at the same time. She has the same wide smile, the same silky, black hair. But her eyes are darker, hollower. She is slower to smile, and up close, her hair is speckled with silver. She sits at the kitchen table, sipping milk tea as if it is the most natural thing in the world.

He blurts out, "Where's my mother?"

She looks at him, considering. "Out."

"Out?"

Aisin stands up. "Your sister had to go to the hospital."

"The hospital?"

She watches him. "That's what I said."

A lump forms in his throat. "Why the hell are you here?"

"I think," she says slowly, "You already know the answer."

He does. But he is stunned by her audacity. She has always loved his father. The extent of their relationship he doesn't know.

"I will always be here for your family," she says. "They have shown me a kindness few have." Aisin pours herself more tea. Only now does he see how her back is bleeding, the angry red welts on her arm.

It isn't the answer he wants, but he suspects there's some truth to it. His mouth is dry. Something is more important than Aisin right now, more important than his wariness towards her. "Is Gerel all right?"

She pours him a cup of tea.

"She's visiting a man who was shot by officers. He died a few hours ago. Your mother is trying to convince her to leave."

"Someone we know?"

Aisin looks at him carefully. "No. Not anyone you'd know."

"Then why—"

"Your mother is concerned it's dangerous." She pauses. "For your sister."

"Is it?"

"Maybe," she admits. "I did what I could. We left the market as soon as—"

"Who was shot?"

"A monk."

"A monk," he repeats in disbelief. "My sister isn't even religious."

"When you see someone shot and killed in front of you—"

He scoffs. "She doesn't even know this man."

Gerel has always been the brave one—there's no doubt about that. The shining star of their family. He often wished he were as brave as her. But she can also be rash, foolish. And this time, it's not only her life she's putting at risk.

Quatan is torn between worry and anger at how reckless she's become. And he knows they are no longer close enough for him to make her see reason.

It's another way their family is broken and becoming more so day by day.

The irony is that Aisin—the woman who has never belonged, whom he should hate— seems to be the only one trying to hold them together.

Aisin lifts her head, and under her uncannily familiar stare, Quatan feels chilled.

"You didn't know my uncle when you contacted him," she says.

"I knew him before—"

"No," she says stiffly. "And you still don't. He's dying, you know. He didn't deserve that. It isn't his fault."

"No," Quatan agrees. "It's yours. And my father's."

She sets her cup on the counter, and tea splatters over the stone. "This isn't the time."

"When is the time, then?"

"I don't know. But your sister needs you."

"Yes," he says. "My sister."

To his surprise, Aisin begins to cry. It makes her look breakable, human, and he forces himself to look away.

"Fine," he says.

"After, we'll talk," she promises.

At the hospital, they can't find her. They search the lobby and ask one of the attending nurses. The halls smell like wax and cleaning supplies, and Quatan's head aches.

Back in the waiting room, a nurse assures them she'll look

for Gerel, but the description Aisin has provided could fit anyone, she says.

"Quatan! There you are!"

He turns. His father is there, his receding hairline glistening under the dim lighting, his dress shirt disheveled. He doesn't seem to notice Aisin.

"Father?"

As he approaches, Aisin stands. She exchanges a long look with Ganbaatar.

"I have to go." She brushes off her skirt, her brows furrowed. She glances at Quatan, as if expecting him to say something.

Quatan opens his mouth, but no words come. He waits until Aisin disappears, then turns to his father.

A few nurses pass by, then a flutter of activity as a stretcher is carried in. Quatan glimpses a young man, chestnut hair plastered with blood to his scalp, Chinese. His chest rises and falls slowly under the blankets.

"Another one," his father murmurs.

"You asked Aisin to come?" Quatan asks.

"I had to make sure someone was here."

"Or you could have been here, been a father for once," Quatan says, spitting out each word.

The older man blinks. "You're right. I've made many mistakes. Maybe one day, you'll see."

"See what?"

His father's gaze is broken, wounded. "You can love, or try to love, and still make mistakes. Or make mistakes because of that love. But you – you and your sister – perhaps you will not repeat my mistakes."

It's the closest Quatan will ever get to an apology or

confession, and the men fall silent, as if finally acknowledging the inadequacy of their words.

Gerel comes home two days later, her face blank and pale as the moon, her hair matted and uncombed. She smells like hospital scrubs, antiseptic, and cleaning supplies. She talks little and eats even less, refusing the dumplings Mother fries on the stove and even the lavender tea Aisin drops off.

Quatan wants to ask her what happened, why she stayed so long. But he has spent years distancing himself, and his sister is not much more than a stranger, posing as a young woman who resembles the child who once egged him on by stealing his favorite toys, who raced him around the *ger* and narrated stories about imaginary horse racers. She has lost her chubby cheeks, her quick laugh. She is a woman now, long-limbed and confident, even in her sorrow. As always, she is more certain of her place than he will ever be.

Except.

She pulls at her hair and paces. For the first few days, she runs a fever, sips hot broth, and does not attend school. Whenever their mother tries to talk to her, she rolls onto her side and pretends to be asleep. Their father gives Gerel space, becoming nothing more than a transporter for her food and water. This painfully monotonous and indeterminable pattern continues for nearly a week.

On the sixth day, her fever breaks. She rises in the morning, drinks milk tea, and eats a hearty portion of leftover mutton cutlets as if nothing has happened. Bright-eyed, she bids their mother and father good day before they leave. When she sees Quatan is staying, she frowns. "Aren't you going to see your fiancé?"

　　　Erin Jamieson

He freezes. "Gerel, we—"

"Oh. yes. I'm sorry."

"It's nothing to be sorry about."

"Well, aren't you off to work?"

"Quit my job," he says, staring at the floor.

"Oh." She sets her bowl down and wanders into the next room, where she buttons up her winter coat and throws a scarf around her neck.

He stands up. "What are you doing?"

"Going to school."

"No, you're not."

She blinks. "If I miss anything else, I'll fail."

"Gerel, you aren't being reasonable. You've been extremely sick."

In the morning light, her skin is sickly pale, her body painfully thin. "Doesn't matter."

He catches her arm. "Yes, it does."

"Since when did you care so much?"

He lets her arm drop. "I've always cared, Gerel. I'm your brother."

"Tell me why you decided not to marry her. And don't pretend to be too upset to talk about it, because we both know that's not true."

He wants to tell her. He wants to tell someone. His chest hurts as he looks at her. Her hair is still short as it was when she was a girl. He can still envision her sneaking into the pastures to feed treats to the goats. They would watch the sunset, drinking in the fading, summer air before winter hit.

Those are days that will never come back again. "I'm sorry," he says finally.

"I went to the market because I was looking for someone,"

Gerel blurts. "I thought I'd find her there. And I did, that day the monk was shot."

"Who were you looking for?"

She narrows her eyes. "Mother's cousin."

"What?"

"Mother's cousin. I thought she said something about her cousin who lives here. She used to know Grandfather, and even liked him. I thought she could help us find him."

Instead of feeling relieved at her explanation, Quatan finds himself speechless. "You're trying to contact Grandfather? But we write to him—"

"Not that grandfather."

And then he understands. "Gerel, he doesn't even know about you. He hardly knows about me. The few times Father mentioned him, I could see how much it upset him."

"But what about me? What about us? Don't you care about meeting your own grandfather?"

"Not if it hurts Father!"

"Right. Because you care so much about sparing every-one's feelings. Are you going to tell me your little secret? Now that I've told you mine?"

"Gerel—"

"Forget it." She swings open the front door.

Frigid air enters the house, the taste of ash and snow. Quatan approaches his sister. Somewhere in the distance, a car horn beeps; a bell signals the start to a day at the cloth-ing factory, where their mother is now, bending her already aching back. Nothing improves; they repeat the same cycle in and out, day after day.

"Wait," he says.

Gerel stops, one foot on the cracked concrete of the

Erin Jamieson

doorstep, another inside. "What? Are you going to tell me what you've been doing?"

He clears his throat. "Visiting that monk was really dangerous." He'd meant to say brave. He isn't sure about what she did or what happened to the monk, but everything he says turns to ashes on his tongue.

"You think he deserved to die?" she asks.

"I didn't say that."

She shakes her head. "At least he stood for something. At least he had something that meant that much to him. Do you have anything like that, anything you'd die for?"

"Why does that matter?"

She stares at him for a long moment before slamming the door in his face.

Quatan does want to feel something, as the monk did. He wishes he had something he cared about so much that he would sacrifice anything to have it. But he doesn't. Nothing is ever enough. His beautiful fiancée, with her gentle voice and intelligent eyes. The admission to the university, or the fine clothes mother bought him as a present.

Maybe that's what's led him to where he is now, wandering a dimly lit alley in the middle of March, as snow drifts off heavy banks; his cheeks are numb and his breaths tight and congested. He passes grim-faced street sweepers with graying hairs and bent backs and clothes thin as a whisper. He passes the market where the monk was shot, where Aisin appeared back in their lives.

Aisin. She hasn't come by their home again since Gerel started improving. Had she returned to the Gobi? She must have. She wouldn't have stayed. And Quatan couldn't blame her. There was nothing to stay for.

He hesitates before turning around to stop at the first vendor. A wizened man of forty is selling goat milk curds. Quatan haggles down the price to half the original cost. He pops one of the curds into his mouth and swallows mechanically. He hasn't eaten since last night, and his stomach is an empty cavern. The curd is tasteless, nothing like his mother used to make year-round. He eats a few more curds before stashing them in his pocket. He feels them crush together, oozing onto the handsome silk of his pants, the pants he was supposed to be wearing to an interview today. The interview he would have had if he hadn't broken off the engagement.

A lone bench overlooks one of the main streets, where men and women commute to and from their workplaces, some holding briefcases, their expressions strained, and bodies burdened with invisible weight. Quatan feels as if he could melt into the concrete, as if his skin has already become synonymous with the ash, the ash from the chimney smoke and the exhaust of cars and buses, the ash from grimy bodies that have not been cleaned for some time.

This is all that's left. The sun rises in the background, but its light barely penetrates the smog, providing little warmth. He is colder by the minute, but where is he supposed to go? Several days ago, he knew where he was headed. Everything he'd assumed, the secrets he'd buried inside himself, had turned into nothing. And the only person who could have helped never would now.

Grandfather. Gerel has been trying to contact their grandfather. That astounds Quatan more than her visiting the monk, or a million other brave things she has done. He has never been willing to look for someone who might reject him.

   Erin Jamieson

He thinks of his father, shutting himself away, with no friends or family aside from mother and Gerel and Aisin. All because of his hand, and a stupid rift with his own father.

Like father, like son.

"Are you lost?"

Yes, he is. He turns and sees a woman around his mother's age, with a pinched face and molasses dark hair, speckled with white.

"No—"

But then he realizes there is someone else, a small child next to her, thumb in his mouth. Quatan realizes she wasn't talking to him. Like everyone else, she hadn't seen him at all. With his head bent against the wind, he presses on.

TWENTY-FIVE

May 1943
Ulaanbaatar

AISIN STAYS SEVERAL weeks past the monk's assassination. She lingers in the capital, living in a makeshift *yurt* on the edge of town, selling goods her uncle sends and working as a housekeeper for wealthy homeowners. She begins visiting in the evenings, arms full of goods from the market: crisp, fresh apples (a heavenly respite from all the heavy meat they consume), choice cuts of venison, a handmade clay bracelet for Gerel, and a chain for Quatan's pocket watch. As she was in the Gobi, Aisin is like an aunt to their adult-yet-not-adult children—compassionate, enthusiastic, encouraging. As Ganbaatar works longer and longer hours, Aisin and Bolormaa become closer, sharing their deepest regrets and secret frustrations.

Bolormaa has come to anticipate her time with Aisin. One afternoon, as she hands Aisin a tall glass of water, she has a passing thought. "Don't you mind it?" she asks.

Aisin takes a sip from the glass. The water is cloudy and tastes like dirt, but everyone insists it is safe to drink here. "Mind what?"

"Living alone."

Instantly, Bolormaa regrets the question. "I'm sorry," she murmurs, clamping a hand to her mouth.

Aisin looks at her carefully. "Sometimes I do. But I have my uncle back there, and my friends." She smiles. "Haven't you ever lived alone? Or wondered what it would be like?"

No, Bolormaa hadn't. She had never been able to imagine—

But maybe she had. That far off, tiny seed of an idea. Seeing the world or studying in Ulaanbaatar—the irony isn't lost on her.

How funny, she thinks, that we often get close to our dream, but in an entirely different way. And maybe, you can no longer recognize what the dream had once been.

"You would make a good mother," Bolormaa finally says

Aisin laughs. "I'm not like you. When you were getting married to Ganbaatar, I was still behaving like a child. I still do. I was racing horses, showing the world how brave I could be. And damned if I could trouble myself with settling down."

A few years ago, Bolormaa would have believed her. But she has come to notice Aisin's subtleties: how her eyes darken, and she looks just over someone's shoulder when she's not being honest. But she also sees the way she gazes at Gerel and Quatan sometimes, the way she settles into the home she and Ganbaatar have built.

"It's not too late," Bolormaa says.

For some reason, Aisin tenses. "Awfully noisy, isn't it?" She paces and pulls back the blinds.

Once, Bolormaa had spent so much time worrying about

what was between Aisin and Ganbaatar. Now she wonders—even if what she felt was true, even if something had happened—what had Aisin gained? Hadn't they been cheated out of any possibilities, in a way?

It is a warm and glistening summer day, the kind that makes you gasp, even in Ulaanbaatar. The sun breaks through a fine veneer of white clouds, and the sky is not as gray as usual, a blue like pressed blueberries. Children chase each other in the streets, tossing a ball back and forth or sharing a rusty bicycle. Quatan and Gerel used to play like that, Bolormaa remembers. Gerel would steal one of her brother's favorite books and make him chase after her, until they both fell. The girl would laugh so hard she'd forget to breathe, and her brother would smile in spite of himself.

She can't remember the last time she saw either of her children laugh, let alone together. What had happened? When had their family started to erode? Ganbaatar works longer hours and now, they only see each other on the weekends, when he is too exhausted for anything more than a faint hello or "How was your day?" She can't remember the last time they kissed or touched, and it has been over a year since they made love.

Gerel moves around the apartment like a ghost, quiet and sullen after the monk was shot. She still attends school, but Bolormaa doubts she is doing well. At almost seventeen years old, Gerel expresses no interest in finding a suitable mate.

Quatan, by far, is managing the worst. After he broke off his engagement, he also declined his scholarship and took a shift at the same factory where Bolormaa works. He, too, becomes grimmer by the day, and less sociable. Now, at Ganbaatar's bidding, he has started searching for another job, but his efforts are half-hearted and lethargic. When Bolormaa

     Erin Jamieson

asks him about the university, he shakes his head and mutters, "What's the point?'"

If Bolormaa was a good mother, she would have insisted to know what was troubling her son, or why Gerel continually declares she will never marry. But she deals with her own portion of daily stresses. She doesn't understand herself, much less her husband and kids. She realizes, with a start, that she never has, and therein lies the problem. She never had time to prepare to be a mother. Some days, she wakes feeling like the nineteen-year-old bride, uncertain, afraid, wanting to please her mother and father, and helplessly in love with a man she does not really know.

"Where have you gone?" Aisin stands with the sunlight behind her.

Bolormaa shrugs, tapping her fingers on the table. It is her day off from the factory, and she can't leave the confines of this apartment, with its worn carpet, broken kitchen cabinets, and stained walls. Things they can now afford to fix, things they likely never will.

"I was thinking about how much things change," she says.

Aisin lays a gentle hand on her shoulder. "Gerel? Quatan?"

"My parents," Bolormaa whispers. "I wish Mother had told me about Father."

"I thought you said his decline was sudden."

"It was. But I wish I could have been there."

"Would it help to visit your mother?"

Bolormaa shakes her head. Her mother is frail, thin as a shadow, her walking slow and her mind slower. She forgot the children's names long ago, and sometimes she cannot remember Ganbaatar. Bolormaa offered to take her in, but even with her aging mind and body, she refused. She said she would die in a place like Ulaanbaatar much faster than in the Gobi, where she was born, lived, and loved. When Bolormaa begged Ganbaatar to move out of the city so they could take care of her mother, he refused.

"We can't simply leave," he said. "We have jobs here."

"And we have family there," she answered.

"No," he insisted quietly, "You have family there. Our family is here. But obviously, you don't see that."

Secretly, Bolormaa worried he was right. She never adjusted to life in the city, to breathing in the dust from car exhaust, the smoke from factory chimneys and worn furnaces. She hasn't gotten used to the feeling of four walls around her, of waking to a gray, hazy sky or walking to a market where the meat is pre-butchered and portioned.

But most of all, she misses the air after a hard rain, the contented bleating of goats as they graze, the summer sun spilling over the canvas of blue sky. The sounds of crickets in the thick of evening and camels snorting and spitting. The feeling of felt, carefully rolled, or the gurgling of milk as it is churned into curds. She misses sleeping under a blanket of stars, bleaching her skin, and the sound of a silent night, with no one else around for miles.

Here, with neighbors above, below, and beside her, Bolormaa feels more alone than she ever has. It is a pronounced but chronic loneliness, a constant unease that stays with her every day as she rises and retires. Still, she has never complained, not as her husband spends less and less time with her, or as her son gives up on both his career and love, or as Gerel becomes more and more distant. She has never complained, because she has been taught to endure, to accept. Isn't that how she first fell in love with her husband, by accepting and enduring what at first felt monumentally oppressive?

But her mother. She should be there for her. Lately,

     Erin Jamieson

Bolormaa feels old herself and understands her mother's resistance to move. Her back aches from the hours feeding machines at the factory, her hair is more silver than chestnut, and her hands are a map of veins and wrinkles from years in the sun. She has become old overnight.

Aisin sees her inspecting her reflection in the window. "You look fine."

"I look old."

"The way I see it, we have two options. Aging is better."

Bolormaa shakes her head. "Easier for you to say. You barely look a day older than when we met." And it's true: though she is less free-spirited and a bit more defeated than she was, Aisin's skin is still radiantly smooth, her hair long and shining with health, her figure sturdy and shapely. As if time has not touched her at all.

"You're being too hard on yourself." Aisin hesitates at the front door. "Why don't you go by yourself to see your mother?"

"I'm too old to make that journey alone."

"Nonsense." Her eyebrows rise. "You can come with me. I'm going back."

Bolormaa stares. "You're not staying in Ulaanbaatar?"

"I've been here for months. That's more than enough. City life isn't for me."

"It's not for me, either. There are benefits, though."

"Like the air quality." Aisin laughs.

"And the spacious living."

"Free alarm clocks! If you miss the sounds of the first automobiles, you'll be sure to hear everyone walking to work."

"See? I can't see why you won't stay."

"I can't," Aisin says, suddenly serious. "But my offer stands."

Something passes over Bolormaa's face, as if she's considering. "I have to be here for my family," she says.

"I thought you might say that. Remember, your mother is family, too."

"Will we see you again?"

Aisin crosses the room, embraces Bolormaa, then pulls back and meets her eyes. "Things have a way of working out, my friend."

"Will you see Ganbaatar before you leave?"

Something flickers in Aisin's eyes. "No, but please send him my best."

Her tone grows sharper, but Bolormaa is afraid to ask what Aisin is unwilling to tell her. "Are you sure you have to go?"

Aisin studies her, as if committing her face, this room, to memory. "I can't live here anymore," she says, but this time her answer is a thread of a whisper and becomes lost in the noise of the streets below.

That night, dinner tastes like ashes.

"Pass me the stew," Ganbaatar says, wiping his lips.

"How can you stand to eat it?" Gerel demands. Her hair is in a careful braid, with wisps that frame her forehead. Her long eyelashes are prominent, and her chin juts stubbornly. She looks nothing like Bolormaa, but she has some of her father's mannerisms, such as the way she bites her lip when she's impatient, as she is now.

"Gerel!" Bolormaa says.

"I'm sorry, but it's terrible. You said so yourself, didn't you?"

She had. But her daughter's remark stings. "No one is forcing you to eat," she says calmly.

     Erin Jamieson

Their daughter, who is volatile about anything from the weather to someone washing her clothes differently than she likes, slams her chair back into the table and wordlessly disappears into the next room.

Ganbaatar, incredibly, is still eating. He notices Bolormaa staring. "What?"

"Gerel."

He shrugs and brings another generous spoonful to his mouth. "She has a point."

Bolormaa sighs. "It was all I could find."

He lifts a spoonful and looks at the watery, grayish-brown matter floating in the broth. "May I ask what it is?"

"Marmot."

He takes a bite. "Not sure about that."

"That's what the butcher said. I'm not good at picking things out. I never have been."

"Don't worry. It's edible."

Edible. Bolormaa spent an hour looking at the meat. For the past month, Aisin has helped her select the choicest cuts, and they've enjoyed the best suppers since they moved to Ulaanbaatar all those years ago. They've become spoiled.

"Bolormaa, what's wrong?"

She lets her spoon clang against the bowl. She's been waiting for him to ask for so long. And he is looking at her, maybe not passionately, but with concern.

"I'm worried," she says.

"About Gerel?"

"And Quatan."

"Ah. I don't think there's anything to worry about."

"She's been so moody lately."

Ganbaatar smirks.

"What?"

"Nothing."

"No, tell me."

"Well. You weren't exactly even keeled when I met you."

"One minute you couldn't stand me," Ganbaatar says, smiling, "and the next you were certain you wanted to marry me."

"And you're upset?"

Ganbaatar is still laughing. "I was lucky."

She looks up. "Lucky?"

"Yes," he says quietly, "though it took me a long time to figure it out." He thinks of the beginning, all the way back to their first meeting. The moments that seemed to promise something more. The night when they looked at the stars and shared their dreams. Before things became complicated but also very full.

Maybe some of this misunderstanding is his fault. Maybe he is unhappy because he isn't willing to see what's right in front of him.

Maybe he could try harder.

"Do you want more stew?"

He reaches for the pot the same instance she does, and their hands brush. "Let me clean up for a change," he says.

Bolormaa bites her lip. "Thank you," she says.

He squeezes her hand. "Quatan will find his way."

"I don't like him living by himself."

"He's old enough."

"I know." She shakes her head. "But since he broke off the engagement, he's been different."

"Our children are growing up."

"I think there may be something else."

"'Bolormaa, come over here."

Surprised, she walks to the sink where he is scrubbing the bowls clean.

 Erin Jamieson

"You worry too much," he says. And then, tentatively, he wraps his arms around her waist.

She's forgotten how he smells—sun and grass, only now punctuated with smells of the trains and the grimy streets and the apartment. His skin feels smoother than she remembers, and his hair has grown gray; in fact, his hairline has receded, and he is nearly bald. His midsection holds supple fat where it used to be trim, and his muscles are loose instead of wiry. But it is still him, her husband. It is still Ganbaatar, the man who raced in his youth and fathered two children, the man who has been here all these years. He is still the man whose touch she misses, who used to tell her about his secret fears under the cover of darkness as they lay down for the night.

He kisses her cheek. "You don't need to worry about the children."

And because she wants to, because her body feels heavy and he is supporting her, because she cannot imagine an alternative, she believes him, just as she believed things would be better in the city.

He is strange, familiar, cradling her chin with his hands, kissing her hair, her eyes, her nose. It is like their wedding night, only now his lips are thin and chapped, kissing her silver hair, her creased skin. She is not beautiful, and he does not tell her she is. She is not young, but with him, she does not feel she needs to be.

As they lie side by side in the dark, her chest feels as if it will burst. Who knew that their children, in their divisiveness, would bring them together again? She nestles beside her husband and in her sleep, he wraps his arms around her. His stump rests on her hip. That damage he's tried to hide his entire life is beautiful to her. Despite his injury, he is the strong man she first met. His hand has been a source of shame, but it only reminds her how resilient they both are.

Ganbaatar rolls over and murmurs something about oranges. Oranges? Thinking it must be a childhood memory, she waits for him to speak again, but he doesn't.

Instead, he starts to cry. She tries to soothe him, but he is still asleep, sobbing. Perhaps he needs her as much as she needs him. Why doesn't matter, only that he does. Only that she is needed, that he is needed. And somehow, the rest doesn't matter.

❦

Gerel pushes aside the porridge her mother woke up early to cook. "It's cold. And thick."

"Suit yourself," Bolormaa says, taking the bowl.

"That's it? You aren't going to yell at me?"

"Why would I do that?"

Gerel looks at her with narrowed eyes. "I don't know. You usually do."

That isn't true, not really. Bolormaa occasionally loses her temper lately, but today, she is too happy to care whether her daughter eats or doesn't.

"Are you all right?" Gerel asks.

Bolormaa laughs. "Yes. Why?"

"You've been really upset and now you're—" She stares. "Are you wearing perfume and lipstick?"

Bolormaa ducks her head. "So what if I am?"

"You never do."

"Well. Find something else to eat or get ready. You don't want to be late. Finals are this week, aren't they?"

"I'm not sure."

     Erin Jamieson

"What do you mean?"

"I'm not going to school."

"Don't be ridiculous."

Gerel meets her eyes. "I'm serious. There's no point."

"You don't mean that. I thought you valued education."

"I would if that's what they were offering. But we spend all day learning about Russia and China, just like in the Gobi. I barely have time to work on anything else."

"I'm sure they have their reasons for the curriculum," Bolormaa says stiffly. "Even when I was a student, we learned about Russia. It's good to be aware of the world. There's nothing terrible about it."

Gerel rolls her eyes. "I knew you'd say that."

Bolormaa bites back a reply, takes a deep breath. "You may feel that way, Gerel, but that doesn't mean you can just—"

"I stopped attending two months ago," Gerel interrupts.

"What?"

"Look. You think you can run my life and Quatan's, but you can't. And I'm doing something important now."

"Important?"

"Raising awareness."

Chills hit Bolormaa. "About what?"

"About how stilted our education is, about the hundreds of people executed or exiled to Siberia for having a different opinion."

"Gerel."

"What?"

"This is dangerous."

"And life here isn't? Haven't you heard about the war? Do you think it isn't going to affect us? We're puppets to the Soviet Union's will! And the Japanese are putting on an aggressive front."

Bolormaa closes her eyes. She's heard about the Mongolian and Japanese troops fighting along the Manchurian border and how the Soviets stepped in to protect against an impending Japanese invasion. Some say the Soviet Union is the only entity saving them. Others say Mongolia, sandwiched between two powers, is being used.

That their culture will be erased, their autonomy gone.

But maybe, Bolormaa thinks, that's the price that must be paid. The collectives took away their freedom of independent ownership, but they also made it easier to survive. War echoes across nations, but at least Mongolia is protected. She wants to believe this; she needs to believe it.

Others can talk big and protest. They can hate what's happened. But Bolormaa knows everything comes with a price.

The world is not neatly divided into black and white as she once believed. She wants to explain this to Gerel, the way the world will make you see all the grays. But by the time she blinks her eyes open, her daughter has already left.

Erin Jamieson

TWENTY-SIX

1945

Outskirts of Manchuria

QUATAN HAD SOMETHING at last.

Do you have anything like that, something you would die for?

His sister's question has burned into him for many years. Long years of failing repeatedly, of breaking his mother's heart and disappointing his father. Years of working in sooty factories, unable or unwilling to continue his education. Years of half-hearted dates with women whose names were a mystery, with lovely laughs, beautiful waists, straight teeth, and whose words remain no longer than a summer breeze. Years of wrapping his arms around a warm body only to feel alone afterwards, of changing job locations and becoming whatever he needs to be—a street sweeper, a janitor, a vendor, a teller.

Many times, his mother has looked at him, her eyes cloudy with cataracts after years working in thin light, and asked whether he'd consider finishing school as he planned.

But now he is twenty-five and feels far removed from school. He cannot imagine sitting in class next to fresh-faced, hopeful young men, having to explain how his life has been derailed by a single person. He cannot imagine taking exams when the questions that matter have no answer key.

But now, he does have something he would die for. It is not for the Soviet Union, attempting to recruit men to attack Japan's front on Manchuria. It is not his mother or father, who have both loved and failed him, or the absent grandfather Gerel still seeks, who is probably long gone by now. It is not even the comfort of a wife and a family, or a home where the carpets do not smell like rodent droppings and the sink has running, clear water.

He sits up, his back in knots and head still buzzing from the night before. Beside him a naked young woman stirs in the sheets and moans softly as he gets up. But she doesn't wake up. Good. He hates looking a woman in the eye in the morning and admitting to himself he doesn't quite know who she is; he hates himself in those moments, too.

He fixes a leftover bowl of beef broth and drinks none of it. He opens the newspaper and closes it. He peers back at the bed, the makeshift cot, where the woman turns in her sleep. Now that Mongolia is aligned against Japan, his feelings about Chinese women have changed. He feels a stab. Aisin. It had been six-and-a-half years. Where was she now? What was she doing? He was certain she had never visited his mother again—that would have been mentioned in the hasty letters his mother sent over the years, letters meant to somehow make up for the fact that her son no longer came to visit.

"Quatan?"

Someone is outside the tent.

     Erin Jamieson

He pokes his head out. The vodka is still in him, making his throat sting and his vision cloudy. "Yes?"

A Russian officer he doesn't recognize stares at him. "You need to report."

Quatan glances down at his nightshirt, stained with alcohol and mutton juice, acutely aware of his unshaven face. "Report?"

"Dumber every minute," the officer murmurs. "Yes. Beds need cleaning."

"Where?"

"Main tent. Now."

"Yes sir," he says, resigned.

He trudges into the sticky air. The sun has barely risen, but already it is stifling and difficult to breathe. When he first came to Manchuria, it was almost a relief. The air quality in Ulaanbaatar had been almost unbearable. Manchuria was a far cry from the fresh, open air of the Gobi, but it was, at least, an improvement.

He'd stumbled upon this appointment two months earlier, on his commute to the local market. He'd worked a variety of odd jobs during the years following his decision to break off the engagement and his ties. He did menial factory work like his mother and tutored the most privileged children in the east, those whose parents could afford to worry about their offspring learning Russian, manners, and social conduct. He hated all the jobs because he could have done something professional if he had completed his schooling. He hated each job because he could not face his own parents, knowing he had disappointed them.

But this had been different. He'd seen a flier, posted not long after the Soviet Union had announced its entry into the war. The sign, written in Russian and imperfect English, called for medical assistants for troops stationed near Manchuria. Speaking Mongolian was not required, though he can count on his hands the number of people who can fluently converse in either English or Russian and are older than twenty-one. He'd nearly walked away, until he'd seen the note at the bottom: no experience necessary.

He isn't being paid. He's a volunteer, and that suits him fine. His days are preoccupied with cleaning bed linens, bringing sterile water, and transporting meals to officers and soldiers. Nothing of consequence has happened, but he still feels somehow, he has a purpose here. Unbidden, his sister's words come back to him: *Do you have something you'd die for?* This isn't that, certainly, but at least he has a purpose. At least, even if he is doing nothing of consequence, it is better than doing nothing back in Ulaanbaatar, where the city swallows him whole, and he might disappear without anyone noticing for weeks. Here, he would be missed. Here, his duties would not be fulfilled, and someone would notice the lack of water or the uniforms that hadn't been laundered. He can be replaced by anyone, but at least for one day, someone would notice.

Officer Bogdin is situated at his splintered wooden desk, sipping slowly from a mug. He doesn't turn around. Quatan's nostrils are instantly filled with bitter coffee grounds, brewed so long they have burnt.

"Sir?"

The officer continues to sip from his mug, gazing at the backdrop of the tent.

"Sir? You wanted me?"

He turns slowly. His face is blotchy, eyebrows furrowed, his belt threatening to burst over his generous girth. An overgrown, rust-colored beard frames his beefy face. "*Kto ty?* Who are you?"

     Erin Jamieson

Russian has never come easily for Quatan. He detests the way the syllables vibrate on his tongue. "Quatan. *Ya chishche.*"

"A cleaner. And a Mongolian."

He feels his cheeks flame.

"Why were you sent?"

"I don't know," he admits.

"Well, then. You will deliver a message for me. You're a trustworthy boy, yes?"

He isn't a boy. Quatan grits his teeth. "I suppose."

"Good. Deliver this to Artur. He's in the next tent." He hands over a tightly wound scroll.

"Anything else?"

The officer studies him. "Have any family?"

He thinks of his mother and father, how aged they were the last time he saw them, his father's body shrunken to finally suit his bad hand, his mother's shoulders forever slumped in defeat.

"No," he says finally.

"Good," the officer answers. "Good."

The Japanese have been severely weakened. Quatan has heard rumors about a bomb in Hiroshima, but now the officer confirms they are true. An atomic bomb, he explains, dropped in the heart of the city. The Soviet Union has hoped it will force the Japanese to surrender, but, despite the chaos in Hiroshima, despite the thousands wounded or dead or affected, there is no sign this is Japan's intent.

Which is why they are stationed here, just outside of Manchuria. A surprise invasion, he explains, as he draws invisible demarcations on the creased map with his stubby, coffee-stained fingers. Invading the northern region of Japan will involve expertise, but he is confident a surprise attack is the key.

"If they don't see us coming, they can't prepare."

⁓

Under cover of night, Quatan stirs restlessly in his cot. Thinking about the post was one thing, but being here amid troops is another reality. It had been an escape, an excuse to avoid the war without risking the reputation of purposefully hiding from it.

He is a coward. He can stay here, and he will be a coward. He can desert, and he will be a coward. There is no home to return to, no one to return to. For his entire life, he has been running, back when he was a small boy and his father wanted him to race horses, to when he became engaged to a girl he hardly knew, to now, cowering under thin sheets, blinking at the darkness, when hundreds of men are getting dressed and preparing to invade and fight, with no promise they will ever return.

He throws the sheets off and stretches. His skin is as sticky as the summer heat. He hears distant grunts as men step into their shoes and uniforms. What is the point of uniforms when darkness is their only companion? What are the men thinking about as they line up outside? Are they casting last glances at the beds they inhabited, whispering prayers to whatever god they believe in, kissing the pictures of loved ones back home?

No. It is numbness. He's sure numbness compels these men forward. The ability and art of not feeling at all. It's a tactic he knows all too well.

Out in the darkness, he follows far behind. It is half-past eleven, and the stars are barely visible. As he walks in the wet grass, his legs brush something soft.

A uniform. Somehow, a uniform was left outside.

　　　　Erin Jamieson

He does it without thinking. He slips the pants on over his own, and even then, the waistband is too large. He has not eaten well for weeks. The shirt fits better, though the sleeves drape around his thin arms like curtains.

He means to go back, but when has he ever made a sensible choice? Instead, he wanders into the darkness until he finds the line of soldiers and takes a place among them. He shakes from head to toe.

"Excited?" someone nearby asks.

"Something like that," Quatan mumbles. And then, as if his legs are no longer his own, he continues on the order to march.

TWENTY-SEVEN

August 1950
Eredet, Mongolia

IT HAS BEEN five years since Gerel's brother went missing. Tonight, she stands in front of a full-size mirror, studying herself, looking for his face on her own. A hairline crack runs down the center of the glass, forcing her to lean either to the left or right to fully see herself. She looks as divided as she feels, the splintered part of the glass bisecting her chest in two. Her cheeks are flushed pleasantly, her lips painted crimson. After spending an hour on her hair, it lies in limp curls at her shoulders, a stylish, short cut her mother cannot stand. The thick eyebrows she inherited from her father. With the same stubborn jaw and small frame, she feels like a child in a woman's dress.

Self-consciously, she runs her hands along the bottom of her dress skirt. The dress has a fair amount of silk in a delicate pink her mother said brought out Gerel's "natural glow." She grew accustomed to western dress, the petal skirts and button-up blouses she wore to lectures and class presentations. But tonight, her mother has insisted she wear something that makes her feel—well, Mongolian. And as strange as it feels, Gerel agrees with her mother's choice.

It has been five years since her brother disappeared and nearly five since China recognized Mongolia's independence. And yet. Over the course of these years, while attending classes at the University of Ulaanbaatar, balancing writing speeches and term papers, and holding a waitressing job at a local sandwich shop, Gerel has not noticed any changes. A sense of national pride has her people holding themselves higher. On the avenue by the college, several stores have closed, no longer supported by the Soviet Union's treasury. But relationships, for what it's worth, are either the same or worse. A Chinese man on a street will walk circuitously to avoid a Mongolian man. Russian vendors are mistrusted. A Mongolian girl is exposed to advertisements in Russian featuring women with high cheekbones, wide eyes, and pale complexions.

Which is why, despite herself, Gerel continues to harbor anger at their circumstances. The truth is, Mongolia is independent in name only. They are still controlled by the whims of the Soviet Union, from their economy to the mandated educational system to religion—or the lack thereof. She clasps a hand to the cross necklace she is wearing, hidden under the front of her dress. Wearing it is foolish, but she doesn't care. Her mother would be horrified; the danger, she insists, "isn't worth it." She simply doesn't understand. "How can you want to be something other than Buddhist?" she'd pried.

Her mother insists that attending the university has filled Gerel's head with frivolity, but they both know that makes no sense. The university is inundated with the Soviet Union regime's influences. Classes run on strict schedules and teach a curriculum slanted to the will of Russian, rather than Mongolian, history and tradition. And most notably: no one attends services of any kind. No one so much as mentions religion.

That's why Chingis caught her eye—he had an air about him that suggested he would bend rules when necessary. Stocky, with a crooked nose and too large ears, he is not exactly handsome. But the first time they sat beside each other in class, he confessed that she intimidated him. "You're so certain of yourself," he'd said. "You know what you want to do in life."

Over time, she started to trust him enough to share that, yes, she did know. After a dinner of roasted sheep in orange curry sauce, she showed him outlines for speeches she kept hidden, speeches that were dangerous and spoke of religious freedom.

He also longs for a day when religion can be practiced openly, but she's not sure whether he's religious or not. They talk about theories, about oppression.

Gerel is certain of one thing: she will not grow up like her mother, trapped in a still life where all her dreams and desires become buried under the weight of another's.

There is a rap at her apartment door, and she answers, fumbling for the lock. "Just a min—" The door swings open, and she steps back. "By all means, don't wait for me to let you in."

Chingis raises his eyebrows. "Someone's in a mood."

"It's been a long day."

He studies her before kissing her cheek.

The royal blue *deel*, complete with a gold sash and a repeating pattern of pink blossoms, brings out the flecks of hazel in her eyes. Her hair is pulled into a long plait, worn long and over her shoulder.

     Erin Jamieson

"You look beautiful," he says.

"Is that your way of saying, 'What are you doing dressed like that'?"

"No," he says, frowning. His *deel* is plain in comparison, brown and loosely fitting, falling below his knees, with silver embroidery as the only embellishment.

"You aren't surprised?"

"Maybe curious. But I mean what I said. You do look beautiful."

"Don't I always?" Gerel jokes.

"Yes."

But he doesn't smile. "Come on. We're going to be late."

"Let me grab my coat."

"It's nearly eighty outside."

"Just in case."

He shrugs. "Hurry!"

What is wrong with him? Ordinarily, he is patient to a fault. Gerel grabs the camel's hair coat her mother bought two Christmases ago. Or was it three? Since her brother disappeared, holidays have blended together, subdued visits to a house filled with incense, where her mother tends the altar of lighted candles. They celebrate the winter solstice, although Gerel always labels it as Christmas in her head. She doesn't tell her mother, of course. She doesn't tell how she has managed to find a religious book in the underground market, how she skims through Latin passages she sometimes understands and sometimes does not.

Most of those cold months are spent traveling to and from her parents' house, wrapped in a facade of joy. Her mother makes or buys Gerel things she can never use or possibly want— handwoven placemats for four, long gloves someone might have once worn to a formal event, back when there were such things, delicate, silver hair combs that must have cost a month's salary. These gifts Gerel keeps on a high shelf, a memorial of how tenuous their family has become. She doesn't understand the extravagance. She lets the gifts collect dust, fine as a first snowfall, because if she takes them down, she'll have to admit these items have replaced the things she desperately needs and longs for: conversations with substance, warm embraces, and feeling as if she still has a home.

"Gerel?"

"Coming" she says. In her haste, she leaves the coat draped over a chair.

The hall is crowded, the air stifling. Gerel taps her feet without realizing it, until Chingis lays a gentle hand on her shoulder.

"Sorry," she whispers.

But he's already turned his attention to the front of the room, where a young man is speaking.

"The religious freedom we deserve!"

There is thunderous applause, and people begin to stand, mostly men with a sprinkling of women, all in black despite the heat. That way, in the darkness, they might be less easy to spot. That's the theory at least.

"Hungry?" Chingis asks.

Gerel shakes her head. "More nauseous."

"Let's get some air."

He leads her outside, where the night is painted with a smattering of stars, barely visible in the always hazy, ashy, charcoal skies. They hold hands, walking in silence, before Chingis suddenly stops.

"Thank you for coming."

She gives a short laugh. "Shouldn't I be thanking you?"

"True. You're the one who told me about these meetings." He pauses. "Do you think it's worth it?"

"The risk you mean?"

"Yes."

"Obviously. Would I come otherwise?"

"Your faith must be very important to you."

It is said in such a formal tone, she stiffens. "You're having doubts?"

"Sometimes. About attending, I mean."

"You've never mentioned—"

"I'm afraid, Gerel." He glances at her, looks away. "I've always been a coward."

She squeezes his hand.

"I watched someone die."

She waits.

"I saw a man shot for his faith."

In a flash, Gerel sees it again, the monk wandering the market, the gun pointed at his chest, the blood covering the cracked sidewalk.

"I have, too."

He doesn't seem to hear her. "It was awful. He didn't deserve to die."

"Does anyone deserve to die?"

He considers. "Yes. There are evil people in this world, people who persecute others. They deserve to die. The people who decide that other lives are disposable."

Something strange flutters in Gerel's chest. "Nothing will happen to us," she says.

"You don't know that."

"I don't. But all this time–"

He stops abruptly in the street, cupping her chin with his calloused hands. "We've been lucky."

She pulls away. "So that's it, then? Do you want to stop going to the meetings? I didn't think you'd give up like that."

He closes his eyes. "I don't want anything to happen to us."

"You don't want anything to happen to you," she says. "Don't you see? This is so much bigger than us. So much more important."

He blinks, stunned as if she's slapped him. "I love you, Gerel," he says huskily. "Don't you know that?" He folds her into an embrace, and she smells fresh rainfall, a touch of the ashy sky, and cloves. It is a scent that feels like home, a fragrance that calms her instantly. She wraps her arms around his neck, willing the street to disappear, willing everything to disappear but him and this moment.

When she pulls away, he is staring at her. "Gerel, I wanted to ask your parents. But you've never offered to take me."

Her eyes widen.

"I'm tired of sneaking around," he says. "Aren't you?" He moves his hands to her waist. "I was going to ask your parents for your hand in marriage."

A roll of thunder erupts. The skies seemed to have drifted into a deep periwinkle.

"I wanted to do it correctly," he says. "I think that's the right way, asking permission? My parents married by arrangement."

Gerel is silent for a long moment. She should feel a rush of excitement or happiness, but she only aches. She has witnessed how things happen, how they deteriorate. Part of her wants to rewind to several moments before this moment, before things shifted in a way that can't be shifted back.

 Erin Jamieson

"My parents had an arranged marriage also," Gerel says.

"It's good to have a choice now," he says, "but people are sure to mess it up."

Gerel thinks of Quatan and his broken engagement. He was never the same afterward, as if a part of him had been shut away forever. Her brother had collected secrets the way others might memories. And she hadn't lived much differently.

She still doesn't. What is she hiding under all this devotion to religious freedom? How strong is her faith and her desire for freedom for her people, or is she merely avoiding herself? She feels nauseous. Would Chingis want her if he knew her completely? She looks up, realizes he is slipping something cool onto her finger.

"Will you marry me?" he repeats.

She glances at the plain, silver band, which she knows cost him all that he'd saved from odd jobs. It is beautiful, simple, and perfect.

"I—"

"Promise me we'll tell your parents."

"Of course," she says.

And then he's beaming. "See. We won't need this anymore." He kisses her full on the mouth, shamelessly.

She looks up from the ring on her finger. "You expect me to stop coming to the meetings?"

"Is that so much to ask?"

"Yes," she says softly, Once, years ago, she had asked her brother if he had anything he'd die for. She wants to believe that Chingis is one of those things but working toward this goal has given her life. Why does she have to choose?

It begins to rain, fine and misty, like gentle kisses on her skin.

"Gerel?"

"Don't make me decide between you and what I believe," she says.

He squeezes her hand. "I'm asking my fiancé not to endanger her life."

"What are you doing?"

"I don't know," she admits, removing the ring. "I don't know."

"Gerel, don't do something you'll regret."

He says it kindly, pleading, but she hears something else. A life unlived. A life spent fretting over what one is supposed to do. A life meant to avoid risks—only to face those challenges anyway.

"I don't want to regret another time I should have done more than I did." She never said goodbye to her brother, that last time. She abandoned her search for her grandfather. She stopped trying to connect with her mother and shut herself away. She stopped writing letters to Aisin when life got in the way.

"I love you," she says, "but not enough."

And then another clap of thunder swallows the silence, and he is walking away before she can change her mind. She watches as he becomes a shadow in the night, a brief flicker that might have been nothing or nobody at all.

 Erin Jamieson

TWENTY-EIGHT

GEREL'S MOTHER IS still awake. Gerel can see her slightly stooped back, her shadow fluttering like the dying embers of a candle inside the darkened kitchen. The shades are drawn except for one, small window that has been crawling with mildew since she moved out years ago to attend college.

It is almost midnight, but Gerel ascends the creaking stairs. The door is still the same rusty hue, but now the paint is peeling and faded to a fleshy salmon color. She knocks once, too softly for the dead to hear, then a second time. At first, she thinks no one has heard, but then her mother peeks through the window, opens her mouth in surprise, and disappears for a minute before she swings the door open.

"I hope I didn't wake you or Father," Gerel begins.

"Nonsense. I couldn't sleep. Your father, on the other hand, could wake a city with his snoring."

Gerel smiles; she can hear the buzz, even from the front entrance.

"Don't stand there," Bolormaa says. "Come in."

The kitchen is warm, damp, and smells of cumin, garlic, and pepper. Gerel nearly trips over the tile floor, which is starting to wear down to the original foundation and is uneven in many places. The counters are meticulously clean, though, and a tiny calendar is hung on the wall. Gerel fights the urge to look at the squares filled with writing.

What exactly did her parents do, anyway? Ever since her mother had fallen last year and quit her job, Gerel cannot imagine what she does to fill her time, especially with Quatan gone. She visits only a few times a year. Her father, she knows, still works, but he has reduced his hours to twenty, thirty hours a week at most.

It's the natural order of things, she supposes. Last week, she accepted a position at a marketing firm on the outskirts of Erdenet. It is monotonous work, mostly filing papers and typing, but at least now she can afford a few luxuries, like new clothes for the upcoming winter, a welcome mat for her apartment, and the handsome painting she hung in the front hall.

Sometimes, she compares these luxuries to the quilts and rugs they made for their *ger*. She thinks of the altar her father kept with care, of the modest pots her family used to cook with.

Mostly, how endless the sky looked on a cloudless day.

The heaviness she's been trying to ignore fills her now, as if a balloon had suddenly been placed inside her chest. She sinks into a chair at the kitchen table, exhausted.

"Gerel?" Her mother's hand is light on her shoulder.

"I shouldn't have come," she says. She lifts her head and sees tears in her mother's eyes.

"You're always welcome here," Bolormaa says.

Gerel doesn't answer. This isn't her home, and it never will be. It will always be the place where they fell apart, where she stopped talking to Quatan and let bitterness fester inside her, where her father grew more and more detached, and her mother tried unsuccessfully to patch them together. And now it is easier, with the peeling paint and the blistered floors, the home that appears as worn and broken as she feels. It is easier, finally, to stop pretending.

"You and Chingis," her mother begins.

Gerel stares. "How did you know?"

She smiles sadly, peeking outside at the silvery sliver of moon. "Your brother had the same look when he broke off his engagement."

Gerel didn't come here to talk about Quatan. She reaches for the cross necklace under her dress and pulls it out. Her mother's eyes darken but she says nothing.

"He didn't share my views," Gerel says.

"But you love him."

"Maybe."

Her mother nods. "Can I get you something? Tea?"

"Why do you always do that, change the subject?"

"Gerel, I'm too tired for this."

"You think I'm being foolish."

"I can't pretend to understand. I wish you happiness."

"What do you know about happiness?" Gerel regrets the words the instance she's uttered them.

"I used to be happy," her mother says quietly. "Losing your brother—"

"That was a long time ago."

The kettle on the stove begins to whistle. Did her father really sleep so soundly?

"Don't say that."

"He was hiding something," Gerel insists. "He shut us out for so long. Didn't you ever wonder?"

"Why does it matter now?" her mother sighs. "He wasn't happy. I know that. He felt too much pressure. Sometimes I worry it was our fault, that we were bad parents."

Gerel pours a cup of tea for her mother and for herself. "I used to believe that, but life isn't so simple. When we moved into the city, everything changed."

"Yes," her mother says, "It did."

"I wish I knew what Quatan was looking for back then."

Her mother shakes her head. "Let's not talk about that." She lifts the cup to her mouth.

And just like that, the subject is closed. In the past, this would have made Gerel angry, but now she feels the weight of resignation.

She gazes at her mother's creased face, the map of veins running down her arms and legs. At her hair, now completely colorless, her faded clothes. When did her mother become so old? Did it start the Christmas after Quatan disappeared, when, despite pleas, Gerel did not come? Or had it been sooner? She tries to remember, tries to remember the quiet but strong mother who had once spent her days laying out goat's milk to form curds, who'd helped transport the *ger* from location to location, who'd brushed horses' manes and fed the goats.

Tears sting her eyes, and Gerel isn't sure if she's upset about her brother, her mother and father, her brief, broken engagement, or something else. Maybe it is everything. When she lifts her head, a hundred stones press her chest, and it hurts to breathe.

"We should have never left the Gobi."

Bolormaa looks up in surprise. "As you say, it isn't that simple."

But what is simple? Love isn't simple. Even having something to die for isn't. Gerel lowers her head, accepting and knowing that her mother doesn't have answers to satisfy her.

  Erin Jamieson

"I have to go," she says, draining her cup. "Thank you for the tea."

"It's the middle of the night," her mother says with a strained, hurt voice. "Surely you can stay one night?"

There is nothing Gerel wants less right now. The house smells of memories: the flat cakes she and Quatan baked for their mother's birthday, the leather horse gloves their father gave them both, although neither would ever need them. The cinnamon, hard candies Aisin brought on a cold, February night when the streets were obscured with gray sleet and despair.

"I can stay," she says finally, squeezing her mother's hand.

"I'll set up something for you."

"If it's all right, I'd like to sleep on the floor. On a mat like we used to."

Her mother nods. "We can do that. Sometimes, that's where I'm most comfortable, too."

TWENTY-NINE

1960
Gobi Desert

IN THE END, their lives were nothing more than a smattering of stars in breathtakingly endless skies overlooking wide, open lands. Full of possibility, full of pits to sink into.

Bolormaa is dressed from head to toe in a soft, black, silk dress, western-style, which smells of the cooking she and Gerel did earlier that morning: roasted tomatoes with wild rice and braised mutton and pan-seared horse meat with sage. And *buuz*, the same kind they had the first day she met her husband.

There is little need for ceremony. She walks beside Aisin, who, even at her age looks regal, holding her shoulders even and her head high. Aisin points to a lone figure in the middle of the open plain, and Bolormaa nods.

Although it has been fifteen years since they last saw each other, the women have picked up where they left off. Like dear friends, Bolormaa realizes. Like she used to be with her younger brother, Batbayar, before they parted ways.

It hasn't been easy. Aisin sent a letter seven years ago, explaining why she never returned to the city. She had never felt right about being in the same home as Ganbaatar, she wrote, and she had loved him her whole life at the same time she had cared for and respected Bolormaa.

Quatan had suspected. That's as much as Gerel and Bolormaa can gather. He hunted for a woman his father loved, trying to protect their family.

Bolormaa would like to believe he would have returned, especially now. But that means she may believe her son is dead. So she continues hoping, and praying to a god she is still unsure of—is it the Christian god, or one she has constructed? She isn't sure. She's still working on that, and maybe always will be.

"Are you ready?" Aisin asks.

Is she? She knows she isn't. Gerel stands beside her with red but dry eyes, her husband Chingis on the other side, and their seven-year-old daughter fidgeting against her father's grip. Her granddaughter looks, Bolormaa thinks, like Gerel did at that age. So hopeful. So naive. But so alive.

They scatter his ashes across the soil. Ganbaatar has finally come home to the place he loved, the place where he cut off his father and spent the rest of his life regretting it.

It is also the land where they married, too young and foolish to admit neither was prepared. Quatan and Gerel were born here, and they built a life together in a series of makeshift *gers* before each collapsed only to be built again.

Except. Gerel's daughter gives a squeal of excitement as, after the ashes have blown and the blessings have been said, Aisin leads a horse. It is painted, majestic, and marches proudly towards them. The animal's demeanor is gentle and accepting as its soft, brown eyes blink at them. Gerel mounts as gracefully as someone who has ridden her entire life. She lifts her daughter onto the saddle beside her, to which Chingis protests.

"She'll be safe with me," she assures him, smirking. "Do you think I'm a bad rider?"

"For heaven's sake, Gerel—"

"Let them," Aisin interrupts.

Chingis turns with pleading eyes to Bolormaa.

But for once, the older woman finds herself agreeing with Gerel and Aisin. "Let them ride. Your daughter is old enough to ride on her own now."

And she will be, soon. Gerel's daughter doesn't have her mother's temperament; like Quatan, she has little interest in racing. But she does want to ride.

They watch as Gerel steers the horse in a luxurious lap around the field, with her daughter gripping tightly to her waist.

This morning as she'd dressed, Bolormaa had dreaded this moment, this day. But the air is fresh, breathing life into her lungs. The sun is warm on her tired back. The home in Ulaanbaatar has been sold, along with all but a few of Quatan and Ganbaatar's things. She no longer feels anger. She no longer feels afraid, or even sorrowful.

The wind blows again, and she knows the physical being of her husband is gone, forever gone. But they say the skies are infinite in Mongolia. She stares up at the breathtaking, piercing blue, one of the last, warm days of the year before autumn hits.

She's home, in a way she has never felt before.

Aisin squeezes her hand as they watch the horse with its graceful riders. "He loved you," she says.

Even a year ago, this would have hurt her, knowing what

　　　　　Erin Jamieson

she did about Aisin. But she nods and pats her friend's back. Ganbaatar did love her—at times, romantically, but always kindly and loyally. He tried so hard.

She thinks about the nights they danced. The times they laughed. The cold spells where it felt as if their lives would continue to fracture until there was nothing left.

The sun is setting and Gerel and her daughter are returning, both sweaty and flushed. This land is hers, but it is also theirs, under this colorful, ever-changing sky.

Bolormaa walks toward the golden horizon to meet her daughter. They have a long walk back to the *ger* before night falls.

Just for a moment, a shadow catches Bolormaa's eye. Her breath catches in her chest, spreading warmth as she leans forward, straining to see. She watches as the shadow sharpens and takes the form of a slight figure. A figure with a subtle limp and a posture she knows like she knows her own, coming towards them, moving over the demanding land of their ancestors, trying to find a way through the fading light of dusk and back to them.

ACKNOWLEDGEMENTS

Without many people, this novel would not have been possible. First, thanks to Dr. Marcia Frost, Emerita Associate Professor of Economics at Wittenberg University, whose course first sparked my interest in Mongolian history. Thanks to the faculty within the MFA program at Miami University, especially Joseph Bates, Brian Roley, and Cathy Wagner. Thanks to Mary Vensel White and the team at Type Eighteen Books for not only giving this novel a chance, but also for helping to shape it into the best version possible. Thanks to all my family and friends, who have always supported my writing, even when I doubted myself most. And finally, I would not be here today—let alone have a novel published—were it not for my faith in Jesus Christ.

ABOUT THE AUTHOR

Erin Jamieson (she/her) holds an MFA in Creative Writing from Miami University. Her writing has been published in over eighty literary magazines, including a Pushcart Prize nomination. She is the author of a poetry collection (*Clothesline*, 2023) and four poetry chapbooks. She's taught writing at universities in the Midwest and in her spare time, she loves hiking, visiting museums, and spending time with family.

She also produces gaming commentary for life simulation games on her YouTube channel, Simmer Erin. Find her there, or on X (Twitter): @erin_simmer.